Vicious Scars

JANE BLYTHE

Cover designed by RBA Designs

❀ Created with Vellum

Acknowledgments

I'd like to thank everyone who played a part in bringing this story to life. Particularly my mom who is always there to share her thoughts and opinions with me. My wonderful cover designer Letitia who did an amazing job with this stunning cover. My fabulous editor Lisa for all the hard work she puts into polishing my work. My awesome team, Sophie, Robyn, and Clayr, without your help I'd never be able to run my street team. And my fantastic street team members who help share my books with every share, comment, and like!

And of course a big thank you to all of you, my readers! Without you I wouldn't be living my dreams of sharing the stories in my head with the world!

CHAPTER One

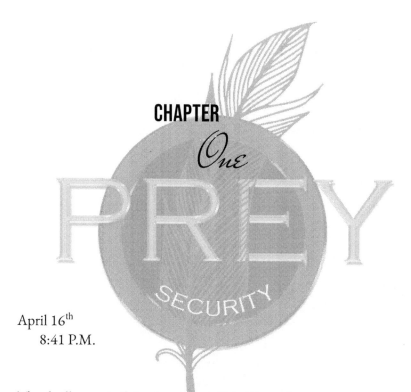

PREY SECURITY

April 16th
8:41 P.M.

The shrill sound of the alarm ripped him from sleep.

Years as a Delta Force operator and Gabriel "Tank" Dawson was instantly awake and fully alert, every one of his finely tuned senses honed.

They had an intruder.

A quick glance at the clock told him it was a little after twenty-thirty. He'd only been asleep for a bit over thirty minutes, but already he'd tossed the covers off. They lay in a tangled heap at the side of the bed, and he stepped over them as he reached for a pair of sweatpants that he'd tossed onto the chair by the bed.

Sleeping naked had its advantages—he didn't sweat so much when the nightmares came—but it also had its disadvantages—it took longer than it otherwise would to be ready in an emergency.

Still, he didn't waste much time shoving his feet into a worn pair of sneakers and grabbing his weapon and comms unit. Neither was very far away. He and his team were a paranoid bunch.

They had reason to be.

After breaking up a notorious trafficking ring a few years back their cover had been blown and targets painted on their backs.

Living with a threat like that had pretty much terminated their Delta Force careers, but they had been lucky enough to be offered jobs by the revered Eagle Oswald at his world-renowned security and black ops company, Prey Security.

Now he and his team lived on a remote compound deep in the woods. They never had visitors. Well, other than the occasional one by Eagle, but the billionaire former SEAL spent most of his time in New York with his wife Olivia and their two children, three-year-old Luna and three-month-old Apollo. Most of their correspondence was done by video call because the man knew they didn't like people in their space.

There was zero reason for anyone to have set off one of the alarms lining the property's perimeter.

Especially at night.

"Check-in," he demanded as soon as he had the comms in and was heading out his door.

His team immediately checked in.

"Rock," Sebastian "Rock" Rockman said.

"Scorpion," Mason "Scorpion" Markson said.

"Damn, spider," Patrick "Trick" Kramer muttered, sounding more horrified than he should for a former Delta turned Prey operative. "Beast was right beside the doorhandle, almost touched it."

They could all but hear Trick's shudder, and Tank rolled his eyes.

"Computer already up and running," Rafe "Panther" Neal said.

"I'm here," said Axel "Axe" Lindon. Axe had been their team leader up until eight months ago when his wife was snatched on what should have been a routine trip to the grocery store. Tank had stepped up when Axe had asked him to, and although it still felt odd to be the one in charge, he respected the man who, in his mind, would always be their leader for stepping away when he knew he couldn't give one hundred percent.

"Alarm was tripped in the 2-C quadrant. You're closest, Tank," their computer guru Panther informed him.

When they'd first moved to the remote compound, they'd split the seventy acres into seven distinct sections. They each had ten acres that was their own personal space, and the remaining ten had a communal building they shared along with a large training ground so they never had to leave except when they worked a mission.

His ten acres were designated 2, and C meant it was on the acre closest to the fence.

A barbed wire fence that should be enough to deter anyone who happened to wander too close to the remote compound.

Obviously, this intruder hadn't gotten the memo.

Only someone who knew they were here should be determined enough to make it up and over that fence.

Which meant bad news for him and his team.

"I want him alive," Axe's cold voice came through the comms. Their team leader had changed a lot in the last eight months. Losing the woman he loved had come as close to breaking Axe as Tank had seen in the almost decade he'd known the man.

Already outside, Tank made quick work of closing the distance between his cabin and where the intruder had set off the alarm. Although there were cameras in the woods, they couldn't put one on every single tree, so as much as he would prefer to have a visual before heading in, he had no choice but to go in blind.

Not that he was worried.

He was highly trained and able to take on and eliminate any threat. Whoever had broken into the compound tonight had no idea just who they were up against. Taking on six former Delta Force operators who chose to lock themselves away from the rest of the world was not a smart move.

Tank was closing in on acre number three when he heard the sound of heavy breathing. It was obvious whoever had breached their perimeter wasn't highly trained. Anyone who was, wouldn't be running as though they were being chased by the devil, taking no care to attempt to hide their location.

It was almost like they wanted to be found.

Remaining on high alert in case this was a trap, Tank judged the location of the sound and the direction the person was running, then hid himself behind a tree and waited.

A minute later, a figure dressed in white rushed past.

One smooth move was all it took to get the intruder pinned against his chest with an arm banded around them, holding their arms immobile at their side.

Despite their small size, his captive fought hard. Thrashing and screaming, flinging their small body about to the point where he actually loosened his hold because he was afraid they were going to hurt themselves.

That was when he saw it.

The long golden-brown locks, now tangled and knotted.

The wide doe brown eyes, now filled with pure, undiluted terror.

The slim body that belonged to a woman was now gaunt and much too thin.

"Please!" she sobbed hysterically, "don't hurt me. *Please*, don't hurt me. Not again. Please, please, please," she chanted over and over again.

It wasn't possible, and yet …

Here she was.

Fighting against his hold as though her life depended on it.

"It's Beth," he said into the comms. He wanted to adjust his hold on her, offer comfort to a woman he considered a sister, but he was afraid if he let go, she'd be off running again, and even in the dark, she looked like a strong breeze could blow her over.

For a moment silence met his words.

Then he heard a choked sob.

"Beth?" Axe asked as though hardly daring to believe that his wife who they had searched tirelessly for these past eight months, had randomly turned up here on the compound.

"Yeah, man," he said gently, unable to comprehend the mess of emotions Axe must be feeling in this moment.

"Is she … okay?"

How could he answer that question?

No.

The simple answer was that the woman struggling against his grip was nowhere close to being okay.

In fact, she was the opposite.

She was much too thin, dirty, barefoot, covered in blood and scratches. But he didn't want to say all of that when he knew Axe was holding on by a thread.

"Just get here, man, yeah?" he said.

For the next several minutes, he alternated between making sure Panther was doing everything he could to trace the path Beth had taken to get here in hopes of finding a lead on who had taken her and where she'd been held and attempting to calm the hysterical woman in his arms.

Nothing he said seemed to work. Beth was too trapped in whatever nightmare she'd somehow managed to escape to hear a word he was saying.

It wasn't until Axe screamed her name that she finally went still.

As soon as he reached their side, Axe grabbed Beth and hauled her into his arms. His friend was openly crying as he clutched Beth and rocked her, holding her like she was the most precious thing in the world to him.

Because she was.

When Axe finally loosened his hold on Beth, her soft voice spoke words that stunned them all.

"Who is Beth?"

They all exchanged confused glances.

Axe's hands framed Beth's gaunt face. The woman looked so fragile, so very breakable. "*You* are Beth."

Her brow furrowed. "And who are you?"

"I'm Axel. Your husband." The pain in Axe's words about broke Tank's heart. He'd been searching relentlessly for his wife, and now that he had her back, she didn't seem to remember anything about him or herself.

"Husband." Beth echoed the word like it was foreign to her, had no meaning, no context. "Who are they?" she asked, looking at him and the rest of their team gathered around the couple.

"They're my team. My friends. Your friends. Sweetheart, what *do* you remember?"

"Fight," Beth replied immediately. "To survive you have to fight."

The words meant nothing to any of them, but Tank knew that

finding out what had happened to Beth and making sure the person responsible was punished was all of Bravo Team's top priority.

~

April 16th
   10:02 P.M.

New house, new name, new life.

Tallulah "Tillie" Russel looked around the small, empty cottage. It was old but nice and in reasonable condition, and she'd certainly lived in worse places growing up. Downstairs, there was a kitchen that opened into a dining room, a lounge room with a large fireplace that she intended to make good use of next winter, and a tiny office that she already had plans to turn into her own little library.

There were changes she'd make, the dark brown floorboards were nice, but she hated the white walls, they were so ... plain. Plain was something she'd been called enough times in her life to have developed an aversion to it, and her first job here would be painting all the walls bright, vivid colors.

Pinks, and purples, and blues was the color pallet she always gravitated toward, and even though she was supposed to be a new person now with a brand new bought and paid for by the state identity, there were some parts of herself she just couldn't let go of.

This was one of them.

It might be a new life, but it was still a life she had to live, and that meant some things weren't negotiable.

So much was lost to her. The social worker job she had adored and worked so hard to achieve, as well as her volunteer work fostering puppies and kittens and other animals that had been neglected and abused. That was something she always identified with, whether it be a child or a pet, and she wanted to do her part to ease that suffering since no one had ever been there for her or cared about her own suffering.

As weird as it was being away from everything she had ever known, and the life she had built for herself, at least she was alive.

When it all boiled down to it that was what mattered the most.

"To new beginnings," she whispered aloud, not that there was anyone to hear her.

Alone.

For now, she had to rebuild her life alone.

Still, at least she had a life.

And it wasn't like being alone was anything new for her. She had basically been on her own since she was three years old. Growing up in foster care was a hard enough way to live out your childhood and adolescence, but when you had a family history like hers, it made it that much worse.

She was the kid nobody wanted to get too close to for fear she would turn out like her father.

No matter how hard she tried to shake off that weight hanging around her neck, she never seemed to be able to actually do it. Tillie had worked so hard in school, got perfect grades, played several musical instruments, sang in the choir, performed in school plays, and was good at sports, but none of it ever changed where she'd come from.

Even as an adult that stigma was still there.

At work, people gave her wary looks when they thought she wasn't looking. No one could deny she was good at her job, that she had a way of making abused kids feel safe enough to admit the truth of what their lives were really like, but that doesn't mean her colleagues liked her. Or trusted her.

There was always that doubt.

Maybe there was some of her father in her that she hid behind her long blonde locks, big turquoise eyes, and freckles.

Maybe if someone said or did the wrong thing, that evil monster would come out.

Only there was no evil monster lurking inside her.

She carried her father's DNA. Yes, of course she did. But that didn't mean she carried the demons that had plagued him for a lifetime.

At least her book club friends hadn't treated her like a freak. Okay, so they had never known that the Tillie they knew who loved anything with a romance arc but was partial to suspense, mystery, thrillers, action, and military romances, was really Tallulah Russel, but it was so nice to be treated as just her and not Frank Russel's daughter.

Now Tallulah Russel didn't exist.

She had become Matilda Malcom. Still Tillie to anyone she would meet in this new life, but no longer the woman with the infamous father.

In a way it held—or should hold—a kind of freedom she'd been lacking for almost thirty years.

All things considered, she knew she had a lot to be thankful for, and she better start remembering that instead of the things she had lost.

To that end, Tillie straightened her spine, set down her suitcase—packed with the only things she had been allowed to bring with her—and headed for the kitchen. She had brought one bag of groceries on the way here, she'd make a late dinner and then sleep in the sleeping bag on the floor.

Tomorrow she'd hit up some charity stores and try to find some cheap furniture to get her started. She had a little money to get by, but she was going to have to find a job, and quickly. Since she couldn't go back to being a social worker, she was going to have to look for something else. Likely something where she couldn't use her skill set because if anyone was looking for her they'd be looking in those very places.

Working in a library had seemed like a good compromise since she couldn't do social work or really any work with kids. But the agent assigned to her case had told her that possibility wasn't on the table.

She'd tried arguing for a job in a bookstore, something to give her some sort of connection to who she really was, but that had been vetoed as well.

Probably she'd end up working in a bank, or a supermarket, or something else equally boring.

There was nothing wrong with those jobs they just weren't her.

Tillie knew she was a little odd. Growing up shunned the way she had she was often awkward in social settings. Dealing with traumatized kids was fine, she was comfortable in that work because she related to them. The same when it was other bookish people, they had something in common, something she could connect to.

But making small talk?

That was her kryptonite.

Since she didn't really have a lot of options, she was going to have to find a way to make it work. Right now she just needed *a* job. There were bills to pay plus all the expenses of starting over from scratch.

Furniture wasn't all she needed. Clothes, sheets, blankets, towels, cutlery, plates, bowls, pots, pans, oven trays, casserole dishes, toiletries, a vacuum cleaner, mop, broom ... the list went on and on and on. Everything a home needed she would have to purchase. All she had with her were a few outfits, a couple of pairs of shoes, and one or two mementos from her old life she had been allowed to keep.

It was overwhelming, and she was way too tired to obsess over it now, so Tillie deliberately shoved away her worries, and set the bag of groceries on the counter.

Getting out bread, cheese, and butter she set about making herself a toasted cheese sandwich, the ultimate comfort food for her and one she had basically grown up on. Also something she could make in the tabletop oven that had thankfully been left behind by the previous owner.

Comfort food was going to be featured quite heavily in her diet for the next few weeks. Anything to help make this transition as easy as it could be. Macaroni and cheese, mashed potatoes, spaghetti and meatballs, lasagna, chicken pot pie, mmm ... her mouth watered just thinking about it.

And ice cream.

Lots of ice cream.

Cookie dough ice cream was her favorite. She'd even been known to make her own when she had the time.

Actually, just cookie dough on its own was comfort food-alicious. As much as she loved freshly baked homemade cookies, any time she went to bake some she usually wound up just eating the raw dough straight out of the bowl.

Mmm.

Delicious.

Too bad she hadn't thought to pick up any baking ingredients when she'd stopped by the supermarket on the way here. Still, she had bought a big tub of ice cream, one she was going to devour as soon as she'd eaten her toasted cheese sandwich.

The light in the cottage was dull, coming only from a couple of old-fashioned wall lamps, and Tillie was distracted, bustling about the kitchen unpacking her meager supply of groceries while her sandwich toasted so she didn't see the figure creeping quietly through the house.

It wasn't until a hand closed over her mouth and she was yanked back against a rock-hard chest that she realized her past had just caught up with her.

What was that saying?

No good deed goes unpunished.

Well, she was about to pay for her good deed with her life.

CHAPTER

Two

April 16th
10:34 P.M.

Tank hated it when cases were women.

Especially petite women like the one making the sandwich in her kitchen, completely oblivious to his presence.

She really should be paying more attention to her surroundings. Just because you were indoors, it didn't mean you were any safer than if you were outdoors. Perhaps if more people realized that there would be less crime.

Still, less crime meant less business for him.

As much as he found this particular case to be distasteful, he had been paid to collect the woman, so that was what he'd come here to do.

What he was going to do.

Like it or not, it didn't make a difference. You did the job you were paid to do, and as much as he hadn't wanted to take on this particular case, when your boss gave it to you that was that.

It wasn't just that Tank didn't want to be here to grab the woman, it was that he wanted to be with his team right now. They needed him,

Beth's shock return with zero memory of where she had been for the last eight months or who she had been before had rocked all of them.

He should be there.

Supporting Axe, supporting Beth.

Tank couldn't imagine how hard this must be for either of them. Beth was clearly terrified out of her mind to the point where they'd wound up giving her a sedative just before he left to come here. And Axe had been searching for the woman he loved—a woman who had already survived more than most people would ever have to endure—for eight long months only to lose her all over again when he did finally get her back.

Being here felt wrong, but Eagle had insisted this wasn't something that could wait.

This woman had gotten herself mixed up in something bigger than she realized, making her a threat to many.

Meaning there was no choice but to do what he'd been sent to do.

Many years of training meant he knew how to move without making a sound and he moved across the kitchen, never alerting her to his presence.

She was humming softly as she put away the meager groceries she'd brought with her to the empty house. She sounded good, could carry a tune, and he knew from the intel he'd scanned on the way here that she was musically talented.

There had been a time—that felt like another lifetime—when he'd wanted to be in a band. With supportive parents who encouraged their kids to find what they were interested in and run with it, he'd taken lessons. He'd learned to play the guitar, the saxophone, and the piano before his life was irrevocably changed.

As change often was, it was hard to go back, and those dreams had fallen by the wayside in place of the practicalities of trying to survive.

Being reminded of his long-forgotten dream was the last thing he wanted when he was already not pleased with being given this case. Tank let a small sigh puff through his chest as he came up behind the still-oblivious woman.

When he grabbed her, yanking her up against him and pinning her arms by her sides, he felt her freeze for a moment as the expected fear hit, that moment of terror that would be threatening to overwhelm her. Learning to work through that fear took time and practice, but it was essential to survival.

Only the little blonde pixie did something he hadn't been expecting.

Instead of trying to brute force her way out of his hold by thrashing about, which would have been impossible, she immediately put her hand between his legs, grabbed his crotch, and twisted.

The pain was instantaneous and did exactly what she intended.

Instinct could be hard to fight against, especially when you weren't prepared for something, and her actions caused him to release her as his hands automatically pressed against his throbbing length.

Again, the blonde pixie surprised him when she quickly grabbed the tub of butter off the counter and swung it at his head.

Tank wasn't so incapacitated that he couldn't duck, and the butter glanced off his skull.

There was no hesitation on the pixie's part, she immediately dodged around him, sprinting for the door.

If she got through it, she'd get away.

The pixie was smart, with a solid head on her shoulders. She wasn't going to panic. She knew the best moves to make to ensure her survival. As soon as she got herself outside, she would scream for help, alerting the neighbors.

That would throw a spanner in the works.

Wouldn't stop him from doing what he'd come here for. He wasn't leaving until he had the woman in his possession.

Moving faster than the little blonde pixie could ever hope to, Tank reached out and snagged her again. For a tiny little thing she fought like her life depended on it.

Because she knew it did.

Since she was much smaller than his six foot eight, three-hundred-pound frame of pure muscle, keeping a hold of her was easy. Still, he had to give credit where credit was due, and he respected the hell out of her for fighting with everything she had.

Too bad it wasn't going to do any good.

Keeping a hold of her, he twisted his body so that she couldn't get in another attack and pulled out the syringe.

"Good try, little pixie," he murmured as he pierced her skin and delivered the sedative.

As the woman's fighting slowly faded until she hung limp in his arms and he swung her up, Tank decided he hated this case more than any other he had worked. The little blonde pixie didn't deserve what she had coming.

But it wasn't his job to input his personal opinion into this mission.

Get the girl, take her to the cabin, keep her there.

That was what he had been ordered to do, and that was what he would do.

Hefting his small burden over one shoulder, he grabbed the sandwich she'd been making and took a bite. Perfect. The cheese was melted just the way he liked it, and the bread toasted just slightly overdone but not burned.

Because he didn't want to catch the attention of any neighbors still up and about at this time, he shifted the pixie so she was cradled in his arms. That looked a lot less suspicious, and he'd done it for that reason alone, but when he looked down at her blonde head resting against his shoulder, he felt an odd stirring of ... something in his chest.

Dismissing the feeling as nothing more than the shock they'd all had earlier tonight and his reluctance to break into this woman's home and abduct her, he went to the freezer, grabbed the ice cream, and then headed out the front door.

The neighborhood was quiet as he carried her to his SUV, parked in the street a couple of houses down from the pixie's. Once he'd opened the back door and laid her small body out on the backseat, Tank grabbed some zip ties.

"Sorry, pixie," he apologized to the unconscious woman as he cuffed first her wrists together and then her ankles. He didn't want the spunky pixie to get any ideas about making an escape before he got her to the cabin. If his few minutes in her company had taught him anything it was to expect the unexpected. He certainly wouldn't put it past her to throw herself out of the moving vehicle if she regained consciousness too soon.

Couldn't have that happening.

With the woman restrained, he closed the door and got into the driver's seat. To be safe, he engaged the child locks. If the woman did wake up in the car, she'd have to go through him to get out and that certainly wasn't happening.

"Package is secure," he said when he dialed Eagle and the other man answered.

"Get her to the safehouse ASAP," Eagle said.

"Will do."

"And, Tank, nothing can go wrong," his boss warned.

"I know."

"Stakes are high on this one. She's sweet and innocent looking, beautiful, too, don't let that interfere with what has to be done."

Tank glanced in the rear vision mirror, looking at the pixie passed out in his backseat. She did look sweet, innocent, and she was definitely beautiful. But he'd been with enough pretty women to know they were more trouble than they were worth, and this one was holding a metaphorical live bomb just waiting to go off and take out anyone too close to her as collateral damage.

He had no intention of being blown up along with the pixie.

"Hear you loud and clear, boss. This is just another case."

And if there was a tiny voice in the back of his head calling him a liar, Tank ignored it as he set his phone on the passenger seat and drove off into the night to the cabin where his little blonde pixie would be kept for the foreseeable future.

~

April 17th
12:15 A.M.

Tillie woke slowly, feeling like she was encased in some sort of fluffy cloud.

It filled her head, filled her mouth, and coated her body in a soft cocoon.

For one beautiful second it felt so nice, so freeing, like she was flying high across the huge expanse of inky night sky.

Then reality settled in.

It took several long moments for her memories to come back, but when they did, she bolted upright and launched to her feet.

Well, she *tried* to launch to her feet, but something yanked on her wrist making her fall backward onto the bed.

A bed?

In a panic, Tillie looked around. She was in a bedroom in what appeared to be a cabin, if the wooden floors, walls, and furniture were anything to go by. The bed was big, with a heavy oak frame and a soft mattress. A pair of handcuffs ran from her left wrist to the headboard, and she was ... in her underwear.

Tillie leaned over the side of the bed and promptly threw up.

Had she been raped? Was her kidnapper some sort of deranged sexual predator who intended to keep her locked up as his personal prisoner?

This wasn't her new house.

It wasn't her old house.

It wasn't any place she'd ever been before.

She'd been kidnapped.

Abducted.

Maybe raped.

Panic flooded her system. Her heart beat so hard and fast inside her chest that it physically hurt, and her breathing increased until she was panting for air, sounding like a dog who had just gone on a ten-mile run.

This couldn't be happening.

They'd assured her she was safe.

Promised her if she told what she knew they would give her a whole new life.

A life that was supposed to be safe.

Yet clearly it wasn't.

Twelve hours—or at least twelve hours to when she'd been standing in her kitchen making a toasted cheese sandwich—that was all it had lasted.

It wasn't fair.

She hadn't even done anything wrong, and yet she kept getting punished over and over again.

Yanking on her bound arm, Tillie spent the next several minutes locked in a battle with the immovable handcuffs. By the time acceptance sank in, she was exhausted, and her wrist was bruised, swollen, and aching.

Curling up against the headboard, she pulled her knees to her chest and hugged herself. How could this be happening? She was supposed to be safe. Witness Protection had set her up with a whole new identity, and yet here she was, a prisoner chained to a bed.

Had her new identity been breached? Was the man who had drugged and kidnapped her one of O'Riley's?

He had to be, right?

Who else *could* it be?

Wasn't like she had a whole bunch of targets on her back.

Well, unless she included all the people who hated her father. But how would any of them know about her new name?

They wouldn't.

This had to be the work of O'Riley.

Tillie cursed the day she'd first heard his name.

She'd been warned, but she'd been cocky. Thought that it would all work out the way it was supposed to.

How very stupid and naïve she'd been.

But this wasn't something you could take back. It wasn't something that learning a lesson would magically undo.

This was her life now, and even if by some miracle she survived whatever was going to happen to her here, it didn't mean she was free and clear. Her choices would follow her for the rest of her life, whether that be a short time or a long one.

Worst of all was knowing that even if it was possible to go back in time and have a do-over she would only do the same stupid thing all over again.

Damn her too-sensitive heart.

It just couldn't stand the thought of someone hurting, she had to do something about it, even if in doing so, she got herself into hot water.

No, not hot water.

Boiling water.

Tillie was stuck in a big pot of boiling water that she was only going to splash around in and then drown.

Tears burned the backs of her eyes, and although she fought them valiantly, wanting to put on a brave front for her captor and try to convince him that she wasn't afraid and would find a way to outsmart him, they leaked out anyway.

All of a sudden, the door to her room opened, and a huge man walked through.

Man or mountain?

At the sight of him, her mouth dropped open and she stared in horror. He had to be close to seven feet tall and three hundred pounds of solid muscle. He was built like a tank and any hopes she had of escaping bled away.

There was no way she could ever hope to defeat him.

Even if she wasn't mostly naked and cuffed to a bed, she couldn't take him down. No amount of self-defense training—and she'd been taking self-defense classes for years—could overcome this kind of size difference. She just managed to clock in at five feet tall and didn't even make it to triple digits in weight.

She was a gnat to his grizzly bear.

He stood there in the doorway, lounging against the frame like he didn't have a care in the world, and eyed her for a moment. Tillie could have sworn she saw something like regret in his dark eyes, but she had to be imagining it.

While she could hope he felt guilty after delivering her here—wherever here was—she knew men like him didn't have it in them to feel guilt. The mountain of a man didn't care if he was handing her over to someone who would love nothing more than to see her suffer and then die. Most likely a long, painful death.

Didn't care if she was raped and humiliated, and would probably stand by and take his turn if he hadn't already. After all, she was nothing but a traitor to a man she had sworn no allegiance to.

All her life she had practiced showing the world a calm face, not letting them get a glimpse of the pain and insecurity she carried inside.

Never before had it been so difficult to keep hidden the absolute blinding terror she was feeling right now.

Still, she was no coward.

Gathering the courage that was the only thing that had kept her alive this long, Tillie looked back at the big man. "Who are you and why did you bring me here?" she demanded. No way was she cowering in front of him no matter how scared she was.

After a long moment with them locked in a silent battle of wills, he inclined his head once, sending a shock of black hair over his eyes. "You'll get your answers soon enough, little pixie."

With that, he turned and walked away leaving a hint of a memory tugging at her mind. Pixie. He'd called her a little pixie right before he'd administered a drug to render her unconscious. What kind of kidnapper called his victim a pixie?

And what kind of garbage answer was that?

She'd get her answers soon enough.

Who was he to determine what soon enough was?

She was the one sitting in here, chained to the bed, in her underwear, helpless and powerless to change her circumstances. He was out there, wandering around, free and no doubt pleased with the payday he'd be getting when he handed her over to Mac O'Riley. Of course, he felt no compulsion to tell her anything.

But that wasn't good enough for her.

Tillie was so absolutely sick to death of people playing with her life like she didn't even deserve to have one.

That was it.

She'd had enough.

Reached her breaking point.

"I want to know where I am," she screamed at the top of her lungs. No doubt they were someplace secluded where nobody would hear her cries for help, but she wasn't so stupid that she wasn't going to try to alert anybody close by. "I want to know who you are. I want to know who you work for. I want to know what you did to me while I was unconscious. I want to know what you're going to do to me. I want answers, and I want them now!"

If she could, she would have stamped her feet to emphasize her point, but of course, she couldn't do that because she was cuffed to the damn bed.

Anger and fear waged a desperate battle inside of her, attempting to determine who would come out on top.

In the end, it didn't really matter.

Big always beat small, her mountain of a captor was the one with all the power here and he'd use that power against her. He would rape or torture her, and then he'd hand her over to the true villain of her story, who would do so much worse.

For once she wished that the little guy could come out on top.

But wishes were like puffs of smoke, gone before they'd ever really been there, no substance, nothing really to them, certainly nothing that could change the world.

If she was going to survive, she'd need something a whole lot more than a wish.

CHAPTER Three

April 17th
2:42 A.M.

This sucked.

The quicker Tank could pass off the little blonde pixie the better.

There was something about her that he respected. No, it was more than simple respect, there was something about her that he actually liked.

Although there was a hell of a lot of respect there too.

Even though she was clearly terrified of him, she hadn't backed down. Of course, he'd noticed the tear tracks on her cheeks, and the way she'd bruised her wrist trying to yank it free from the metal cuff—clearly a pointless task, yet she'd been determined in her attempts.

When he'd entered the bedroom, she'd met his gaze squarely, and while there might have been a quiver in her voice, she had demanded answers to the dozens of questions that must be swarming inside her head. In fact, she'd continued screaming questions at him, along with a litany of threats of what she would do to him if she got her hands on him until her voice had gone hoarse.

As amused as he'd been by some of those threats, he'd respected that she hadn't let her fear get the best of her.

Tank was sure when he did tell her why she was here she was going to be none too pleased with him. And worse than that, he would actually feel bad about it.

There was no reason to. He was only doing the job he'd been given, and it was no one's fault but her own that Tallulah Russel had gotten herself into this mess. Good intentions or not, she'd gotten in way over her head, and now she had to live with those consequences.

No reason at all for him to feel bad.

Yet he was pretty sure he would.

Which was exactly why the sooner he could hand her off and go back to his team the better.

Walking through the cabin, Tank grabbed a bucket from under the kitchen sink, filled it with water, grabbed a towel, then stopped in the laundry room to collect the clothes from the dryer. When he walked back into the bedroom, he found the blonde pixie right where he'd left her, curled up against the bed's headboard.

Even with the death stare she threw his way as soon as he stepped through the bedroom door, she was a pretty thing. Long blonde locks that he already knew felt like silk. Huge turquoise eyes that were framed by some of the longest lashes he'd ever seen. She had a few freckles across her nose, giving her a sweet and innocent look.

When their gazes met, some of her bravado faded, and she shrunk away from his large, intimidating frame. Her anger and fear morphed into confusion when he tossed her the clothes and got down on his hands and knees to clean up where she'd been sick all over the floor. Tank made a mental note that sedatives made the pixie sick.

"Are these my clothes?" Tallulah asked, sounding shocked.

"You got sick all over yourself on the ride here. I threw them in the washer and dryer for you. They're done," he answered, finding himself amused by her utter confusion. It seemed it didn't matter what emotion the pixie was throwing at him, he enjoyed them all. Despite knowing who she was and the choices she'd made, there was an innocence about her that was refreshing.

Too bad she wasn't his to keep.

Not that he did long-term relationships. They weren't his thing. There were plenty of women around who would be happy to warm his bed, although mostly he took care of his needs himself.

Easier that way.

"What are you doing?"

"What does it look like?" he asked wryly, riling up the pixie was a habit he could find himself addicted to. Probably wasn't nice of him considering she'd just been snatched from her home, but she wasn't in any danger from him.

Others, yes.

But him, no.

He didn't hurt women.

"I don't understand," she said, sounding lost. He didn't like that, it made him want to make things better for her, but that wasn't his job. His job was to keep her here by any means necessary until it was time to hand her over. Hence the handcuffs.

Because if there was one thing Tank knew it was that Tallulah wasn't staying here if he asked her to.

Nope.

She'd be out the door so fast his head would spin.

"You will."

"You said that before, but I want answers now," she demanded, her voice strong again despite her obvious fear and confusion.

"Patience, little pixie."

"Stop calling me little," she growled. Yep, actually growled, and he couldn't help but quirk his lips up into a smile. Damn, she was adorable.

Too adorable.

The kind of adorable that got its hooks into you and before you knew what you were doing, you were developing feelings.

Feelings he didn't want.

He looked over at her to find that she had managed to pull her legs into her yoga pants, pull the sweatshirt over her head, and slip her free arm into it all with one hand still cuffed to the bedframe. Adorable, determined, and tough.

The trifecta of doom as far as he was concerned.

There was so much indignation on her face that he huffed an amused chuckle. No amount of indignation was going to get her what she wanted. For now, there wasn't going to be any answers, nor was she leaving here any time soon.

There was something else in her expression. The way she'd cocked her head to the side like she was trying to figure something out told him that she'd noted there was something strangely familiar about him. Not that she'd ever seen him before he'd snatched her from her new home.

"Not my fault you're a tiny little thing," he said with a shrug as he dumped the towel into the bucket of now dirty water and stood.

"Please," she begged as he walked toward the door. "Let me go. I won't tell anyone what you did. I promise."

Tank laughed outright at that.

They both knew it was a lie.

If he let her go, the first thing she would do was run straight to the cops.

Couldn't let that happen.

"Better get yourself used to the accommodations, pixie. This is going to be home for a while."

"You can't just keep me here," she shouted.

"You going to stop me?" he asked with a laugh.

"Stop laughing at me." She huffed. "There's nothing funny about kidnapping someone."

"Depends on who you kidnap."

"Is this just some joke to you?" she shouted, but it ended on half a sob. Credit where credit was due, she managed to drag in the sob before it escaped completely.

"No joke, pixie."

Her gaze narrowed, and because he saw the sob retreat further, he curled his lips into a smirk, and like he'd flipped a switch, annoyance sparked in her blue-green eyes making them look like blue flames.

"I want to go home," she insisted, but she stumbled over the word home, and he knew because he'd read her file that she didn't really have a home and never had.

"Not going anywhere, pixie," he said. Whether he thought the pixie was cute, beautiful, smart, strong, or spunky it made no difference. The ball had already been rolled, and now, unfortunately, she was paying the price for those choices.

Pulling the key from his pocket, he held it up. "Can I trust you?" he asked. "Not to run and to do exactly as I say?"

There was barely a hesitation before she nodded. "Yes."

This time Tank threw back his head and laughed. He didn't trust the pixie as far as he could throw her. "Think you're lying, pixie, and I don't like liars. I think we'll leave you right where you are until you can tell me the truth."

"You can't do this!" she screamed, wrenching her bound arm and wincing as she obviously caused herself pain.

"Might want to stop doing that, pixie. You're going to hurt yourself."

"Like you care." She huffed.

"Wasn't hired to hurt you, pixie. I'll get you an icepack for your wrist."

"I don't get you. You break into my house, drug me, bring me here, keep me chained up, and tell me you won't let me go. Yet you washed my clothes because they got dirty and cleaned the floor, and now you're offering to give me an icepack. I don't understand," she finished helplessly.

She was begging him to reassure her, give her something to hold onto, an answer that made some sort of sense.

Since he couldn't offer her any of those things, Tank slipped the key to the handcuffs back into his pocket, took his bucket, and left the room. Having some fun with the pixie while they were stuck here together was one thing, but feeling sorry for her wasn't in his job description. Fate had already dealt her a hand. What was done was done, there was no changing it, no changing what lay in Tallulah Russel's future.

He'd do well to remember that.

∼

April 17th
    1:28 P.M.

. . .

She needed to pee really bad.

Like *really* bad.

Actually, Tillie was surprised she hadn't already wet herself.

Talk about having all the motivation in the world to hold it in. If she did pee all over herself who knows what her captor might do. Just because he hadn't hurt her so far didn't mean he wouldn't. There was every chance he'd be angry with her for soiling the sheets.

Even if he wasn't, knowing Mr. Clean Freak he'd likely strip the bed and her so he could wash everything.

It was bad enough he'd seen her in her underwear, she definitely didn't want him to see her naked.

Squirming uncomfortably, Tillie tried to find a position that didn't make her arm feel like it was about to pop right out of its socket. Too many hours cuffed to the bed had her muscles cramping as well as her bladder screaming at her.

Honestly, if she pressed her thighs together any tighter, she was going to leave bruises.

Thankfully, she hadn't drunk all that much yesterday because she'd been so intent on driving out to the new house. Still, it was enough that she was pretty close to bursting.

Sooner or later her handler in the US Marshalls would realize that she was gone. If she was lucky, it would be as soon as she missed the first check-in. She was supposed to make contact later today to let them know she had made it safely to the new house.

But even if they realized something was wrong when she missed that first check-in, it would still take them days at the very least to find her. Holding on for days wasn't even inside the realm of possibilities.

Which meant she only had two options.

One, wait as long as she could until her bladder gave out and pee all over herself, risking both her captor's anger and his cleanliness.

Or two, surrender her pride and ask him if she could use the restroom.

Neither of those options sounded particularly appealing.

When the door to the bedroom opened, Tillie startled, quickly trying to pull herself together. Even though she knew that he knew she was terrified of him, she wanted to try to put on a brave face. There was no need for him to know that she found him as attractive as she did scary.

No need for her to acknowledge that fact out loud either.

Best not to think about his inky black eyes that reminded her of the night sky, or the way his muscles seemed to have their own muscles which also had their own muscles. There was something about his cocky confidence that was both infuriating and strangely attractive.

Obviously, she was having these lustful thoughts for her abductor because almost all medications made her go loopy as well as throw up.

"Finished admiring the view, pixie?"

Averting her eyes quickly and praying that he didn't notice her flaming cheeks—which, of course he would because her skin was so pale there was no way anyone couldn't notice when she was blushing—Tillie huffed. "I wasn't admiring you. You kidnapped me. What possible reason would I have to admire a single thing about you?"

"What about this?"

Even though she didn't want to engage with him in any way, shape, or form, the warm, toasty fragrance drew her attention, her nose having a mind of its own as it led her face toward the smell. Her abductor held a tray in his hands. On the tray was a plate of toasted cheese sandwiches, a glass of water, and a small vase of flowers.

This guy was some twisted kind of monster.

Flowers?

Really?

This wasn't the morning after a date. The last thing she wanted was flowers, what she wanted was to go home.

"Thought you might be hungry, and your stomach has probably settled by now."

"Like you care if I'm nauseous or not," she shot back, mostly because it looked like he did care and that was just too disconcerting to deal with.

Ignoring her snarky comment, he continued, "I know you like toasted cheese sandwiches, so that's what I made. Probably not as good as yours though."

Her mouth dropped open.

Was he kidding her right now?

"You ... you *ate* the sandwich I was making when you kidnapped me?" she spluttered. "Isn't that against the kidnapper code or something?"

More annoyingly, he laughed like they were friends just hanging out. "Good one, pixie."

"It wasn't a joke," she snapped.

Ignoring her again, he said, "Brought you some water, too. You'll be dehydrated from being sick, so we need to attend to that."

"And who's fault is that?"

"Don't think you would have said yes if I'd strolled in and asked you to come with me, pixie. Once we have you rehydrated there's soda and juice in the fridge."

"Are you my nurse or my kidnapper?" she growled. How could he be standing there chatting away to her about beverages while she was cuffed to the bed?

"I can't be both?" he teased.

"You're insane."

"Maybe," he agreed cheerfully.

"I'm not hungry," she said when he moved to set the tray on the bed beside her.

Her traitorous stomach chose that exact moment to grumble loudly, making her captor arch a dark brow. Why shouldn't her stomach call her out on her lies like this infuriating man had earlier this morning?

Why should anything go her way?

For once in her life, she'd like fate to shine a little sunshine into her world instead of constantly raining down a torrent with some thunder and lightning thrown in.

"You sound hungry," he said with a smirk.

What she wouldn't give to smack that smirk right off his face.

"Well, I'm not. I don't want anything." Tillie would much rather starve than eat anything this man prepared for her. She'd almost rather he torture her or lock her in a cage or anything other than cooking her meals he knew she'd like, preparing it on a tray with flowers, and worrying about the fact she'd gotten dehydrated from throwing up.

This was messing with her head.

Blurring the lines.

"Don't want anything, huh?" he repeated. "Not even this?" He held up a tub of her favorite ice cream. There was no way he could know that cookie dough ice cream was her favorite. He must have taken it from her freezer.

Tears blurred her vision. "Why are you doing this to me? Do you get some sort of sick pleasure out of taunting me?"

Something flitted through his eyes that she didn't understand. It kind of looked like regret, but he had nothing to regret. He'd already admitted that this was a job to him, and he was merely keeping her here until it was time to hand her off.

"No pleasure, pixie, thought you'd like the ice cream."

Thing was, she actually believed that. His expression said that he had brought it with him to be nice to her.

What did she make of that?

He wasn't her friend. Not even close. He worked for Mac O'Riley, as soon as things died down no doubt he would hand her over to him. It was smart of O'Riley to hire someone to get her, it meant when the US Marshals investigated her disappearance, he could honestly say he didn't have her.

"Actions have consequences, pixie."

Well, she couldn't argue with that.

It was her own naivete and stubbornness that had gotten her into this predicament.

There was no time to worry about it, her bladder was screeching now and she couldn't ignore it any longer.

Time to suck up her pride.

"May I please use the restroom?" she bit out through gritted teeth.

Amusement sparked in the man's eyes. "Sure thing, pixie. I'll go with you."

Tillie froze. "What do you mean?"

"I mean, I'm not uncuffing you and letting you go in there by yourself. You think I'm stupid as well as handsome, pixie?"

Throwing her best glare at him, she straightened as much as she could. "I never said I thought you were handsome."

"You do though," he goaded. "But it's up to you, pixie. You can either go with me or you can go right in the bed. My vote is you go to the bathroom with me, save me having to wash all the sheets and your clothes again."

The heat in his eyes told her that he found her attractive, but so far he hadn't done anything about it.

She didn't want that to change.

"I can't pee with someone listening," she protested, praying he'd take mercy on her. As busting as she was right now, she'd even promise not to try to run and mean it.

"Then I'll go check I have plenty of laundry powder."

When he turned to walk away, Tillie knew she just had to do it and get it over with. "Wait."

"Yes, pixie?" he said, turning slowly, the smirk back on his face.

"Fine."

"Fine what?"

"I'll go to the bathroom with you," she growled. He just had to make this as humiliating as he could for her, didn't he.

"Knew you would, pixie."

"Stop calling me that." It was a stupid nickname, and she didn't look like a pixie at all.

One of his large hands curled around her wrist, and she noted that he seemed to take care not to touch the bruises she'd gotten from fighting against the metal cuff. His grip was tight enough that she couldn't pull free but not tight enough to hurt, as he uncuffed the end from the bedframe and snapped it around his own wrist.

"Your throne room awaits, pixie."

"I really hate you."

Her obnoxious captor just threw back his head and laughed like she was the funniest thing he'd ever heard.

Yep, she hated him.

Absolutely hated him.

CHAPTER

Four

April 17th
   2:42 A.M.

Tank was pretty sure this was going to be as hard for him as it was for Tallulah.

Being attracted to the pixie was a bad idea.

A *really* bad idea.

This wasn't a date, and it wasn't a vacation, this was work. She was a job, one that wasn't supposed to involve him taunting her because he knew when she was annoyed with him, she wasn't thinking about how scared she was. Fire danced in her eyes every time he got her riled up, and he much preferred it to the stark terror that told him she knew she was about to be paying for her sins.

Not that they really were sins.

Tallulah Russel's only sin was being too naïve. Thinking she could go up against a well-known crime boss and come out on top.

Unfortunately, she'd learned the hard way that good intentions didn't always equal a good outcome.

Not only had she not achieved what she set out to, but she'd thrown herself into hot water.

The kind of hot water that got you killed.

There was no way she would believe him if he told her right now that his job was to make sure she *didn't* get herself killed. Letting her go on believing that he was the bad guy might seem cruel, but it was necessary if he wanted to keep her alive. The pixie was the kind of woman who, if she knew how big the danger swirling around her actually was, she'd do something stupid like try to toss herself into the middle of it to fight for her causes.

She had a lot to learn about how the world worked.

More than she should given her family history.

But it was that very spark of determination to go up against an enemy she had no chance of beating because it was the right thing to do that drew him to her. She was sassy and spunky, she didn't let her fear control her, and she was the most beautiful woman he'd ever laid eyes on, but she wasn't his.

Was never going to be his.

Playing with her, keeping her distracted, that was one thing, but he had to be careful not to let it go beyond that. When she learned the truth, the pixie was really going to hate him.

Besides, it wasn't like anything real or lasting was going to happen between them. The pixie had too much on her plate, and he had been turned off from letting anyone get too close when he was forced to listen to his parents be horribly tortured and murdered.

Shutting off the cabin lights, Tank sent a quick text to Eagle to let him know that everything was still quiet, then one to Axe to ask if there was any improvement with Beth. They all kept hoping that she would just snap out of it and her memories would all come back, but so far, that hadn't happened.

If anything, she was getting worse.

With no memories of her husband, the compound, or any of Bravo Team, she didn't feel safe there. It was no longer her home.

Watching the people you loved suffering was worse than suffering yourself. It left you feeling helpless.

Helplessness was a feeling Tank avoided at all costs.

Ever since he was eleven and his parents were murdered. Those hours had been pure hell on Earth, and something he never wanted to repeat, and yet here he was again, watching the people he loves suffering with no way to make it stop.

After a last check of the locks and the surveillance system, he headed for the bedroom.

When he opened the door, the pixie turned to look at him. There was the usual fear he was used to seeing, along with her anger. Making her use the restroom cuffed to him might have been mean, but if he hadn't done it, she would have tried to escape.

Safehouses were safe but they weren't infallible.

Especially when the man you were hiding from had a lot of resources.

Along with the fear and anger was a hint of hopefulness, and Tank didn't bother to hide his smirk because he knew exactly what she'd been hoping for.

"Told you when I brought you dinner, and you refused it that the kitchen was closed for the night," he said as he went to the window and closed the blinds.

"I don't want anything you cooked anyway." She huffed with a haughtiness that made him laugh. The pixie had obviously learned young never to let anyone think they had a leg up over you. Anything someone could use against you would be used against you in the pixie's mind, and Tank couldn't say he disagreed with her thinking.

"No? Going to lie and tell me you're not hungry?"

Another huff, this one sending a lock of blonde hair puffing up. Her hair was so long, so silky soft, and he couldn't help but think about what it would feel like wrapped around his hand as he pounded into her from behind.

Totally inappropriate so he quickly shoved the thoughts away.

"Just so you know, I ate all the ice cream."

"*My* ice cream," she fumed. "I bought it for myself, as a treat, because it's my favorite and I needed something good. But no, why should I have any pleasure in my life."

There was pain in her words that ran a whole lot deeper than a tub of cookie dough ice cream.

Now he felt bad for eating it.

It had been good, too, and he didn't usually like cookie dough, but that brand had been delicious.

"What are you doing?" Tallulah asked in a strangled voice when he grabbed the hem of his T-shirt and pulled it up over his head.

"What does it look like, pixie?"

"It looks like you're undressing."

"Knew you were a smart one," he teased. There hadn't been fear in the pixie's voice over the idea of him undressing. If anything, there had been heat there. Wasn't like he didn't know that she found him physically attractive, but he also knew that he was in a position of power here and he didn't intend to abuse it.

"Why are you undressing?"

"Getting ready for bed."

"You're ... sleeping ... in here?" she asked, sounding positively horrified by the notion.

"Only the one bedroom in the cabin, pixie."

"But ... but ... you can't ... I ... are you going to ...?"

"I'm going to sleep, pixie," he assured her.

When he unzipped his jeans and let them fall down his legs, the pixie let out a strangled gasp, and he fought a smile. Seemed like his pixie was a bit of a prude. Kind of made her more appealing, he wanted to peel away her layers until he found the real Tallulah, the fiery beast she'd be beneath the barriers she used to protect herself.

"What are you doing now?" she shrieked when he shoved his boxers down, letting them join his jeans on the floor.

"Pretty sure that's obvious, pixie."

"You're naked," she squeaked like she'd never seen a naked man before. Given that she was thirty and attractive he doubted she was a virgin. Was she just this freaked out because of the situation or was the sight of a naked man that unsettling to her?

"Hot sleeper," he said as a way of explanation.

"But you can't ... sleep in here naked."

"Pretty sure I can, pixie." Stalking over to the bed, Tank hid a smile as he watched her gaze travel across his chiseled chest, over his six-pack, and linger on his length. It took some effort to make sure he didn't grow hard, he didn't want to freak his pixie out.

She was still staring at him in open-mouthed shock as he unlocked the end of the handcuff attached to the bed and snapped it around his own wrist.

The sound of the cuff closing drew her attention.

"What are you doing?" she demanded.

"Making sure I get some sleep. I don't want to be worrying about you trying to escape all night. Thought this would be more comfortable than you being cuffed to the bed, but if you'd rather ...?"

There was indecision in her gaze, but she didn't ask him to cuff her back to the bed, so he stretched out, bringing Tallulah down the bed with him. Snaking an arm around her shoulders and settling her against his chest seemed like the most natural thing in the world.

At least to him.

Tallulah's breathing accelerated, and he could feel her heart rapping out a panicked rhythm in her chest.

"Sleep, pixie," he murmured as he placed their hands that were cuffed together on his chest where it would be comfortable for her.

It took a long time for the pixie to relax enough to go to sleep, even longer for him to push away the sense of peace holding this sassy woman in his arms out of his mind for him to join her in slumberland.

~

April 18th
    8:22 A.M.

"You can't do this."

"You going to stop me, pixie?"

Tillie growled. "Would you *stop* calling me pixie?! It's a ridiculous name. I do not look like a pixie, it is not an appropriate name for a kidnapper to call his victim, and it makes me sound like I'm four years old."

"Definitely don't think you're four years old ... pixie," her ridiculously annoying abductor said with a smirk.

Damn, he was an irritating mix of arrogant, infuriating, and dangerously sexy when he smirked like that.

It never failed to make her want to smack it right off his face as it was her least favorite expression, but she couldn't deny he was sinfully sexy when he looked at her like that. There was a spark of amusement in his eyes. He knew he was getting to her, and he loved it, not what she expected from a man holding her captive.

Which was what made him so dangerous.

He was attempting to lull her into a false sense of security.

Tillie knew that, but it was damn hard to resist softening toward him when he teased her and acted goofy.

They weren't friends, he wasn't on her side, he was an enemy. She had to keep her wits about her and let him think he was getting to her so that he would lower his guard. Easier said than done since his act *was* getting to her.

Lowering her defenses was only going to wind up with her getting hurt. Sooner or later, he'd grow tired of playing with her and move on to torturing her in a more painful way. That or it would be time for him to hand her over to Mac O'Riley. Once that happened the arrogant, smirking man mountain cuffing himself to her while she slept would seem like a walk in the park compared to what O'Riley would put her through.

Maybe she could encourage the man—who refused to tell her his name—to keep her as long as possible. Delaying her fate wasn't going to stop it from coming, but at least it would put it off for a while longer.

The desire in his eyes as he looked at her confirmed what she already knew. He was attracted to her. Each heated glance he threw her way all but screamed it, but so far, he hadn't done anything about it and she was so very grateful.

Just because she found him physically attractive didn't mean she wanted him to touch her.

Nothing changed the fact that he had drugged and kidnapped her, and she hated him.

"So, what's your decision, yes or no?" he asked, tapping his toes on the floor as though impatient for her to make her choice, but from the amused glint in his pitch-black eyes, she knew he was just toying with her. Again.

"Why are you being so stubborn?"

"I'm not the stubborn one, pixie."

"I can't shower with you in the bathroom with me." Tillie might not be a virgin, but she hadn't had a lot of boyfriends, and the ones she'd had left when they learned who she was related to. Doing intimate things like showering with a boyfriend in the room was totally different than doing it with a stranger who had abducted her, listening and watching.

"You said that about peeing and sleeping in the bed with me," he reminded her with another of those obnoxious smirks. "Seems to me you managed to do both just fine. Should give yourself more credit, pixie."

Shooting him her best glower, it was ruined when her stomach made a loud growling grumble.

Her abductor snickered. "And who's calling who stubborn? You're the one who refused to eat lunch or dinner yesterday, simply on principle, even though you're clearly starving."

What could she say to that?

That was absolutely what she had done.

Eating the sandwich he'd made because he knew she liked it and then cooking her homemade mashed potatoes and fried chicken felt too intimate.

So, she'd refused.

Because she hadn't wanted to accept any kindness from him given what he had done—was doing—to her.

Petty.

Given her situation, it was stupid and petty. Keeping up her strength should be a whole lot more important than her pride and feeling uncomfortable accepting anything from him. If he was stupid enough to keep her strength up by feeding her, then she should run with it, because first chance she got she was getting out of here.

"Fine," she huffed, somewhat ungratefully considering he didn't have to offer her a shower. Keeping her fed was one thing, Mac O'Riley wanted her alive, but he certainly didn't need her clean.

"Wasn't so hard now, was it?" he asked cheerfully as he uncuffed her from the bed and snapped the cuff around his own wrist. That cheerfulness always sounded so genuine. What kind of mercenary, or bounty hunter, or whatever his job title was, was he?

Since there was no good comeback to that, she pursed her lips together as he walked much too fast for her smaller legs to keep up with, toward the bathroom.

Honestly, this man couldn't be more annoying if he tried.

His cheerfulness continued when they entered the bathroom. "There's shampoo and conditioner in the shower, body wash, too, and a new loofah. Clean towels, too, for when you're done."

"Umm, thanks," she said, uncomfortable again. It made zero sense for him to be this nice to her. She kept waiting for the catch.

There was *always* a catch.

"You're welcome."

Tillie rolled her eyes, but the sight of the huge, tiled walk-in shower was too enticing for her to stay mad for long. It wasn't a big deal in the scheme of things, but a shower would do wonders for her morale.

"Strip, pixie."

Although it was inappropriate, the blatant sexuality in his words, backed by the fire in his dark eyes, did something to her insides.

Made them go soft somehow.

Total Stockholm Syndrome.

"Turn your back," she ordered, but her voice was shaky, not really a command.

Still, he complied, and she quickly shimmied out of her leggings and sweater, tossing the pants and her panties on the floor, the sweater hung from the cuffs binding her to her kidnapper.

"Going to turn around now, pixie," he said, his voice low and deep, rumbling over her and making her skin break out in a mass of goosebumps.

"But I'm naked," she protested weakly.

"Gotta cuff you to the shower rail."

"Then I won't be able to wash properly.

"You'll make do. Can't have my pixie flying away now, can I?"

She wasn't the one with the power in this situation, so all she could do was angle her body away from him as best as she could and cover the apex of her thighs with her free hand.

To his credit, her captor had his eyes closed when he turned, unlocking the cuff with ease and closing it around the shower rail.

Then he walked over to the counter and jumped up on it, lounging against the wall, eyes still closed.

"Go ahead, pixie, enjoy your shower."

Yeah.

Like she was going to enjoy it with him sitting there.

Best to pretend he didn't even exist.

Turning on the water, she got it as hot as she could bear and then stood under it for what had to be a solid five minutes. It felt so good, so normal, and for a moment she was able to pretend she wasn't being held prisoner and about to be handed over to a dangerous crime boss.

The shampoo and conditioner were the ones she'd had with her at her new house, he must have brought them along, too, and it was kind of nice to have something of hers here. Awkward as it was one-handed, Tillie washed and conditioned her hair, and then grabbed the loofah and squirted on a generous amount of body wash. No telling when he'd let her shower again.

"Enjoying yourself, pixie?"

Tillie hummed her pleasure as she ran the loofah across her chest. "Oh, yeah." Deciding to give him a taste of his own medicine, she added, "Cleaning my breasts right now, and it feels amazing."

"I bet it does," he agreed. She was sure he was watching her, but when she peeked out at him, his eyes were still closed. "Your skin's petal soft, isn't it, pixie? Like silk. Bet your nipples are sensitive, aren't they? Would they pebble as I brush my calloused fingertips over them?"

She pressed her legs together as a rush of heat pooled low in her stomach.

Oh, yeah, they would.

Not that she was going to tell him that.

This erotic game they were playing was dangerous.

For her anyway.

He could force her if he wanted to, and she couldn't stop it from happening, and even though she didn't want to have sex with him, her body responded to his voice, his words, his touch. It wanted him even if her mind didn't.

"Bet I'd make you feel better than any other man ever has," he said, his voice still pure seduction and so arrogant it was like he had a doctorate on the subject.

"You're an arrogant pig, you know that?"

He tossed his head back and laughed like she was some big joke.

Tears pricked her eyes. She was sick of being a joke. Neither what she'd lived through as a child nor what she was going through now was funny.

She didn't deserve this.

Then again, life didn't care what you deserved, it expected you to just take what it gave you.

CHAPTER *Five*

April 18th
6:03 P.M.

"Can't we just ...?"

"Nope."

"But I didn't even ask yet so how can you say no?"

"I know what you're going to ask, pixie."

"Well, I think since you kidnapped me and brought me here against my will, you could at least have the decency to let me finish my questions," she snapped with all the haughtiness of a queen over her subjects.

"Ever going to stop throwing that in my face, pixie?" he teased. Tank *did* feel bad about how this situation had to be handled, but the priority was keeping Tallulah alive. She was important to a whole lot of people, and if he didn't play this one the way Eagle wanted, she might not live long enough to do what they needed her to do.

The pixie arched a brow. "Would you?"

What he would have done was kill anyone who was stupid enough to attempt to abduct him. Since the pixie didn't have the same skill set he did, that wasn't an option for her. So, no, if he were in her shoes, he wouldn't stop throwing in his abductor's face that they'd taken her against her will.

"Okay, pixie, ask your question." He knew what she was going to ask, a variant of the same question she'd been asking all day, but he indulged her anyway.

Despite the fact the look she gave screamed suspicious, she asked her question. "Can't you just unlock the handcuffs while we cook dinner?"

"Nope."

"But it's impossible to cook joined together like this." She held up her cuffed hand and jiggled it.

"We were doing okay before you stopped to complain." When he'd asked her what she wanted to eat, she'd said spaghetti and meatballs. They'd already chopped the onion and garlic, then mixed them with the ground beef, breadcrumbs, milk, egg, and parmesan. They'd argued over how much salt and pepper—he wanted a lot, her just a little—and what herbs to use—him oregano, her parsley. She had won both arguments, but now she was back to begging him to uncuff her hand from his.

"I can't roll the meatballs while we're joined together. Your arm is like a tree trunk, it weighs a ton."

That made him chuckle. "Sounds like a compliment, pixie. Trying to butter me up?"

His joke earned him an eye roll. "There's no way I could make it out of the cabin without you stopping me. You're bigger, you're stronger, you're—"

"Smarter," he inserted with a grin, garnering another eye roll.

"If there's no way for me to run then there's no point in keeping yourself cuffed to me."

"Maybe I like being cuffed to you, pixie. Ever think of that?"

"Would you be serious for just a moment?" she snapped. "My life isn't a joke."

"Never thought, or implied, it was."

"Yet you're playing games with it as though it were."

That was a sensitive issue for her. It wasn't the first time she'd mentioned her life not being a joke. Given what he knew about her infamous father, and the documentaries, movies, books, and TV shows about what he had done, it wasn't surprising that she felt she wasn't taken seriously.

As much as he wanted to make her time here as comfortable as possible, there were some things he couldn't compromise on.

This was one of them.

"I've been more lenient with you than I needed to be. Didn't have to clean your clothes, didn't have to let you use the bathroom, didn't have to let you take a shower, didn't have to give you the privacy of not watching you shower, and I didn't have to let you come and hang out in the kitchen so close to the knives."

From the guilty look she shot the knife she'd been using earlier to chop the onion, Tank knew she had considered using it on him.

"I've gone above and beyond, and if I hear you ask again to be uncuffed, I'll put you back in the bedroom and leave you there. Do I make myself clear?" Tank hardened his voice, reminding her with his tone that he wasn't a man to be messed with. Just because he'd taken pity on the pixie and allowed her more freedom than she deserved and gone out of his way to make sure her stay here with him was as pleasant as it could be, even doing his best to ease her fear, he was still the one in charge.

Tallulah gulped and gave a small nod, her body shrinking away from his even as she remained cuffed and at his side.

Now that he had her put back in her place, Tank softened his voice. "Now, I'm sure we can figure out how to roll the meatballs without it feeling like you're pulling a tree trunk along with you."

A small smile curled up her lips, and she gave another nod. "I *guess* we could make it work, but I don't know how."

Turning her so she was facing the wooden countertop, Tank moved in behind her. With their joined hands in front of her, he made sure he stretched his much longer arms so that the pixie was comfortable. Also allowed her to use both of her hands to roll the meatballs with relative ease.

"How's that?" he asked, his breath stirring her hair as he dipped his head until his lips were close enough to her neck that he could touch kisses to the slender column.

When she trembled slightly, Tank knew it was because she was affected by his nearness. Flirting with her wasn't fair. Her life was about to go through another major upheaval, and he had no intention of crossing the line from flirting to acting on his attraction to the alluring pixie, but he couldn't seem to help himself.

Damn temptress, that's what she was.

And she wasn't even trying to get to him.

Well, nothing other than her too-cute attempt at ruffling him by mentioning her breasts. He'd turned that one around on her real quick. Wasn't hard to do when just the thought of touching those delectable breasts of hers had him growing hard.

"Umm, yeah, I guess I can make it work," she said nervously.

"Course you can. How about I help." Scooping up some of the meat, Tank set it in the pixie's left hand—the one cuffed to his—then used his free hand to hold her left wrist. When Tallulah sucked in a breath as his large hand gently circled her wrist, he whispered against her ear. "Just helping, pixie. Eliminating the tree trunk problem."

Her hand shook as she lifted it, pressing the meat between both her palms. As he helped her roll it into a ball, Tank allowed his fingertips to caress the sensitive skin on the inside of her wrist.

With each meatball they rolled, the pixie's breathing increased, and she began to squirm. With each wriggle of her tight little backside against his groin, Tank grew harder. Because part of him liked the idea of the pixie being attracted to him—okay, so he was every bit as arrogant as she accused him of being—and he didn't want to move her out of the blissfulness of being turned on to fear that he was going to take things further than she was comfortable with, Tank shifted away from her.

Since they were joined together, she turned as he did until they faced one another. Tallulah's gaze was fixed firmly on his chest, her own rose and fell with each pant of air she took.

Slowly, that gaze lifted till her turquoise eyes looked into his.

Light and dark.

While it was true they had both lived through dark childhoods, she had come out of hers with a lightness to her that most people wouldn't be able to understand. On the other hand, he had come out every bit as dark as one would expect of a child who had lived through what he and his brother had.

Something passed between them.

There was still major distrust on the pixie's part, well-deserved mistrust since he hadn't told her anything, but there was also a heavy amount of attraction.

Her brain might be ordering her to stay away from him, but her hormones were telling her the opposite.

Would she let him kiss her?

Chances were, if he tried, he'd end up with a pixie-sized red hand-print mark on his cheek. Again, totally deserved.

Still, the desire dancing in her blue-green eyes told him she'd kiss him back before her brain overrode her hormones, and she delivered that slap.

"Pixie?"

The tip of her tongue darted out to run along her bottom lip. "Yeah?"

"We better put the meatballs in the oven and get the spaghetti cooking before your stomach starts grumbling again." His pixie would never believe it, but he was one of the good guys, and he wasn't going to take advantage of Tallulah even if she let him.

~

April 19th
2:36 A.M.

Red.

It was her favorite color.

The color of a heart.

Tillie liked hearts. She wanted someone to love her.

Her daddy didn't love her. If he did, he wouldn't scare her all the time by screaming and hitting Mommy.

Mommy didn't love her either, because if she did, she'd take them both away from Daddy.

Lots of times she'd asked Mommy if they could leave while Daddy was at work, but Mommy always said no. Mommy said it was too dangerous, but Tillie didn't know what that meant.

What she did know was her house was scary and she didn't like it.

Now she didn't like red anymore either.

There was too much red in her house.

It was all over the floors and walls.

All over her mommy.

All over her daddy, too.

All over the houses on her street.

Too much red.

It wasn't her favorite color anymore.

She wanted it to go away.

But instead of going away, there was more and more.

Too much.

Make it stop.

Daddy, stop.

Please stop.

Stop.

Stop.

STOP!

"Pixie."

The hard voice calling her name in a command even her subconscious seemed to know to obey, snapped her awake because there was only one person who called her pixie, and he wasn't there the day it was red.

"Pixie, open your eyes for me. Now."

Open her eyes?

No way.

The last thing she wanted was to see more red.

"Wake up, pixie. Now. Damn it. Tallulah, wake up."

Tallulah?

Only her daddy called her that.

Was he here?

Panic flooded her system.

Her daddy was big, and she was small, but she fought with everything that she had. She didn't want her daddy to make her red like all the others.

Fighting was pointless when Daddy was so big, and she was pulled up against something hard, her arms pinned by her side, and held immobile as she sobbed for her life.

"Please, Daddy, please, don't kill me. Please, Daddy, I'll be a good girl, I promise. I won't be bad like Mommy. Don't hurt me, Daddy," she sobbed and pleaded, begging with everything she had as her chest heaved and her breath caught.

Something shifted her, and she felt like she was floating. Then she was tucked against something so warm she couldn't not burrow into its heat. She was so cold, her entire body shivering violently now as it felt like she had been encased in ice.

"Damn, pixie, hurry up and come back to me," a voice whispered against the top of her head. She could feel warm breath, the steady thumping of a heartbeat, and miles of smooth, hard muscle.

Her abductor.

All of a sudden, everything came slamming back into focus, and she choked on another sob. Escaping one nightmare only to wind up trapped in another didn't seem fair.

"You with me again, pixie?" her captor asked as he shifted, and a moment later, covered her in the soft blanket that had been on the bed.

Talking was beyond her at the moment so she simply gave a nod and did her best to get her crying under control. It was mortifying enough to know she'd shown such an enormous weakness in front of a man who would use it against her. The last thing she wanted to do was sob in his arms as he held her on his ...

Lap?

Seriously?

He had her cradled on his lap, the blanket tucked around both of them. One of his large hands cradled her cheek, his fingers gently caressing the back of her head. His other arm was wrapped tightly around her, not in a constricting way but as though he were trying to anchor her to him so she had something to hold onto through the storm of her nightmares and the resulting terror.

Their hands that were cuffed together rested on her lap, and he had entwined their fingers, again offering her a buoy to hold onto as her emotions raged around her.

It was sweet and confusing, and yet instead of pulling away, she sank deeper into his hold.

"You okay, pixie?" he asked a few minutes later.

"Yeah," she whispered.

"One hell of a nightmare."

"Not the first time I've had it." It had been a recurring one ever since she was three years old, and her life went from regular old abusive family to worldwide news story. "Sorry for waking you."

A chuckle rumbled through his chest. "Not worried about the lack of sleep, pixie, I've gone weeks with less than this a night. I'm worried about you."

"Worried about me?" she echoed. How could he be worried about her when he'd abducted her? That very clearly screamed that he cared nothing about her or her feelings.

"Sounded like you were living through hell."

"I was," she murmured. Her very own personal version of hell. One she lived through again and again at least once a month.

"Nightmare about what your dad did?" he asked quietly.

Tillie froze.

Every cell in her body went haywire at someone actually bringing that up to her face.

Sure, people talked about her behind her back all the time. Tallulah Russel, daughter of the infamous Frank Russel, she was probably carrying around her father's evil genes. After all, he hadn't killed her along with everyone else and there had to be a reason for that.

There was, but it had nothing to do with her father sparing her life because she was going to become his protégé.

"I ... umm ... why ... it's ..."

"It's okay, pixie," he soothed. "Might help to talk about it. Don't think you've done a whole lot of that."

"Never had anyone to talk to," she admitted. No one wanted to get close to the girl whose father went on a murderous killing spree lasting six hours and leaving almost three dozen innocent people dead.

"You have me."

She was about to scoff about how she absolutely didn't have him, but there was a seriousness in his tone that stopped her. "I ... don't remember that night."

"Then what was the nightmare about?" he asked, sounding confused.

"Red."

"Red?"

"All I remember."

"Red the blood?" he asked gently.

Tillie nodded. "All I remember from that night is red. Everywhere. Over everything. So much red. Cops tried everything to get me to give them a statement about what my dad did. They acted like I was deliberately keeping it from them, but I was *three*. Three years old. A baby. I didn't tell them anything because I couldn't. All I could see was the red."

"They had no right to be treating you that way."

A small smile curled her lips up at the indignation in his tone. "It's okay, I'm used to it. Been that way all my life. I never really stood a chance."

"Don't say that." The vehemence in his tone shook her. "You have made something of yourself. You graduated high school, went to college, got a job helping other kids in the system. What you've done matters, *you* matter. You're more than your father and what he did."

The reality of his words sank in slowly.

While she actually did appreciate his vote of confidence, she realized that he didn't just know about Mac O'Riley but every single thing there was to know about her.

"Y-you know who I am? I mean all of me. Not just why you kidnapped me."

"Of course I do. Never take on a job without knowing everything there is to know about the target."

Job.

Right.

For a moment she'd forgotten she was his prisoner. This wasn't a safe place, he wasn't a friend to confide in. Just because he'd been sweet when he'd woken her from the nightmare didn't mean he cared about her, it was just another way to mess with her head.

When she went to pull away, move off his lap, and put some distance between them, he tightened his hold, keeping her right in place.

"Not yet, pixie," he whispered, tucking her close again.

Since she couldn't fight him off, she had no choice but to stay right where she was.

Right where she didn't want to be.

The longer she spent trapped here at the cabin with this man, the more he started to feel like an ally of sorts instead of the man who would one day soon hand her over to someone who wanted nothing more than to punish her for attempting to interfere in his illegal business dealings.

"Name?" she asked.

"Hmm?"

"What's your name? You know absolutely everything there is to know about me and all I know about you is you took a job to find me, kidnap me, and give me to O'Riley. I deserve something. Give me your name at least."

After a long moment of silence, he replied, "Tank."

"Tank?"

"What everyone who knows me calls me."

Tank. How appropriate. The man had certainly barreled into her life like a tank leaving her battered and broken in his wake.

CHAPTER Six

April 19th
11:41 A.M.

"You are a cheater."

Tank grinned at the pixie who was pouting adorably. "You're just a sore loser."

"How is it losing when you keep cheating?" she sputtered as mad as a honeybee whose hive you disturbed.

"Six games in a row now I've won, pixie. That makes the score six to zero," he taunted because she was too cute not to. Their unusual relationship was confusing him every bit as much as it was her, and he was both looking forward to and dreading Eagle calling to say it was time to make the exchange.

Life hadn't been fair to the pixie, but the saying was true, if you played with fire you were going to get burned, and Tallulah had gotten herself good and burned.

"You haven't won a single game without cheating. Using the hand cuffed to mine every time I try to remove a piece from the tower to bump me so I knock it down doesn't mean you won and I lost. Just means you can't play fair."

"Never claimed to play fair, pixie." Tank had noticed yesterday that she no longer corrected him when he called her pixie and complained about the nickname. She seemed to have accepted it in the same way she had accepted her fate.

Didn't mean the pixie wouldn't do whatever she could to escape if he gave her half a chance. At heart, she was a fighter who'd had to fight harder than most to get to where she was. But she also knew she had no one to blame but herself for the mess she found herself mired in.

Good intentions were one thing, but to try to take on a man like Mac O'Riley yourself was pure suicide.

Just because she wouldn't believe it didn't change the fact that he was the only thing standing between her and death.

"You're impossible." She huffed.

"So, you don't want to play another game of Jenga, pixie?"

"No, of course I don't want to play another game of Jenga with a cheater," she snapped.

"We are cuffed together you know. There's no reason you couldn't have given me a taste of my own medicine," he teased.

Another huff. "You know I *did* try. But your arms are like tree trunks, and you have shockingly steady hands."

Tank laughed. In his business a steady hand was the difference between life and death. Of course, he could hold steady while the pixie who had arms like twigs was trying to pull on her end of the cuff and make him shake and knock down the tower.

"Want to play a different game then if you're too cowardly to go up against me again in Jenga?" he asked. Since the cabin was regularly used as a safehouse, it was well stocked with games, books, and a bunch of other stuff to keep people busy. He'd chosen Jenga specifically because he knew he'd have fun annoying the pixie by making her knock down the tower.

Anything to wipe away the haunted gleam that had been in her eyes ever since her nightmare.

He'd about had a heart attack when he felt her fist collide with his stomach that first time, sure someone had somehow managed to breach the security system and get inside the cabin. When he realized that it was in fact the pixie who had hit him, his heart rate hadn't slowed.

It was obvious she was trapped in the grips of a nightmare, and it had taken him a solid three minutes to snap her out of it. Her pitiful whimpers, pleading with her father not to kill her along with everyone else had reminded him so much of his little brother's whispered pleas that night when their parents had saved their lives, and paid the ultimate price for doing so.

By the time he finally woke her, he wasn't sure who was more shaken, him or her.

Holding her and comforting her had been as natural to him as breathing, and in the end, she had been the one to pull away not him.

If he was going to do the right thing he really should call Eagle, explain that things had gotten complicated and he was developing feelings for the little blonde pixie, but he was selfish. The thought of one of his teammates coming and spending time with Tallulah sparked a horrible fire of jealousy inside him.

Didn't seem to matter how many times he told himself not to fall for her, he couldn't seem to help himself.

"Come on," he cajoled when she looked at him skeptically. "What about hangman? I can't cheat at that." Actually, he was sure he could figure out a way to cheat at any game, but he wasn't about to tell Tallulah that.

"Well ..." From her expression it was obvious she was trying to figure out what kind of trick he was going to play on her next.

"You chicken, pixie?"

"I'm not chicken, I just don't know if I want to waste the next hour with you behaving like a child and cheating just so you can count up how many times you beat someone at a silly kids' game." The eye roll she gave was epic and made him grin. This woman was way more fun to tease than his teammates. Taunting them meant major payback was on the way, but with the pixie all he was going to get were adorable pouts and eye rolls.

"Sounds to me like you're chicken," he drawled as he reached for the pad of paper and a pen on the table beside where they'd set up Jenga.

"Fine," she huffed. "But if you cheat, I'm not playing any more games with you, and I don't care how much begging you do."

Yep, that sent a jolt of heat straight to his groin.

If these were any other circumstances, she'd be the one begging, and they wouldn't be at the kitchen table they'd be in the bedroom, however, there would be a whole lot of eating going on.

"One thing you should know about me, pixie, I don't beg. Got no problem with someone begging me though." When he threw in a wink, Tallulah's cheeks went bright red and she dropped her gaze to the table, but he noticed the pink tip of her tongue dart out, sweeping across her bottom lip like it had the day before when he'd almost kissed her. His pixie was definitely attracted to him, and Tank knew without a shadow of a doubt if they ever did fall into bed together it would be explosive.

Not going to happen.

Better keep reminding himself of that.

Tallulah cleared her throat. "Hmm, right, okay, well I guess we can play hangman. Do you want to choose a word first or me?"

"I always go first, pixie." Unless it was in the bedroom. Then the woman always came first. Several times.

"Course you do." She gave him one of her eye rolls, and he was grinning as he drew four little lines one beside the other. "A four-letter word?" There was that suspicion in her eyes again. "Tell me you're not so immature that you picked something crass?"

"Crass, nah, definitely too mature for that." True too. He hadn't chosen a crass word, but he had chosen something of a fun nature. By fun he definitely meant sexual.

"Sure you are."

"What's your first guess? Remember you only get ten, then I win."

"Is winning all you care about?"

Actually, it wasn't.

Unless it was a mission, and that was because the stakes were high enough that a loss meant a dangerous person was still free to perpetuate their crimes.

"A."

"Going with the easy guess first, not a risk taker, huh, pixie. Nope, no a."

"E."

He snickered at her sensible, logical approach to the game. "Nope."

"I."

"Ah, got one." He wrote in the letter on the second line.

"I still get eight misses and only three letters left to guess," Tallulah said, the haunted look in her eyes gone, and he was glad his teasing and poking at her had helped to wipe away the horrors she'd survived. Having to relive the most horrific moments of your life in your dreams was the most horrible of tortures. Every day your body needed sleep, so every single day you were leaving yourself vulnerable, with no way to stop the dreams when they came.

"Still think I'm going to win."

"We'll see about that. Mmm, S?"

Her play-it-safe strategy was working out. "Yep, two Ss." He put them in on the third and fourth lines.

Tallulah studied the word for a moment then narrowed her eyes. "You wouldn't, would you?"

"Wouldn't what, pixie?" he asked even as he knew exactly what she was asking.

"K?"

"Ding, ding, ding, ding, ding. We have a winner." Adding the K to the first line he grinned at her. She was staring at his lips, an almost hesitant look on her face.

"Why did you choose that word?" she asked, never lifting her gaze.

"Why not?"

"To mess with my head? Confuse me? Play with me?"

"No, pixie. I wouldn't do that."

Finally, she lifted her eyes to meet his, a vulnerability in them he was surprised she let him see. "Then why?"

"Because I can't stop thinking about kissing you."

~

April 19th
   12:02 P.M.

. . .

Kiss.

That was the word he'd chosen.

Tillie thought he would have chosen some military word, or the name of some weapon, or something she would never guess. There wasn't a doubt in her mind after spending the last few days with him that Tank was some former military turned mercenary. There were so many things he could have chosen that she could simply never get because she didn't know they existed.

Yet he'd chosen none of those.

Kiss.

A simple word but one with so much meaning behind it.

Maybe meaning she could exploit?

He'd said that he couldn't stop thinking about kissing her. Could she use that to her advantage? Maybe if she let him think that she was thinking about kissing him, too, she could convince him to uncuff her.

All she needed was one chance, and she'd find a way out of here.

But what if she had to take it beyond talk?

Could she seduce a man?

It was a good cause. The best. The difference between life and death. But even knowing that, Tillie was hardly a sex siren who was experienced in seducing men. Having some experience with men was not at all the same as knowing how to go about seducing a man like this who had to be so much more experienced than she was.

A man like this probably had a different woman in his bed every night.

Hundreds of them.

Maybe even thousands.

No way he was going to be fooled by her no doubt clumsy attempts at convincing him that she wanted sex with him.

Not even the fact that there was the very smallest, tiniest, most minuscule part of her that *did* want to have sex with him.

Tillie hated herself for it, knew it was because he had been messing with her head by plying her with kindness while simultaneously holding her prisoner.

Shame didn't change that almost carnal desire he stirred up inside her. She might not want those feelings, but they were there nonetheless, and if she made it out of this alive, it would take time to convince herself she hadn't been so insanely stupid as to develop any sort of feelings for her captor.

Turning her hand, the one that was cuffed to Tank's, Tillie traced circles on his palm with the pad of a fingertip. "What would you say if I tell you I keep thinking about the same thing?" she asked, attempting to make her voice seductive but not sure she sounded anything more than nervous and uncertain.

"Hmm, that right, pixie?" Tank's voice, on the other hand, was absolute pure sex.

No way her body couldn't respond.

"Yes," she answered breathily, now sounding more into the idea than she had before, but it had nothing to do with her plan and everything to do with the need he seemed to bring out in her. Needs she'd never had before. Sex with her previous boyfriends has been nice, good even, but never had just a steamy look made her feel so turned on.

"Good to know because I don't think I can wait another second to do this?"

"Do wh—" her question cut off on a squawk as Tank somehow managed to maneuver her out of her chair and onto his lap. His hand that was cuffed to hers rested on her hip, and with the position of the handcuffs, her own hand wound up resting between her legs. Spread as they were as he had her straddling his massive thighs, she could feel her own heat and the wetness soaking through her panties and yoga pants.

Damn her body for doing this to her.

Damn Tank for making her feel like this when she wanted to hate him with every fiber of her being.

Instead, he had her body craving him even as her mind hated him for what he'd done.

"This is what you want, isn't it, pixie?" he asked as his other hand curled around the back of her head, his long fingers tangling in her hair.

A throbbing started up between her legs as her body tossed a dozen images of what those fingers would feel like stroking deep inside her into her mind.

Squeezing her eyes shut in an attempt to block them out wound up backfiring.

Without her eyes, her other senses seemed to grow brighter.

Tillie could hear her uneven breathing and the tightness of Tank's that told her he was holding back. What he was holding back was no doubt frantic, almost desperate kisses, and a whole lot of touching that would definitely involve a lot less clothing than they were currently wearing. The scent of her arousal permeated the room. Draped as she was across his lap, she could feel his impressive length pressed hard against her center, and when it twitched, a needy pulsing pounded through her body. Beneath her palm, his rock-hard pec quivered as his muscles bunched.

Every one of her nerves felt alive, stimulated even by this minor touching, and she wondered how she would even survive sex with this man who was just too much.

And she wasn't talking about her mind.

Or her sanity.

She was talking about her heart.

It was too soft, too big sometimes. The reason she was in this mess to begin with. She was always looking for the good in people even when she was warned that there was none to find.

Now she was trying to do that with this man.

Trying to see him as more than just her kidnapper, as a real person who likely had pain in his past that dictated who he had become as an adult just as she did.

It was so very stupid, but she didn't know how to be anyone but herself.

While Tallulah Russel had plenty of issues, there were parts of herself she liked, and topping that list was her big heart. It proved to her in those moments when doubts that she would turn out to be like her father that everyone else was wrong, that *she* was wrong, because she could never do what he had done.

"Tell me no, pixie." Tank's rough voice drew her out of her own mind, and her eyes fluttered open to meet his intense stare.

Everything about this man was intense.

Too much.

Way too much for her to handle.

She liked peace, quiet, and simple things. She didn't do well with intensity or anything too strong, and this man was all power and strength. More than she could cope with.

Still, the word no didn't form on her lips or even in her mind.

Instead, she just held that deep, black stare.

This game she'd started with hopes of seducing him into uncuffing her and giving her a chance at escape had morphed into something that was all too real.

It was real desire burning through her veins.

Real need to feel his lips pressed against hers.

A real wonder of what it would be like to make love to this man, to feel the fullness she knew he could give her, the strength of the pleasure he would bring her.

When she didn't offer him the response he had asked for, Tank moved in slowly, giving her plenty of time to pull back, to change her mind, to tell him to let her go, that kissing was a ridiculous idea given their current situation.

She did none of those things.

Just waited with excited anticipation.

That moment when his lips finally met hers was as explosive as she had known it would be.

Like the alpha that he was, Tank took immediate control of the kiss, plundering her mouth and filling her body with fire. A good kind of fire, cleansing somehow. Like a forest fire that cleared away the old and brought with it regrowth.

A part of her she hadn't even known existed sprung to life.

For the first time, she felt like her.

Just her.

Not the daughter of the notorious killer who had beaten his wife to death then proceeded to walk from house to house killing the neighbors, dragging his three-year-old along with him.

No one who knew who she was ever just saw her for her.

Not until this man.

She might be a job to him, but he had still managed to see the real Tallulah Russel.

Abruptly Tank pulled back, taking with him the passion, the fire that he'd given her.

Tillie moaned a protest. It was like drowning only to be pulled up long enough to take one beautiful, precious breath of fresh air, to be free, then to be shoved right back down again.

Unfair.

One more unfair moment to be added to the litany that littered her life.

"Shouldn't have let me do that, pixie," Tank growled as he shoved her off his lap.

Before she even knew what was happening, he had the cuff on his wrist unlocked and snapped onto the back of the heavy wooden chair she'd been sitting on while they played games.

Then he was storming out of the room, leaving her staring open-mouthed and in shock at his retreating back.

What had just happened?

How had she let it happen?

And why did she want it to happen again more than she wanted her next breath of air?

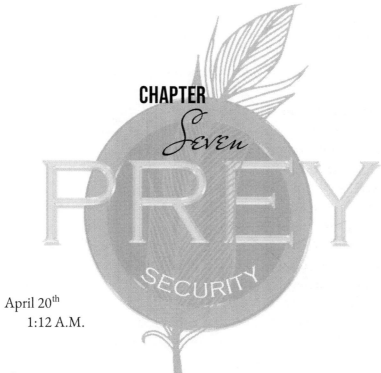

CHAPTER *Seven*

April 20th
   1:12 A.M.

Shame.

Tank had never felt shame like this before.

In his career in Delta Force, he'd done things, horrible things to other people in the name of protecting his country and its people. Same with his work at Prey. Some of the things the job required of him weren't pleasant, but they were a part of the life he had chosen so there was no point in complaining about it.

But he'd never done something he was ashamed of.

What he'd done had always been done in the best interests of his country and those he cared about.

Not this though.

Kissing Tallulah had been a mistake and one he couldn't blame on the job.

On the contrary, Eagle would be disappointed in him to know he'd kissed the woman he was supposed to be keeping alive. Not only was it completely unprofessional and inappropriate, but it could potentially have compromised the mission. If he was distracted making out with the pixie, he wasn't keeping a proper watch on their surroundings.

Just because they were on day four of hiding out at the cabin there was every chance that their location was known. Mac O'Riley was well known for being careful and logical, taking his time, not being emotional, and making smart decisions. One of the reasons he was such a successful mob boss.

That wasn't the only reason Eagle would be disappointed in him making a move on Tallulah.

It had also been taking advantage.

They weren't equals in this situation. He was the one with all the power. There was a lot the pixie still didn't know, didn't understand, and she believed she was being held here in preparation for being handed over to a man she had tried to ruin. A man who wanted nothing more than to destroy her for what she had tried to do even if her motives had been pure.

As much as he'd like to make excuses for his behavior, pat himself on the head and say that she'd wanted that kiss as much as he had, Tank knew there were no excuses to be made.

He'd taken advantage of her and used his position of power to his benefit. Choosing kiss as his word for hangman had been to unsettle her and push her because he was driving himself crazy with how badly he wanted her.

It had seemed like a risk-free idea.

There was no way the pixie would allow him to kiss her.

But then she had.

A ploy on her part, he knew that. Reading her was like reading an open book. She couldn't lie to save her own life, and he'd known when he admitted—truthfully—that he couldn't stop thinking about kissing her that it would throw her.

She thought she had found a way to get an edge, a bit of leverage, something to use against him to even out the playing field just a little bit.

That was when he should have stopped. When he knew that she would willingly offer up her body for a chance at freedom.

Not even a guarantee because she had to know Mac O'Riley would never give up until he had her head on a platter.

That wasn't what he wanted for her. She shouldn't have to prostitute herself just for a chance at living.

Yet wasn't that what he'd made her do?

That kiss had been real from his side, but she'd just been playing along, hoping that she might be able to earn a way out.

It wasn't until that had finally clicked that he'd put a stop to the kiss.

After that, he hadn't been able to face her.

Couldn't stand to see the fear, the loathing, the hatred in her eyes.

How could she not hate him after what he'd done to her?

When she'd said those words to him a couple of days ago, he knew she meant it in a general sense. She hated him because he'd kidnapped her, because he was holding her prisoner, because he kept goading her with his arrogance, she would have hated whoever had been in his position.

Now she had reason to hate him specifically, and that ... hurt.

It upset him in a way it shouldn't given their roles here and the way her future was going to play out.

Despite the late hour, he hadn't yet made it to bed and wouldn't make it to bed. No way he was going into the bedroom after he'd put the pixie in there after dinner. They hadn't exchanged a word since he'd ended the kiss and walked away from her, and if he could help it, they wouldn't exchange another.

They didn't have to talk while he held her here. All he had to do was keep her alive.

Picking up his phone, he punched in Rock's number with more force than necessary. It might be one in the morning, but the man rarely slept. Rock had issues he refused to talk about. A woman from his past he couldn't move on from. One who continued to haunt him, mostly in the early hours of the morning when the world was dark and quiet, leaving you alone with your thoughts.

Thoughts that merely taunted you with all the mistakes you had made.

"Problem?" Rock asked as soon as he answered.

"No. All quiet here. Just wanted to check in and find out how Beth is doing." Tank wasn't ready to tell anyone how monumentally stupid he'd been and that there might be blowback on him, Bravo team, and Prey as a whole when this was all over.

Rock's sigh was deep and full of pain. "No change. She doesn't remember anything. Axe has been trying to show her things from their lives, but she wants no part of it. Poor thing is completely terrified out of her mind and just keeps mumbling about how she has to fight to live. Damn it." Through the phone came the sound of Rock clearly hitting something. "I wish we knew what that meant, but she doesn't remember a damn thing about all those months she was gone. Nothing, man, she doesn't remember anything. Watching her huddle in a corner of the bed because everything is confusing and terrifying to her is hell. It's heartbreaking."

This was where his focus should be right now.

On his family, the people who needed him, not on a woman he was attracted to but who would soon cease to exist.

"I wish I was there," he told his friend. There was nothing he could do. There was no way he could magic Beth's memories back, nor was there any meaningful comfort he could offer Axe who was going through hell right alongside his wife, but at least he'd be there.

Being here when his team was going through something so traumatic not only felt wrong but left him with a sense of helplessness he despised.

Whether or not it would do any good was irrelevant. He wanted to be there, and he hated that Eagle had assigned him this mission when someone else could have handled what amounted to babysitting.

"Nothing you could do here to make it better, brother," Rock said.

"Doesn't change anything."

"Yeah, I get that. So, how's your thing going?" Rock asked.

"It's going," he answered vaguely, hoping he didn't sound like there was a whole lot more going on here than there should be.

"Yeah, that answer's not going to fly."

"What do you mean?"

"A simple text would have sufficed if all you wanted to do was check in on Bethie. You knew if she'd gotten her memory back one of us would have let you know first thing, she's family to all of us. You called for another reason, so spill."

Why had he thought calling Rock was a good idea?

Although pining after a lost love, the man was sharp as a tack and never let anything get by him.

Stalling wouldn't work, Rock was undistractable. The man was seriously like a rock, an enormous bolder who couldn't be moved once he made his mind up about something. Whoever the woman from his past was, she had better look out because when Rock decided it was time for him to make his move, no way was she going to be able to resist when the man went all out to win her back.

"I may have done something that wasn't part of the job description," he admitted.

"You slept with her?" Rock sounded shocked by the idea.

"No. It didn't go that far and it won't, but I did kiss her."

"Kiss her like you felt it was important for your role or because you wanted to?"

"You really have to ask?" None of them used sex as a weapon to keep someone in line, or to get intel from a suspect.

"Sorry, man, I'm just surprised. That's not you at all."

"Tell me about it. I avoid women like her at all costs. Got nothing to offer them."

"Be careful, yeah, man? She doesn't know who you are or why you're really there, once she does, she's probably never going to forgive you."

"Think I don't know that? When the pixie finds out the truth, she'll hate me for real." And the worst part was he cared that she'd hate him.

∼

April 20th
   4:53 A.M.

Fuming.

Tillie was raging mad.

So angry she couldn't even calm down enough to go to sleep.

Okay, so some of that anger was directed at herself for her monumental stupidity, but the majority of it was aimed squarely at Tank.

How dare he.

Wasn't it bad enough that he'd kidnapped her, drugged her, and brought her here? Kept her chained up the entire time, messed with her head, mocked her, flirted with her, only to then kiss her and storm off, basically becoming the invisible man.

After cuffing her to the chair and leaving the room, she'd only seen him three times since then and none of those times had he uttered a single word. He'd taken her to the bathroom and cuffed her to the pipes where she only just had enough movement to do her business, awkward as it was with one arm virtually unusable. Then he'd taken her back, cuffed her to the chair, and given her a sandwich for lunch.

Dinner time he'd repeated the process, a bathroom break, and then a sandwich and glass of water. Looked like the homecooked comfort meals were a thing of the past and now he intended to treat her like the prisoner that she was.

Hadn't made a difference how much she'd railed at him for kissing her and then treating her that way, how many times she begged to be let go, how many times she'd pleaded to at least have the cuffs removed. She had even asked him to at least tell her why he'd kissed her and then acted like he hated her right afterward.

Not that he'd given her an answer or shown her any mercy.

Now she was back in the bed where she had woken that first day, cuffed and uncomfortable, cold, hungry, dirty, confused, angry, and hopeless.

Reality was definitely settling in.

There was nothing to distract her now from the horrors awaiting her as soon as Tank handed her over to Mac O'Riley. Before when Tank had been around, taunting her and occupying all her time with his craziness, it had been easy to forget.

While he was around, she hadn't had the time to obsess over what was coming, but now he was gone and ...

All there was to do was fume about his treatment of her and get more and more afraid of how the last few hours, days, weeks, or however long O'Riley kept her alive would play out.

Tucking herself tighter into a little ball, Tillie stopped trying to fight back the tears. Why bother? There was no one to see them, and Tank couldn't use them against her and make her feel any worse than he already had.

Lost in thought as she was, she startled when the bedroom door opened. She hadn't expected to see Tank again until the sun rose, and he came to get her up, no doubt to give her a bathroom break and breakfast, then leave her alone, cuffed to the chair, until lunchtime.

There was nothing she wanted to say to him, so she merely watched as he walked toward her.

No longer did his presence provide some sort of warped comfort. While she didn't believe he would physically hurt her, what he'd done already—twisting her mind and emotions by playing with her—had hurt her worse than anything else because she had to put some of the blame on herself.

She hadn't been a completely helpless victim, she had played a part in her own demise.

That cut deep.

Tank didn't speak a word as he reached out and uncuffed her from the bed. Guess they were getting an earlier start to the day than she had anticipated.

Because she was so hurt and angry it took a moment to sink in.

He hadn't uncuffed the side of the handcuff that was attached to the bedframe. Instead, he'd removed the side attached to her wrist.

Freeing her.

Her gaze flew to his, only to find he wasn't looking directly at her.

Too many thoughts and emotions bombarded her at once, and it was hard to focus on any one thing.

Run.

Fight.

Move.

The words flitted through her head like butterflies on a summer's day. Even as she knew that just because he had uncuffed her didn't mean he was letting her go, and if she tried to escape, she knew he would stop her, even if that required the use of force.

"Go take a shower," he said gruffly, his voice harder, colder than it had been these last few days.

"A sh-shower? Why?"

"An apology for earlier."

That didn't ring true, but she wasn't going to argue. That very first day, right here in the bedroom, Tank had asked her if he could trust her.

Of course, she had told him he could even though they had both known it was a lie.

It was still a lie.

There was no way she was going to let this opportunity pass her by.

Since she no longer quite trusted Tank—all right, well, she never had completely, but she had allowed her guard to lower—she stuck close to the walls, as far as she could get from him as she inched her way to the bathroom.

He stood silently watching her until she was inside before disappearing from the bedroom. As soon as he was gone, Tillie slammed the bathroom door closed. There was no lock, but she didn't have time to worry about that.

First thing she did was turn on the shower so he would think that's where she was, then she searched the room for a weapon. Every other time she'd been allowed in here, Tank had stayed, so she hadn't had a chance to check it out properly beyond doing her business or taking the one shower he'd allowed her.

When she came up empty, she turned her attention to the small window above the toilet. It would be a tight fit, but Tillie thought she could make it.

Good thing she was small.

Pixie.

That's what Tank usually called her.

It made zero sense.

Why would he bother giving her a nickname when he intended to hand her over to O'Riley?

A lot of what Tank had done didn't really make any sense. He was a walking contradiction, but she had no time to attempt to figure him out.

As she climbed onto the toilet and eased the window open, she could have sworn that she heard another door close.

The cabin's front door?

Had Tank left?

Why would he do that?

He had to know she was going to try to escape.

Footsteps crunched over gravel and she heard a car engine start. He *was* leaving.

Relief hit her hard. She had no idea why he would leave her here alone nor was she going to waste time thinking about it.

It was still dark out, and she could see trees surrounding the cabin. If she could just make it to those trees, then she stood a chance. Cover like that meant it would be harder for him to find her when he came back to discover her gone.

Shoving the window as far open as it would go, she swung a leg up and over the sill and carefully squeezed herself through.

Elation flooded through her system as her feet hit the ground, adrenaline, too. They were in a forest somewhere, she had no idea where or how long it had taken them to get here since he'd drugged her, but she didn't care. However far she had to go to find freedom, she would go.

Tillie took off running, her bare feet stung as they flew over sticks and stones, but she didn't slow down. She couldn't, not if she wanted to live.

She hadn't gone far when a large shadow appeared in front of her. She had no time to change direction, to stop, or even to scream before he was on her. Yanked up against that same rock-hard chest she had actually begun to daydream about, she knew fighting was futile but she did it anyway.

A hand clamped over her mouth, and she was shaken. Not roughly exactly, just enough for him to get her attention.

"Stop fighting, little pixie. I'm not going to hurt you."

Helplessness hit hard, tears blurring her vision. So close. She had been so close to making it out of here and now she was trapped all over again. Tank kept saying he wasn't going to hurt her, and yet he'd kidnapped her, drugged her, and held her against her will, with plans to hand her over to a man he knew wanted to torture and kill her. If he really wasn't going to hurt her, he never would have abducted her. Why wouldn't he just let her go?

As though he'd heard the question even though she hadn't spoken it aloud, he inclined his head at the cabin she'd just fled and the men currently slinking through the dark toward it. "Because of them. Because I'm the only thing standing between you and certain death at the hands of Mac O'Riley."

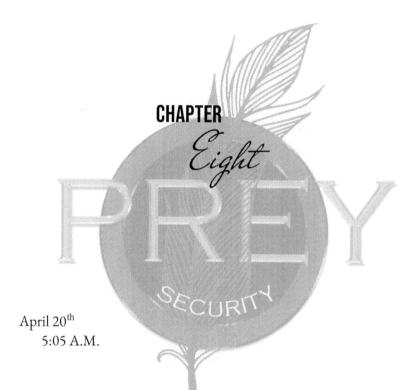

CHAPTER
Eight

April 20th
5:05 A.M.

Looked like the little pixie was going to get her answers sooner than he had anticipated.

Of course, Tank had known she was going to run, he'd been counting on it in fact. Because when someone tripped the security system, the quickest way of getting her out of the cabin without raising suspicion if someone was watching them was to let her do it herself.

The pixie sagged in his hold, and he slowly released her, ready to grab her if she was playing him. While he didn't want to hurt her, his priority was keeping her alive, and if he had to tackle her and leave behind a few bruises, then he'd do it because at least she would still be breathing.

But when he released her all Tallulah did was turn and look up at him.

"You really weren't ever going to hurt me, were you? It's why you washed my clothes and cleaned up after me. Why you cooked for me and let me take a shower. Why you kept being so arrogant and obnoxious, taunting me. You were trying to keep me distracted so I didn't have time to dwell on how scared I was."

Tank nodded.

"I'm sorry. I didn't believe you when you said you wouldn't hurt me," she whispered, dropping her gaze to the ground.

Hooking his forefinger beneath her chin, he nudged until she met his gaze again. "You've got nothing to be sorry about, pixie. There were things I couldn't tell you because I knew how you would react. You'd go running right back to the very place that was going to put you in danger."

"I wouldn't have done anything stupid." She huffed in typically pixie style.

He grinned and huffed a chuckle. "Yeah, you would have, pixie. If I told you what was going on you would have gone right back to witness protection."

Her brow furrowed. "Why shouldn't I do that?"

"Because there's a mole at the US Marshals. You remember Agent Dawson?" When she nodded, he continued, "He's my brother. When he realized that someone had compromised your new identity, and that Mac O'Riley had put a hit out on you, he reached out to me. I work for a group that protects people like you who are in danger. If I'd walked into your house and told you all of this, you wouldn't have believed me. Even if you did, if your house was being watched by a merc and you just walked out with me, they would have known something was up. I had to pose as one of the bounty hunters out to get the money for turning you over to O'Riley."

Tillie's large blue eyes looked almost eerie in the predawn light. He could see her struggling to take all of this in and no doubt regretting her decision to go to the cops with what she had witnessed that night.

But there was no going back. Not for Tillie and not for him. He was in this till he knew for certain she was safe, there was something he didn't understand compelling him to protect her.

"If you'd told me at the cabin who your brother was, I would have listened to you."

A wry grin tugged at the corners of his mouth. "No, you wouldn't, pixie. You would have wanted to go right to the Marshals and try to help them figure out who the mole was." From the stubborn tilt of her chin, he knew he was right. Tenderly, he reached out to smooth a stray lock of soft blonde hair off her cheek, tucking it behind her ear. "Not your job to do that, pixie. Your big heart is going to get you killed one day."

"I don't like other people getting hurt," she murmured.

With her past and the things she'd witnessed as a child, he understood that. While her conscious mind might not remember that night, her subconscious one did, he'd seen those memories play out in her nightmares.

But now wasn't the time for her to play hero.

"I know that, pixie, but sometimes life just happens. You can't keep putting yourself in danger to make up for sins that aren't yours."

Pain flashed in her eyes, but as he watched she shoved it away with a deliberateness that would make a Delta Force operator proud. "Wh-what do we do now?" she asked, with just a tiny tremor in her voice.

Again, the pixie's strength amazed him. She had been through so much, and even though she kept getting knocked down she always bounced right back up again. "For now, all you do is trust me. Is that something you can do?"

It was hard for her, he could see that. Trust wasn't something she could easily hand out, not given how her father had betrayed hers in such epic fashion. But his pixie was a tough one, smart too, and she gave a slow nod.

The gift of her trust meant more to him than it should, and while Tank knew he didn't deserve it, he was going to treasure it, nonetheless.

"Need you to hide, pixie. Up there." He nodded to the tops of the trees above them.

Tallulah gulped. "Up there?"

"Yep."

"Umm ... Tank ... there's something you should know?"

"What's that, pixie?" Casting a glance at the cabin, he saw movement as the men realized it was empty and came outside to no doubt start searching the forest for them. The bounty on Tallulah's head was high enough that any mercenary in the area would be looking to cash in, be the one to find her and deliver her to O'Riley. If it hadn't been for his little brother finding the leak from the Marshals, then the pixie would likely already be in the crime boss' hands.

"I'm afraid of heights."

As much as he wanted to take the time to reassure her, cajole her into doing what he knew she was entirely capable of doing, he didn't have the time.

"You got this, pixie. Use those wings." With that, he grabbed her hips, hoisted her up, and onto one of the lower branches of the nearest tree.

"Tank, I ..."

"You got this," he interrupted. Time was up. If they stayed here and debated it any longer the mercs would find them.

Although he heard her huff, she bravely hoisted herself up onto the next branch and began to make her way up into the treetop.

He prayed it was enough.

Four men, that was how many he'd counted entering the cabin. Taking four men wasn't hard unless they were highly trained. While most mercenaries and bounty hunters had some military or law enforcement training, that didn't mean they were as highly skilled as he was. There was no way to know until he was already engaged.

Even if these four weren't highly skilled, there could be more nearby. No amount of skill in the world could overcome the odds once they got too high.

Trusting Tallulah to keep herself safe and out of sight, Tank slipped away into the shadows. The early hour was working in his favor. It was still too dark for them to be able to see into the forest well, but since they hadn't yet left the small clearing where the cabin sat, he could see them perfectly from the dim light spilling from the building.

The four broke into pairs, and the first was heading right in his direction.

Perfect.

A huge tree trunk provided cover, and Tank hid behind it and waited.

While they moved quietly, the mercs didn't move silently, and he knew exactly when they were approaching.

As soon as the first passed him, he palmed the handle of his knife and prepared to pounce. The second came along a moment later, scanning the area as he went. Dressed all in black as he was, Tank knew he blended into the early morning forest and the man never stood a chance.

One slice of his blade was all it took, and the second of the two men was bleeding out from a cut carotid artery.

Letting the body fall silently to the ground, Tank moved stealthily toward the first guy who had no idea his partner had just been slaughtered.

Luck wasn't always on your side.

Right as he was reaching out to make the kill strike, the man turned, a question dying on his lips as he found Tank standing there instead of his partner.

It only took seconds.

The man screamed and lifted his weapon, alerting his friends to his location.

Tank buried the blade of his K-Bar into the man's neck before he could get off a shot.

That took care of only one problem.

There was no way the other two mercs hadn't heard their friend's shout. They knew where he was, and he was still much too close to Tallulah for his liking.

Which meant he was going hunting. Tank just prayed his pixie didn't spook and stayed right where she was, tucked safely in the treetops.

~

April 20th
    5:19 A.M.

Gunshots.

The sound came out of nowhere, startling her, and she almost lost her grip on the branch she was clinging to with every ounce of strength she possessed.

Tank had asked her to trust him, and she wanted to.

Badly.

Trust wasn't something that came easily for her though. It had to be earned. Had Tank earned her trust?

Now that Tillie knew who he was, she could see the resemblance to Agent Dawson. Agent Dawson had been good to her, kind, thoughtful, compassionate, and he'd gone out of his way to make a terrifying experience as smooth and easy as it could be. She had liked the man, respected him, and he had managed to earn her trust.

Was that another point in Tank's favor?

He, too, had been kind to her when he didn't have to be. His job might have been different from the one she'd first thought, he was here to keep her safe not hand her over to the man who wanted to kill her, but it was a job, nonetheless. There would have been nothing in the job description about cleaning up after her, playing games with her to distract her, and cooking for her. He had done those things because he wanted to.

Because he cared.

A tiny flicker of doubt wavered inside her.

What if he was lying?

What if he was playing her?

What if the men in the cabin were cops come to rescue her from him and he was intent on taking her to O'Riley?

Despite all the what-ifs running through her mind, her gut said he was exactly who he'd said he was. He had taken her for the reasons he'd told her and was currently putting his life on the line for her.

Which had her praying desperately that he hadn't been the one who was shot.

It wasn't just for selfish reasons either. Sure, if he'd been killed she was basically a sitting duck. Even if they didn't search the treetops right away, eventually, they would do a complete and thorough search of the area and find her. If she could even stay up here that long. It was April, early spring, the weather still cold, and she had no food or water, plus sooner or later she'd need to pee.

Without Tank her life was already O'Riley's, but just the idea of him being hurt, or worse killed, left her with a weird, empty feeling inside.

They weren't friends, didn't really know one another, and he'd been lying to her the entire time they'd known one another, but there were also moments that they had shared that felt real. Whether it was just him playing her to keep her in line, make her easier to manage, or they really had been genuine, she couldn't know for sure, but it didn't matter.

Either way she wanted him to be okay.

Crazy as it was, she liked the huge man. Yes, she was attracted to him, but she also felt some sort of kinship she couldn't explain.

Be okay, Tank. Please. Be okay.

Tillie had no idea how long she clung to the trunk of the tree repeating that over and over like some sort of mantra that possessed the ability to protect her.

With each second that ticked by, her fear grew.

Tank must be dead.

If he wasn't he'd be back by now. He was some sort of military man, or former military probably since he said he worked for a group that protected people like her who were in trouble. He knew what he was doing, he'd seemed confident when he left, his hands were steady, his voice didn't shake, and it was like just another day at the office for him.

There was no way those men could take him.

Please let that be true.

Movement close by had her stiffening. Her entire body grew so taut her muscles felt completely tight.

What should she do?

All it would take was one look up and she'd be spotted. Fighting against her fear of heights, she'd climbed as high up as she could get. No one would see her if they were just strolling through the forest, but someone actively looking for her ... they definitely could.

Her lungs tried to expand and contract much too fast, and before she knew it, she was on the verge of hyperventilating.

The panting breaths were not only much too loud considering she was supposed to be hiding, but the lack of oxygen was also making her head spin.

Great.

Not only was she going to give away her hiding spot, but she was going to fall right out of the tree.

Injure herself *and* place herself right at the feet of the men who would take her to a monster.

A monster with a grudge.

Because she had been naïve enough to believe that the truth would prevail.

How she could be that stupid after living through what she had Tillie had no excuse. Her whole life had been an example of how the truth never mattered. People believed what they wanted to believe regardless of whether they were right or wrong.

Limbs shaking, head spinning, breath sawing in and out of her chest, she knew that whoever had been walking past had spotted her because she could hear their voice.

Deciphering the words was beyond her right now as everything that had happened over the last few days crashed down on her all at once.

It was over.

Death was hovering just behind her.

Close enough for her to feel its cold touch.

"Pixie, get your cute little butt down here now."

The words finally penetrated the haze of terror that trapped her in a thick fog, clearing that fog away like the sunshine, and she lifted her head from where it had been resting against the rough bark of the trunk.

"T-Tank?"

"Who else would be wasting their time calling out to you, pixie?" he said, that light teasing tone of his voice pulling a half laugh half sob out of her.

"You're not dead."

"Sorry to ruin your dream, pixie, but you're stuck with me for a little longer."

How could he make jokes at a time like this?

She'd been terrified that he'd been killed, and she was about to be taken to Mac O'Riley to be tortured and murdered, and here he was making jokes like they were back in the cabin playing Jenga or hangman.

"Those men ... are they ... dead?"

"You kidding me, pixie? You think if they weren't, I'd lead them right to you? I'm highly offended."

Tank didn't sound offended, he sounded like he was amusing himself.

Of course he was.

Damn arrogant man.

"Going to make me wait all day, pixie, or are you coming down? Thought you were afraid of heights."

As though reminding her fear that it existed, she made the mistake of glancing down and quickly squeezed her eyes closed. "Why did you say that?" she moaned.

"Come on, pixie. Don't be a baby. You got up so you can get down."

"What would you know? You're not afraid of anything."

"Everyone is afraid of something, pixie," he said, but the lightness was gone from his voice, and she wondered what fears haunted his nightmares.

Slowly, she uncurled her fingers from their death grip on the branch. "If I fall, will you catch me?"

"Every time, pixie."

The confidence in his voice lifted her own. Never in her life had she met a man bigger, stronger, and more capable than Tank.

If anyone really could catch her if she fell, it was absolutely this man.

With more caution than she knew Tank would have used, he would have shimmied up here like he was some sort of monkey or something. No. Not a monkey, he was too big, too powerful, more like a tiger.

Tillie had climbed up higher than she realized and going back down was a whole lot harder. As she moved, she was very aware of Tank watching her every move, it was comforting in a way. There had never been anyone to take care of her before, it had always been her looking out for herself.

Even as a small child, her mom had been too busy trying to avoid beatings from her husband to spend much time looking after her daughter. Then after her father's killing spree, foster parents had treated her like she had been the murderer instead of a traumatized toddler.

If she fell, there had never been anyone there to catch her.

Until now.

Until Tank.

While she knew he meant he'd only be there to catch her every time until they found the mole at the US Marshals and Mac O'Riley was no longer a threat, it was still nice to have someone watching her back.

Something she could get used to.

Something she would have to be careful *not* to get used to.

Tillie reached for a branch only to have it snap as soon as her weight was balanced on it, sending her plummeting toward the ground.

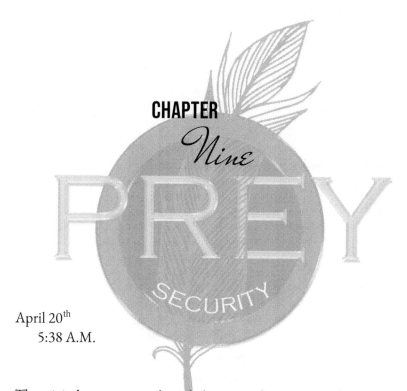

CHAPTER

Nine

April 20th
5:38 A.M.

The pixie better not make a habit out of causing his heart to about hammer its way right out of his chest.

One second she was climbing down with way more care than was necessary, but was understandable given her fear of heights, the next she was plummeting down a whole lot faster than she'd planned.

Although he was sure it didn't feel like it to her, she wasn't all that far up by then, maybe fifteen feet off the ground. Given his over six-foot tall frame, it was only a bit over a seven-foot drop until she reached him, not enough time for her to pick up much speed in her descent.

With a startled squawk, she landed in his arms, and he tightened his hold, not so much because he was afraid of dropping her, not even because he thought she would try to escape his hold as quickly as she could, but because he'd been afraid for her.

Not in the couple of seconds it had taken her to fall into his arms, but when he'd left her alone, knowing there was a chance one or more of the mercs would find her before he could eliminate them all.

Just because all four of them were now deceased didn't mean that they were safe.

On the contrary, now it was common knowledge where Tallulah was. Soon this place would be crawling with mercenaries and bounty hunters, all eager and willing to do whatever it took to be the one to capture her and deliver her for the payout. The mercs who'd found them had disabled his vehicle, and while he could fix it, it would take time. Time they didn't have. Using the mercenaries' discarded vehicle was also out because it could too easily be tracked.

That meant they were going to have to hike out of there.

Usually, he wouldn't mind that, but this wasn't a relaxing stroll through the forest, they'd be hunted the entire time.

"You caught me," Tallulah whispered, obviously shocked.

"Told you I would, pixie." At least after his parents' murders he and his brother had each other. Tallulah had nothing and nobody. Just herself. How lonely an existence that must have been. A terrifying one too. Nobody to turn to, nobody to watch her back, nobody to catch her when she inevitably slipped and stumbled.

Irrational as it was, hearing the surprise and wonder in her voice had him wanting to be that person for her all the time. Show her what it was like to have someone you could count on whenever you needed them, and when you thought you didn't.

But keeping the pixie wasn't in his job description.

Sooner rather than later he was going to have to let her go.

"Thank you." With her hands on his shoulders, she leaned in and brushed her lips across his before pulling back, uncertainty in her turquoise eyes.

If she thought one tiny, chaste kiss was enough to satisfy him she was crazy.

Supporting her weight with one arm, his other palmed the back of her head and pulled her close again, crushing his mouth to hers in a kiss that barely satisfied his insatiable need.

He wanted more.

Wanted to touch and taste every single inch of her delectable silky-soft skin.

Bury himself inside her so deep that he imprinted himself on her body and her soul, so that she could never forget him once he was gone.

Tallulah's fingers curled into his T-shirt, holding onto him as he plundered her mouth. Damn she tasted sweet. Like sugar and honey and syrup all mixed together.

It was an intoxicating combination, and he wondered how he was going to walk away from her when this was done and over.

His pixie would never be free, her choices would follow her for the rest of her life. He had enough demons chasing him and his team, did he want to add to their burden? With everything going on with Axe and Beth, was it fair for him to ask his team to take on the pixie's problems as well?

None of that seemed to matter as her tongue met his, dueled, and he tried to get enough of her to last a lifetime.

By the time his brain kicked back into gear, and he realized that standing here making out with the delectable pixie was using up time they didn't have a lot of to put as much distance between themselves and the men who would soon be coming for them, they were both breathing hard.

"That was ..." Tallulah trailed off, desire evident in her gaze.

"Something I'd love to take further but we have to get out of here." If she gave him even half an indication that she wanted more than just kisses, he was going to take her as many times as she'd let him in every way he could conceive.

"More men are going to come for me, aren't they?" she asked. Like a bucket of ice water had been dumped over her head, that spark in her eyes went out, and she slumped against him.

No use in lying to her, she knew the stakes when she'd started this in motion. "They are."

"They're never going to stop, are they? Not even if O'Riley winds up in prison. If he does, he'll still be able to pay off someone to kill me. He won't care that he doesn't get to end my life himself as long as I pay for what I did to him."

The desolation in her tone, the hopelessness and helplessness, stirred up every protective instinct he had until all he wanted to do was hunt down Mac O'Riley himself and kill the man with his bare hands. Since that option wasn't on the table, he merely nodded in confirmation.

"I didn't even *do* anything," Tallulah said, a mixture of anger and frustration in her voice.

"I know, pixie."

"I tried to help. I did the right thing. I couldn't pretend that I didn't see what I did, that would have been wrong."

"Don't need to convince me of that, pixie." While this mess was one of her own making, the pixie had been trying to do the right thing. The problem wasn't with her, it was with society. Money, more often than not, overruled what was right.

"He has a son. It was my job to investigate the claims of abuse. I had to go in, had to report what the boy told me." The desperation in her tone stirred up the heart he thought he had long since shut up against the world.

The pixie had done everything she could, ignored the warnings of her boss not to proceed with the case, and stayed strong even when she witnessed the maid who had made the initial report of abuse being tortured and murdered.

Now though, it was her life on the line, and Tank found he hated everyone involved in the whole mess who hadn't forced the pixie to back off and keep herself safe.

Didn't she know her own safety should come first?

Hadn't she learned how deep the evil in this world ran?

"Tank?"

"Yeah, pixie?"

When she met his gaze, hers was tear-drenched, and that pierced with more efficiency than a bullet through his chest and right into his heart where it lodged itself. "His son, do you think O'Riley would hurt the boy for talking to me?"

His every instinct demanded that he lie to her and comfort her by whatever means necessary, but the truth was a man like Mac O'Riley would do whatever it took to protect himself, including harming his own six-year-old son to make it happen. Tank didn't know what the child's punishment for talking to Tallulah would have been, but he knew as certainly as he held this trembling woman in his arms that there had been one.

"It's okay," she said softly when he didn't offer her any consolations, and pressed her cheek against his neck, her soft breath warm against his skin. "I know. I know that O'Riley hurt him because of me. Because I wouldn't let it go, I insisted on going to talk to the boy even when my boss forbade it. All I could think of was what that sweet, innocent little child would become if someone didn't help him. I ... had to be that someone."

Didn't need to be a psychologist to know why she felt this driving need to save others when she had witnessed so much death before she was even old enough to start school.

"I can't promise you that I can save the boy, pixie, but I can promise you I'll do everything I can to make sure Mac O'Riley pays for what he's done. And I can promise you I will do whatever it takes to make sure he never gets his hands on you."

Tank didn't make vows lightly, and this was one he intended to keep.

Nobody was going to hurt his pixie.

∾

April 20th
    10:37 P.M.

Weary didn't even begin to describe how she felt.

Tillie had been tired before, what she would have called exhausted even. There had been a few foster homes she'd lived in that had been scary enough that she hadn't felt safe in her bedroom leading to many sleepless nights.

But that was nothing compared to this.

This was a bone-deep weariness that seeped through her every fiber until it felt like her blood had been replaced with concrete, and she was slowly being dragged down.

How much longer until she collapsed?

There wasn't a doubt in her mind that she would go on as long as she could. Giving up wasn't in her nature, but whether her mind remained strong or not, sooner or later, her body would give out.

Inevitable.

No one could keep going forever. Sooner or later, the tank just ran dry.

Well, maybe not *no one*.

Because Tank was plowing along through the forest, walking with a straight back and purpose. He didn't weave and waver as she did. Didn't trip over sticks, roots, rocks, or his own feet like she kept doing.

The man was like a robot.

One who seemed to have a plan. As soon as he'd made his promise not to let anyone hurt her, he'd set her on her feet, taken off his shoes to give her his socks since her feet were bare, and then started them walking.

Apparently, after he'd uncuffed her and sent her off to shower, he'd grabbed a backpack filled with emergency supplies. When she'd asked him why he hadn't got her shoes for her, he'd told her they were in the bedroom beside the bed, and if he'd taken them, it would have aroused her suspicions and he needed to make sure it looked like she escaped to the men approaching the cabin.

It made sense, but she still wished he'd gotten them.

The water and protein bar he stopped to feed her every couple of hours didn't help her poor feet at all. The socks offered little protection, better than nothing, but over hours and hours of walking the material had already begun to wear through.

No matter how long they walked, Tank never seemed to get tired. When they stopped for breaks, she knew it was for her sake, not because he needed a rest. If it was just him then she doubted he would have stopped even one time, and he'd be walking a whole lot faster.

It made her want to apologize for being the weak link.

Something she hated, but there wasn't anything she could do about it.

Facts were, she didn't have the size, strength, or stamina of Tank. Add in the fact that she'd already been existing on mere fumes for months now, ever since she took the report on the abuse of Mac O'Riley's son, and she didn't stand a hope of matching this huge mountain of a man.

Certainly didn't take a genius to figure out where the nickname Tank came from.

As much as she wanted to know what his real name was, maybe it was a good thing he hadn't told her. Already she was struggling to keep a sensible amount of detachment when it came to this man. If she knew his real name, it would increase the sense of intimacy she was fighting against.

All of a sudden, she slammed into Tank's back who had stopped right in front of her.

"We gotta teach you hand signals, pixie," he murmured his voice barely a hint of sound in the silent night.

When she looked at his hand, she saw he had a closed fist held up.

She knew what that meant, she just hadn't been paying much attention to anything other than her thoughts.

Freezing, she looked anxiously about.

To her eyes nothing moved. There were no shadowy forms moving toward them, nothing at all out of the ordinary.

Obviously, Tank saw differently.

"Drop," he ordered.

Tillie didn't hesitate.

As soon as he had his socks on her feet he'd gone through a number of orders. Topping that list was to follow any order he gave her without argument or hesitation.

While she couldn't say she enjoyed being told what to do and when to do it, she was hardly going to argue with a man who was trained to keep her alive when she had zero skills to contribute, that would be stupid.

With her prone on the ground, Tank spun around and fired off three shots behind her.

Three soft thuds followed, and she assumed he had hit all his targets.

"Let's go," he said, reaching down and snagging a hold on her hand, and dragging her to her feet.

Once she was standing, he took off at a pace her much shorter legs had a hard time keeping up with.

After she'd stumbled for the third time, he pulled her around in front of him, without ever breaking stride, and slung her over his shoulder.

Even with her added weight, he was able to increase his pace now that he didn't have to cater to her smaller size. It might not be a comfortable ride, being jostled about on his hard shoulder, but all Tillie cared about was getting as far away from any more men hunting them.

Hunting her.

Tank didn't have to be here.

Sure, it was a job, but he didn't have to promise to protect her no matter what. She was positive that hadn't been in the job description.

The sound of running water got louder, and when she turned her head to the side, she could see them approaching the river.

"Damn."

Tank let out the curse a split second before another shot was fired.

How did he always know when someone was out there? She was the one facing the direction the shot had come from and she couldn't see anyone.

"In you go, pixie." He all but tossed her into a boat and then jumped in behind her.

Another bullet went flying past and Tillie choked on a scream.

No matter what people thought of her based on who her father was, the idea of violence made her feel ill.

While he'd been good about cleaning up after her so far, she doubted Tank would appreciate her throwing up all over his boat.

"You drive, I'll shoot," he told her as he nudged her out of the way.

"Maybe they won't know where we went," she said hopefully as she stepped up to the control panel, steering wheel, whatever it was you called what you used to drive a boat. She'd never driven one before but how hard could it be?

As the engine sprung to life, a bunch of men broke through the tree line, bearing down on them with guns firing. Never once had she regretted going to the cops with what she'd seen that night, not when she had to give up her home, her job, and her life. But in this moment, if she could go back in time, she very well might have heeded the warning of her boss that said pursuing things with the crime boss' son was a suicide mission.

She was going to die out here. She and Tank both. If they were lucky, a bullet would end their lives quickly and mercifully, because if O'Riley got his hands on her then her death would be anything but.

As she did her best to drive the boat away from the shore and the men shooting at them, Tank seemed to fire with ease, taking out their pursuers.

"Wow," she said when he finally stopped firing, totally in awe of everything he'd done to keep her alive so far. "You're good."

"The best," he agreed. "Which is why I was sent to get you. I'm sorry, little pixie, I know that was hell for you."

"You saved my life. I can forgive you for scaring me half to death." She managed a smile for him because she knew without his intervention those men would have come for her when she was alone and vulnerable in her new home, and he appeared genuinely remorseful. "I wish it hadn't had to happen the way it did, but you were right, if I had known there was a mole at the Marshals, I would have done whatever I could to help weed him out."

Tank smiled back and his entire face was transformed. There was no doubt he was pantie-melting good looking, but when he smiled ...

The opposite sex—her included—didn't stand a chance.

An invisible force drew her toward him and she took a step closer.

He moved closer, too, his hands lifted as though he were going to draw her into his arms, then she noticed a loud roaring sound. Startled, she looked around, half expecting to see a helicopter hovering above them, but the sound wasn't coming from the sky, it was coming from the river where a huge waterfall sent water slamming down into the rocks below.

A waterfall they were heading straight for.

CHAPTER

Ten

April 21st
12:21 A.M.

Great.

Just great.

Tank sighed as the boat veered toward the waterfall.

Seemed like everything that could go wrong was going to go wrong tonight. His team hadn't made it here in time, which meant it was just up to him to protect the pixie against any number of mercs and bounty hunters who would do whatever it took to track her down.

Walking had been bad enough because he knew, even though she didn't complain, that every step was torture on her poor feet. If he'd had backup, he would have gathered her up and carried her because knowing she was hurting messed with his head.

The boat had seemed like the ideal solution. It got Tallulah off her feet, and it got them away from the bad guys.

But when he'd told her to drive, he hadn't made sure she knew to take the right side and not the left when they reached the fork. The right side ambled along through the forest, and there was a spot he could stop at with a vehicle parked nearby.

The left side turned into a cascading waterfall.

Which they were seconds away from tumbling over.

"A waterfall?" Tallulah squeaked. Her terrified gaze swung to his and she backed up toward the end of the boat as though that was going to help her. "Tank, I can't do heights."

"Sure you can, pixie," he said calmly, tightening the straps of his pack so he didn't lose it when they went over.

"Can't," she said, teeth beginning to chatter as her fear took hold.

"You climbed the tree. You can do this." Of course, this was a whole lot more dangerous than climbing the tree had been, but he wasn't going to remind her of that and push her over the edge into a hysterical meltdown.

"But you were there to catch me when I fell out of the tree. No way you can catch me here. We're going to die, aren't we?"

"Not going to die, pixie." At least he was reasonably sure they weren't. The fall wasn't really high enough to kill them outright, so long as they got away from the bottom of the waterfall and out from the falling water pushing them down and holding them under, they should be fine.

"I don't believe you."

There was no time to offer any more reassurances because the boat tipped and headed over the waterfall.

For one second, they seemed to hang in midair, suspended over the fifteen-foot drop.

Before they started falling, Tank grabbed at Tallulah, but the forward momentum threw her out of his reach, and he prayed that she knew how to swim.

Then they were falling.

And falling.

And falling.

Even though he knew the drop took all of a few seconds, it seemed so much longer.

More so because he didn't have his pixie tucked safely in his arms.

They hit with a bone-shuddering crash, and the last thing he heard before they were both pushed beneath the swirling water was Tallulah's pained shriek.

Dragging in a deep breath, he held it and didn't fight against it when they were shoved beneath the surface along with the boat. Fighting against it would only tire out his muscles and expend unnecessary energy.

Allowing the water to do its thing, Tank went with the current, and moments later it tossed him out from underneath the pressure of the waterfall's steady stream and he swam for the surface.

Once his head broke above the water, he scanned the area searching for his pixie. Had she made it up? Had the pressure of the waterfall been too much? Had she been too scared to remember to hold her breath before they went under?

Questions ran through his head along with the uncomfortable feeling that he more than liked the little pixie.

Liked her an inappropriate amount.

Enough that he had begun to think of her as *his* pixie.

He was about to dive down and search for her when he spotted her up ahead. She was trying to swim toward the bank but struggling against the current.

Alive.

Relief flooded his system.

They'd both survived the fall. He hadn't lost her, hadn't failed her.

His bigger frame and training meant he could move much more easily through the fast-flowing river, and when he reached her, Tank snagged her hand and reached up and grabbed onto the limb of a fallen tree. Tiny as she was, the pixie didn't add much weight and he was able to easily pull them both up and out of the water.

They were both breathing hard. Tallulah lay pinned beneath him on the large tree branch. The water flowed underneath them and moon-light streamed down upon them, giving the whole setting a romantic vibe even if their reason for being out here was anything but.

Tallulah stared up at him with eyes that were ... soft. Not how he'd expect her to look at him after he'd kidnapped her, drugged her, tied her up, lied to her, and then she had been shot at and almost drowned.

When her gaze dropped to his lips, then rose to his eyes again, he came undone and lost his grip on the control it was even more important that he cling to right now.

But how could he cling to it when she looked at him like that?

Did she want to kiss him?

Heart rate accelerating, pulse-pounding, all the blood in his body surging south, Tank wanted to reach for her, taste her, kiss away all her problems, but he needed to be sure. Already he'd taken advantage of her once, he wasn't going to make that mistake again.

The pixie knew what she wanted, and when her hands lifted, her fingers tangling in his hair, all bets were off.

Crushing his mouth to hers, he kissed her with a fervor he hadn't been expecting. To his body it seemed like this kiss was absolutely pivotal to his survival.

Or maybe it wasn't his body, maybe it was his soul that craved the pixie's touch.

"More," she murmured against his lips as his kisses turned frantic.

"Pixie," he warned, managing to cling to a tiny piece of sanity.

"More," she repeated. Beneath his body, which he had stretched out above her, his weight balanced on his hands so he didn't crush her tiny frame, her legs spread, making it clear where she wanted him to touch her.

"Pixie," he warned again. This had to be the very worst idea ever. Still, he balanced his weight on one hand while his other brushed across her center.

"Mmm," the moan tumbled from her lips, and when he went to withdraw his hand, she grabbed his wrist and held him in place. "Please."

The vulnerability in her stunning turquoise eyes snapped the last of his control, and as his mouth descended on hers, his hand slid beneath the waistband of her yoga pants to find her bare.

"Ah, pixie," he groaned as one finger glided through the wetness coating her center. Wetness that had nothing to do with their crazy dip in the water.

Nope.

This was all for him.

Her hips lifted silently, begging for more, and he grinned against her lips as one finger breached her entrance.

"So tight, pixie, you're going to feel like magic, aren't you?"

Lazily, he thrust that one finger in and out, preparing her to take more. Tank made sure his finger was hooked the right way to graze the spot inside her he knew would soon have her falling apart.

"More," she pleaded again when he didn't increase the pace.

"Say please, pixie."

Defiance sparked in her blue-green eyes, but when he added another finger she gasped, her internal muscles already beginning to quiver. "Please."

"Please what?" Teasing the pixie when he had her spread out like this beneath him was an opportunity he couldn't pass up.

She glared, but when his thumb brushed across her bundle of nerves she quickly said, "Please, let me come. I want to come. I need to come."

Cheeks rosy, eyes glowing with desire, Tank watched every nuance of her expression, memorizing exactly what she liked as he plunged his fingers in and out and worked her bud with his thumb until she was writhing beneath him, hovering right on that threshold of bliss.

As achingly hard as he was, nothing was better than watching his pixie in the moment she tumbled over that cliff.

Pressing harder against her bundle of nerves, he watched in fascination as she cried out, her internal muscles clamping around his fingers, her hips undulating as he didn't let up, stroking, touching, and prolonging her pleasure for as long as he could.

When she finally went completely lax against the tree branch, he withdrew his hand. Bringing it to his lips, he sucked her juices off his fingers, noting the pixie watched him through heavy-lidded eyes still burning with desire.

Big mistake.

Falling for a job was not part of the plan.

One taste was never going to be enough.

~

April 21st

1:02 A.M.

Big mistake.

Falling for Tank should not be part of her plan.

Now that she'd let him touch her, bring her pleasure, she couldn't deny that the bond she felt between them had grown.

Why had she been so stupid?

Tillie wasn't angry with him anymore, nor was she scared of him, but she also knew that he was walking away from her when his responsibilities ended. This was just a job to him, and she had a tendency to let her heart get a little too invested in people who didn't offer her their heart in return.

Attraction was okay, but she had to remember that even though he'd lied to her, he owed her nothing more than to follow through on the job he'd been given. Yet he had gone out of his way to help her, and emotions were riding high. He had saved her life, risking his own in the process. Adrenaline was flooding both of their systems, things were getting out of hand, and she had to be careful.

Making out was a result of their near-death experience.

It didn't mean that he liked her just because she liked him.

Actually, liked him.

Like, *like* liked.

Okay, that made zero sense and made her sound like a lovestruck teenager, but that orgasm had turned her brain to mush.

Stupid as it had been to beg him for more than just a kiss, Tillie didn't regret it for anything in the world. She was always so cautious, so careful, unless it came to her job and the children whose well-being was placed in her hands, she never took any risks.

Making out like this, moments after surviving the plunge over the waterfall, was so out of character for her, but it was a moment she would treasure forever because it had given her a glimpse of the Tillie who would have existed if her father hadn't committed his crimes. The Tillie weighed down by her father's infamy.

For that, she had Tank to thank.

"Thank you." Placing her hands on his shoulders, she lifted her head and feathered her lips across his. The kiss was supposed to be chaste, gratitude for everything he had done for her—the things he knew about, like saving her life and the ones she'd never tell him, like helping her find a missing piece of herself—but it seemed she couldn't pull her lips away from Tank's.

Ending the kiss would be smart.

It would save her heart and her sanity a whole lot of pain.

But just like she couldn't seem to pull her lips away from Tank's, she couldn't seem to pull her heart away from him either. Already he had gotten a fingerhold in there.

Imagine that.

A man who had done all the things to her that Tank had, doing what no one else in her life had ever managed to do. There was just something about the way he took care of her, powerfully, confidently, thoroughly, worrying about the little details like trying to keep her mind from dwelling when everyone else she'd met never even cared about the big things.

Damn.

No matter how hard she tried, she was falling for Tank as hard and fast as they'd gone over that waterfall.

Even if Mac O'Riley didn't get his hands on her, she was in for a world of pain.

"We shouldn't have done that," he said when he pulled away, but his hands were tender as he smoothed a wet lock of hair off her cheek and then helped her to her feet, guiding her off the branch and onto solid ground. "Are you hurt?" He ran his hands over the length of her body, and even though he did it clinically, her body didn't get the memo and heated anyway.

How could she possibly want another orgasm so soon after that mind-blowing one he'd just given her?

Which reminded her …

"I'm okay," she assured him, hoping he thought she was squirming because she was wet and cold and not because of his touch. "But I can …?" She looked at the tent in his pants and then up at his face. No way was she bold enough to say she could get him off with her hands or her mouth, or that her pleasure-addled mind would gladly take a repeat orgasm and they could just have sex.

A tender smile curled up his lips and again he reached out, this time to caress her cheek. "All good, pixie. Raincheck."

"Sure," she agreed, trying to hide her disappointment. They both knew there would be no raincheck. This was a one-and-done thing, which he was right, they shouldn't have done no matter how much she'd enjoyed it.

"We have to get out of here. They'll be coming."

Right.

Of course.

Here she was wanting to waste time making out when they were literally being hunted. The men after her weren't playing around. Money was a huge motivator, these men couldn't be talked into letting her go. They would deliver her to Mac O'Riley and take the payout. The only way to stop that from happening was to avoid them altogether and not get caught.

"Sorry. For a moment I ... forgot. Stupid, I know." It was her life on the line, *she* was the one they wanted. There was nothing stopping Tank from waving her goodbye and getting himself out of there in one piece.

"Love knowing I gave you a moment's peace." Tank leaned in, touched a quick kiss to her forehead, then took her hand and began to pull her along after him.

Time had no meaning as they ran through the forest. Each step sent pain spearing through her feet, spiraling up her legs and hips as her already battered and barely protected feet took another round of punishment.

Wasn't just her feet that were hurting. Her lungs were burning, and she had a stitch in her side. She did yoga every morning, and she went to the gym a couple of days a week to take a cardio class, but she wasn't anywhere close to as fit as Tank was. Just because he was tempering his speed to cater to her substantially shorter legs, it didn't mean that it was easy keeping up with him.

As badly as she wanted to stop and rest, she knew that wasn't an option. So long as Tank kept running, she would too.

This was her mess, and she didn't want Tank to die because of her.

She might be the weak link here, but she was still going to do everything she could to make sure they both survived.

Her eyes brightened when she saw a car up ahead. "Is that yours?" she wheezed.

"Yep, hold on a little longer, pixie, and I'll get you someplace safe."

Safe. Did such a place even exist for her anymore?

As much as she might like to believe there was an end coming, she realized that there likely wouldn't be. What she'd done couldn't be taken back. As long as O'Riley was alive, and maybe even after that, she would have a target on her back.

With a six-year-old child's life at stake, Tillie couldn't say she would take back what she'd tried to do, but she also hadn't realized the magnitude of the decision she was making when she'd defied her boss and gone to speak with Mac O'Riley's son.

They both scrambled into the car, and Tank wasted no time in turning on the engine and taking off through the trees. Despite the fact the ground was uneven and there were trees everywhere, he drove quickly and smoothly, and in no time at all they were on a road.

A tiny flicker of hope ignited inside her.

Just because she might never be completely safe, it didn't mean that Tank and whoever he worked with couldn't keep her alive. Even with their crazy meeting, she did trust him, and she believed him when he said anyone who came for her would have to go through him.

Having someone at her back helped so much.

Because life loved to mess with her, no sooner had she begun to relax a little and allow hope to bubble up inside her, than she noticed the cars up ahead of them blocking the road.

Of course, it couldn't be that easy.

Why would it?

"Tank?" She looked over to find him calmly keeping the car driving down the road, right at the other cars.

"Gabriel," he said.

"Your real name?" She hadn't been expecting him to share that with her.

"Whatever happens, pixie, you fight, okay? Promise me you won't give up."

That was a promise she could make.

She'd been fighting for as long as she could remember. Giving up wasn't who she was.

"I promise."

Gunshots once again pierced the night, and Tillie bit back a scream of fear and frustration. Couldn't for once things go smoothly?

Gabriel threw the car in reverse and started driving backward, and for a moment she thought they might actually get away.

Then she heard his grunt of pain.

Turning, she saw blood blooming on his chest, and all hope died.

Not only was she about to meet a brutal end, but Gabriel was going to die just for trying to save her.

CHAPTER
Eleven

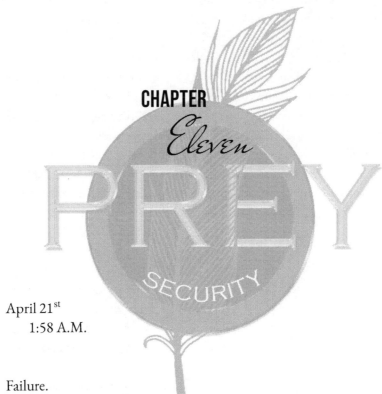

April 21st
   1:58 A.M.

Failure.

He'd just failed the pixie.

It hurt far more than the bullet that had just pierced his chest.

Tank sucked in a pained breath and realized that the panting, near hyperventilating breathing wasn't coming from him.

"Gotta run, pixie," he wheezed. His chances of escaping before the bounty hunters descended on the car were zero. But Tallulah could still run, at least give herself a chance.

Even in his hazy vision, he could see the indignation on her face. "I'm not leaving you alone."

"Tallulah," he groaned. Didn't she know it was his job to protect her no matter what? That he would give his life for hers? More than a job, he wanted to protect her, wanted to trade his life for hers if he could.

It wasn't her job to save him.

"No one calls me Tallulah. Only person who ever did was my dad. I thought I would hate it because I hate him so much, but when you say it ... I more than like it."

He huffed a chuckle then winced. "Not the conversation we should be having right now." Although her admission was sweet, and stirred up more feelings than he should be having right now, he should be attempting to convince her to take her chances and run for the trees.

"I'm not stupid, Gabriel. I know we aren't getting away. Even if I run, they'll only catch me. They're taking me to Mac O'Riley and he's going to kill me. Before that happens, I just want you to know how much I appreciate you trying to save me. I'll do my best to convince him to let you go. I'm sorry, so sorry that you got caught up in this. I don't regret trying to help O'Riley's son, I can't, but I do regret that you're paying the price for me naively thinking the law would trump O'Riley's money."

There were so many things he wanted to say to her.

Assurances, comfort, encouragements, but his car door was yanked open and rough hands grabbed him, dragging him out.

"Hey, be careful! He hasn't done anything wrong. You don't have to hurt him," his crazy pixie said, using her very best indignant and reprimanding tone.

If he could, he would have told her to keep her mouth shut, not invite these men who would take pleasure in her pain and fear to do anything more to her than they'd been ordered to. Angering them was stupid and was only going to wind up causing her more pain than was already coming for her.

But he couldn't.

Because when he was tossed on the ground like a sack of potatoes, pain spiraled through his body with a ferocity that stole consciousness from him.

For a while, everything floated in a pain-filled haze.

There were small grunts and a moan that he knew came from his pixie.

Rough hands lifting, carrying, and dragging.

There was the soft hum of an engine.

Images flashed through his mind sporadically when he assumed he had his eyes open enough to register what was going on around him.

There was the bright, round light of the moon. The backseat of a vehicle. Cold, hard concrete, scratchy beneath his cheek.

And crying.

Quiet sobs like someone was doing their best to make sure nobody heard.

His pixie.

There was not a single doubt in his mind who it was crying. He could feel her pain stronger than he could feel his own.

More than that, he could sense how alone she felt.

How many times had she tried to stifle her tears so no one else would hear them?

Too many to count he guessed.

"Pixie." It came out as barely a croak, but he heard her shuffle closer.

"Gabe?"

"Where ...?" It was all he could manage to ask, the first part of the question, his strength was failing as blood continued to drain from his body.

"I don't know. They put us in a car and drove us here. Looks like some old warehouse or something. Are you okay?"

Why was he not surprised that she was more worried about him than herself?

It was that very same attitude that had put her in this position to begin with.

Sweet as his pixie was, she needed a big dose of self-preservation.

"How long ...?"

"Still dark out so not that long. We've been here long enough for me to pull off your shirt and try to use it as a bandage to slow the bleeding."

Again, Tank wasn't surprised that instead of looking for a way out, his crazy pixie had been more concerned about trying to tend to his wounds.

Time to break some hard truths to her.

Chances were, he wasn't going to survive this wound anyway. Unless they got out of here quickly and he was given blood and fluids, he wasn't going to make it. Doubt he'd even live long enough for infection to set in.

Just because he was going to die here, it didn't mean the pixie had to.

"They hurt you?" So long as she was uninjured, he was going to insist that she do whatever it took to get herself out of there. All she needed to do was find a phone and call his team and they'd be there for her.

Her silence told him everything he needed to know.

Red rage filled his vision.

No one hurt his pixie. *No one.*

Gathering his strength, he lifted his head off the floor to look at her. A visual scan didn't show any obvious wounds, but that didn't mean she wasn't hurt or even that she wasn't badly hurt. Internal injuries could be every bit as serious, often more so. "How bad?"

"Just pushed me around a little." Although she said the words strongly, she wouldn't meet his gaze, and he knew she was downplaying it.

"You have to get out of here." Anger was providing him with a temporary burst of strength that he had to ride out as long as it lasted.

"Can't." Tallulah nodded at her ankle, and he saw that she was cuffed to a pipe. A glance down his own body showed he was similarly restrained.

"Break my foot."

"Huh?" The pixie's brows turned down in the most adorable little frown.

Damn.

He was really messed up if he was thinking about how cute Tallulah was when all he should be focused on was a way to get her out.

"Break my foot," he repeated, attempting to focus his mind when all it wanted to do was memorize every detail about his pixie so he could carry it with him as he crossed over to what lay beyond this life.

"I'm not breaking your foot! Are you insane? Why would I even do that?"

The truth was because he wasn't making it out of there alive, and he wanted to give her every chance of surviving that he could. Adding a broken foot to the chest wound wasn't going to slow him down any more than he already would be, and he was still sure he stood a chance at taking out at least a couple of O'Riley's men and increasing the odds of his pixie escaping.

"Need to get you out of here, pixie."

"That's not the way," she said gently. "I think the bullet might have glanced off your ribs. I don't think you lost enough blood for it to have hit your heart or punctured a lung. I mean, I'm not a doctor or anything, but I think you'd be dead already if the wound was fatal. That means if I can convince them to let you go, that you're just another bounty hunter, and since they already have me there's no need to kill you, then I think you can make it."

Stupid pixie.

Why did she even care?

Had she forgotten everything he'd done to her?

Could she really accept that he'd done it as part of his job and that he felt bad for scaring her?

"Sorry, pixie. For drugging you, kidnapping you, keeping you cuffed. Taunting you."

"You did that to keep me distracted." She gave him a wan smile and then determination filled her pretty face. "I won't let you die for my choices."

The stubborn set to her chin told him it was going to be hard to talk her out of it, but before he even had a chance, a door opened somewhere in the building, and multiple sets of footsteps moved toward them.

"I'll do everything I can, I promise. Thanks for trying to save me," Tallulah whispered before she stood bravely to face the man who wanted nothing more than to punish her for trying to bring him down.

Rage brewed inside him, and Tank assessed how he could best take out any of the men surrounding them. Even one increased the pixie's odds.

That first strike hit him harder than it did his pixie.

Her small grunt of pain, contained for his benefit he knew, threw him back in time two decades.

Awakening at the sound of broken glass.

His mom rushing into the room, grabbing him and his brother.

Although there were enough bedrooms for them to have their own rooms, the two of them were only eleven months apart in age, Irish twins, and very close. They had insisted on sharing a room and loved their late-night talks after their parents tucked them in.

That night, their mom had ushered them into the walk-in closet, where there was a hidden panel that led to the attic.

She'd told them not to come out no matter what they heard.

Easier said than done.

Their parents' insistence that their sons weren't home had caused their final hours to be filled with pain.

Those muted screams still haunted him to this day.

Something he would never forget.

They'd endured horrible agony and then death to protect him and his brother.

A debt he could never repay.

A debt he'd been trying to pay back ever since.

But every life he saved didn't bring them back.

And the one life he wanted to save the most he couldn't.

He was going to lie here and listen to her die just like he had his parents.

If they didn't kill him when they were done with Tallulah, then her final hours would haunt him as his parents' did.

Pain continued to pulse through him, and he gave into the call of unconsciousness, unable to bear a single second more of listening to his sweet, big-hearted pixie suffer.

∼

April 21st
3:27 A.M.

How much longer could she last?

One glance at the man lying still behind her, and she knew the answer.

As long as it took.

Whatever she had to endure, if it meant she might stand a chance at getting Gabriel through this alive, she'd take it.

Deferring to him while they were running through the forest for their lives was one thing, but this was no time for that alpha nonsense he'd tried to pull on her earlier. This might have started out as a job for him, but they'd become teammates now. That meant they had to rely on each other.

Right now, Gabriel was weak and vulnerable. He needed her, and she couldn't let him down.

Stay strong.

Tillie knew she was going to have to say those words to herself over and over again, and in the end, they weren't going to help her get away.

There was going to be no knight in shining armor riding in on a white horse to save her.

Her big, burly, muscled would-be savior hadn't stood a chance against the sheer number of bounty hunters and mercenaries out to get the one-million-dollar reward for finding her and turning her over to the man who wanted her dead.

This man.

Mac O'Riley.

He stood before her now in an expensive black suit with a crisp white shirt and a bright blue tie that matched his eyes.

The Irish crime boss would be a handsome man if there wasn't darkness lurking in those eyes. It was obvious the moment you met him, an evil he didn't bother to hide. On the contrary, he seemed to relish in it, take great pleasure at having people cower in his presence, and bow to his will.

Well, she wasn't going to bow down to him.

At this point, she had nothing left to lose. O'Riley had already decided he was going to make her suffer before he killed her, there was no way her bowing to him was going to improve her situation, and no way refusing to was going to make it worse.

She was sure Gabriel would disagree, tell her to do whatever it took to keep herself alive and in as good a shape as possible, but for what reason?

There were cuffs around both of their ankles, chaining them to the floor. Even if he was free, Gabriel was in no shape to fight or even to run, despite him seemingly thinking differently. They were outnumbered, they were on O'Riley's turf, and nobody was coming for them.

When you couldn't fight, and you couldn't fly, the only option left was to hold onto what you could.

Pride some might call it, but whatever name you wanted to ascribe to it, Tillie knew that the only thing she had left to hold onto was her beliefs.

What she had done was the right thing. Naïve definitely, maybe even stupid, but O'Riley's little boy hadn't had anyone in his corner, and no adult should stand by and allow a child to be subjected to the horrors that little boy had already lived through in his short life, let alone what he would still endure. All in the name of molding him into the perfect heir to take over his father's crime syndicate.

The child deserved better.

All children deserved better.

Innocence and curiosity wrapped up into tiny bundles of energy, children were as close to perfection as existed in this world. Anything hurting them was her limit, and she knew even though it had signed her own death warrant, she had done the right thing and nothing could take that away.

Certainly not whatever was coming next.

Looking her over from head to toe, O'Riley's gaze paused to linger on the bruise on her cheek, then the tear in her oversized sweater from where she'd tried to fight off the men when they dragged Gabriel's limp body into the truck. His men hadn't hurt her badly, a few hits to rough her up but nothing she couldn't handle.

Yet.

It was coming though.

She didn't even need to see the sneer on O'Riley's face as his gaze lingered on her sock-covered battered feet then lifted to meet hers.

"You've caused me a lot of trouble," he said. His cultured voice with the slight Irish accent had an ice-cold quality that told you this was a man with money and power who was used to having his every whim catered to. What he couldn't exhort through fear he bought.

Since there was nothing she could say to that which would be the right thing, she simply said nothing.

Just stood there, keeping her spine straight, her gaze direct, and her expression neutral.

A man like this would pounce all over weakness, and while she was utterly and completely terrified out of her mind, for herself and for Gabriel, she did her best to conceal it. Years of practice hiding her emotions from a world that had already made up its mind about her made it easier.

"Cost me a lot of money." O'Riley took a step closer. It was to intimidate her because she knew he wouldn't dirty his own hands by beating her up himself. That's why he had an army of henchmen standing around.

Whatever he'd spent to pay off judges, cops, and child protective services, and offered as the reward to whoever captured her and brought her to him was nothing but a drop in the ocean compared to how much he was worth. This wasn't about her costing him money or even about his image, this was about her daring to go up against him instead of cowering in fear.

She'd dared to mess with him, and he wanted to make her pay for it.

"How are you going to make up all the time, money, and effort I've wasted?" he asked. A leering gaze settled on her chest, and she had to stiffen every muscle so she didn't attempt to shrink in on herself to hide.

That was what he wanted.

Would he sexually assault her?

Maybe.

But it was giving her the fear that he might that would give him that rush he craved.

"Get down on your hands and knees and crawl to me, beg me to spare you," he ordered like it was already a foregone conclusion that she would do it.

"No." The word came out with more force than she had anticipated, surprising herself as well as O'Riley.

His eyes narrowed, and she expected him to say something, order her again to do what he'd told her, or yell at her for disobeying.

Instead, he nodded at one of his men who moved around and grabbed her from behind, pinning her arms to her sides.

"There is one lesson my father taught me that I always found particularly enlightening. In life there are two roads. The easy road and the hard road. I always encourage those I encounter to take the easy road, but I must admit I find a certain enjoyment in watching them choose the hard road. You, my dear, have chosen the hard road. One thing you should remember is both roads will wind up in the same location. You *will* crawl on your hands and knees and beg me to show mercy."

Over her dead body.

She would never beg this man for anything.

Not for any reason.

Although that was a whole lot easier to think in her mind than it might be to do in reality when the man holding her grabbed her right wrist and held out her hand palm up.

Mac O'Riley calmly removed his belt.

The first strike stung.

The second hurt.

By the fifth, it felt like her hand was on fire.

By the tenth, she was biting on her tongue hard enough to draw blood in her attempt not to scream in pain.

By the fifteenth, blood coated the tender skin of her palm.

When he finally stopped at twenty strikes, she could no longer hold back the tears that streamed down her cheeks.

There was no reprieve.

The man holding her released her right wrist, grabbed her left, and the process started all over again.

Tillie lasted until the fourth strike on her left palm before she could no longer just flinch and whimper at each lash of the belt.

A muted moan turned to a cry and then a sob and then a scream as blow after blow struck her hand.

Although her body attempted reflexively to pull away each time the swish of the belt flying through the air signaled the coming pain, there was nowhere to go. The man holding her was like an immovable rock, his grip on her steady and unbreakable.

Just make it to twenty, she silently pleaded with herself.

Then she'd get a break.

A moment to rest.

Recover.

Rebuild her mental strength for whatever came next.

But her exhale of relief when the twentieth lash came turned out to be premature.

The man holding her shifted her, turning her sideways, arms still pinned to her sides, and before she even had a chance to think about kicking out, another man was stepping up to grip her ankles.

As the blows began to rain down on her knees, Tillie wondered why life never seemed to offer her two choices. Seemed it was always the hard road and nothing else.

CHAPTER
Twelve

April 21st
4:10 A.M.

Was there a more satisfying sound than that of someone shedding tears?

To Mac O'Riley there was not.

Raised by his father to take over the O'Riley empire from the time he was born, he had loved every lesson he'd learned at his beloved father's knee. Everything from how to run a successful legitimate business to keep up the façade, to how to manage the dirtier side of the business world.

Extortion, blackmail, threats, he was more than willing to do whatever it took to get what he wanted just as his father before him had done, and his father's father before that, and his grandfather's father who had created the O'Riley empire from scratch. Built it into something now known—and feared—around the world.

Continuing that legacy was paramount.

After his wife failed to give him an appropriate heir—three daughters were useless as anything other than chess pieces to further extend his family's empire by strategic partnerships—he had turned to a mistress and finally been given the son he craved.

A son the woman crying on the floor at his feet had tried to take from him.

It was well known that his family thrived on corruption within law enforcement and the government. Using it to grow, reach out more tentacles, and expand across the globe until he had connections in every government and every law enforcement branch in every country.

Was there such a thing as too much money?

Too much power?

Mac thought not.

But all the money and power in the world was utterly useless without an heir.

The only key to immortality was through your offspring. No one in this world lived forever, and raised as the Irish catholic boy he had been, he believed in the afterlife but knew it played no part in this world.

A child was your only way to remain alive, part of this world, even after you passed over.

Not just any child.

A son.

Almost forty by the time his boy came along, he'd already begun to feel that strength that came from immortality. A new purpose, a new focus, conquering the business world had gotten old and boring. His failure of a wife was insipid at best, and something better left locked away in his Irish estate along with the three useless daughters she had provided him.

There were plenty of mistresses to fulfill his needs for rough sex, and there was always someone that needed to be beaten into compliance to cater to his need for dominance and inflicting pain. But he lacked a purpose.

Until his boy came along.

Mac O'Riley V.

His pride and joy, the center of his universe, the reason he had worked so hard and expanded what had already been an impressive empire to begin with.

Nobody messed with him, and trying to mess with his son?

That was a surefire way to get yourself to the top of his torture and kill list.

Only now, as he looked at the woman, he realized he might have been premature in making his plan.

She was beautiful in an innocent sort of way. Huge turquoise eyes framed by long lashes, perfectly sculpted lips, and long silky blonde hair. Her frame was tinier than he usually liked, her breasts definitely on the small side, but it was her attitude that had captivated him from the moment they came face to face.

Even trapped in this abandoned warehouse as she was, chained to the floor with no hope of escape, her back had been straight, her gaze steady as she watched him approach.

That attitude would be such fun to break.

It had been a long time since he had undertaken breaking an innocent woman. A way to pass time as a teen and in his early twenties as his father slowly increased the amount he was allowed to participate in the business. Once his father had died when Mac was only twenty-six and he had taken full control, there was no more time for such pursuits.

But now ... and with this woman ...

He was sure he could find the time.

Would be a good lesson for the boy as well.

The child had disappointed him when Mac learned he had told private O'Riley business to the too-nosy-for-her-own-good social worker. What went on in their home was not to be repeated to an outsider, especially a do-gooder one with no concept of how the real world worked.

Threats to her boss hadn't worked, nor had repeated calls to his connections within the police department. Not even threats directly aimed at the woman had stopped her.

But when she'd witnessed the murder of the maid who had made the initial call to child protective services, claiming his boy was being abused, he knew she had become a real problem. One that wouldn't be so easily swept under the rug.

Especially when the FBI became involved.

As their star witness, she possessed the ability to actually destroy him and everything he and the generations of men before him had worked so hard to build.

Tallulah Russel had come much too close to succeeding.

But now she was here. Bloody and crying, helpless and completely at his mercy, and it was time to show his boy how they treated anyone who messed with their family.

"Get the boy," he ordered.

At his words, the woman's head snapped up and her mouth dropped open. He had to give her credit. It was obvious she was more concerned about his son than she was about herself and her own predicament.

He liked that.

She would be a worthy training tool.

It had been the night of his thirteenth birthday when his father first brought him a woman. She'd been innocent-looking like Tallulah Russel —blonde curls, wide blue eyes, dimples, and a smattering of freckles across her cheeks. When she'd been tied to the bed she had begged and pleaded for her life, screamed and sobbed as he used her to become a man, but in the end she had been weak. She hadn't even lasted a week before she was too broken to be any fun.

How long would Tallulah Russel last?

More than a week. He knew that just from the way she narrowed her eyes as his son was marched into the warehouse between two of his most loyal men. Would she last weeks? Months? Years? Could he keep her long enough that the very son she had tried to steal from him could use her to become a man?

"What are you doing?" Tallulah asked, a thread of panic in her voice as his son was brought to stand beside him.

Darting out a hand, he circled her neck, squeezing just enough that she let out a strangled yelp and clawed automatically at his arm. "First lesson is you don't speak without permission. Understand?"

Instead of answering, her gaze darted behind him to where he could hear his boy whimpering.

She was protective of his son, he would give her that.

"Understand?" he repeated, tightening his hold on the slender column of her neck until she was looking at him again.

When she gave a minute nod, he released her and stepped back. Tallulah slumped down but still managed to keep her head up even as she dragged in several ragged breaths.

"I think you're ready to crawl on your hands and knees now," he said smugly. Then he pulled out his weapon and handed it to his boy.

"No, Daddy," the child shrieked, shrinking away from the gun.

Disobedience was not to be tolerated. Already he had been much too soft on the child, coddling him because the boy was exceptionally handsome, and the thought of marring that gorgeous face, a face that could only help him succeed in whatever he did, was an unappealing one.

But it was time to toughen the boy up.

He was six years old now. Old enough to start learning the ropes so he could take over the business one day.

The slap echoed through the room.

"Leave him alone," Tallulah yelled, lunging forward only to be stopped by the chain around her ankle.

His son began to weep, but he ignored it and once again held out the weapon. "Take it," he ordered.

Instead of immediately grasping the gun, the boy looked to Tallulah who nodded at him. Then his small, shaking hand wrapped around the grip.

With slow, deliberate movements, Mac unzipped his pants and pulled his erection free from his boxers. "You crawl toward me on your hands and knees, show me how grateful you are that I have spared your life, or the boy shoots the bounty hunter." He nodded at the prone body of the man who had been brought in with Tallulah. Having lost enough blood that he wasn't a threat even if he hadn't been chained up, Mac wasn't sure yet what he would do with the man when he left here. Perhaps bring him along. If he could be saved, he might prove to be a useful member of Mac's security team given the right motivation to join.

Resignation filled those turquoise eyes.

There was no way the woman would refuse to comply when it meant the child would have to shoot someone.

Mac had been around the boy's age when he had first participated in enforcing the rules, and that first initiation had been with a gun. While he had an affinity for knives, guns were often the more practical choice. This was the way O'Riley men were raised, and this was the way his son would be trained. The boy was his, and he and he alone would make the decisions when it came to what to do with him.

"Ready to crawl?" he asked, already knowing the answer.

With a defeated nod, Tallulah crawled on her bloody and torn hands and knees to kneel before him then took his hard length into her mouth. Power surged through his body. He was in control of his universe and everybody who entered it, and soon enough, Tallulah Russel would learn that lesson.

Better than that, in a delicious twist of fate, she would play a crucial role in teaching his son the O'Riley way despite her efforts to have the boy taken away from him.

CHAPTER

Thirteen

April 21st
6:20 A.M.

Wet drops began to land on his cheeks.

Tears.

Crying.

Someone was weeping.

Tank groaned as his body was jostled, the pain so excruciating that he couldn't fight the black tide of unconsciousness that swept over him.

Even then it poked at him.

Relentlessly.

Pressure on his chest prodded him awake, but even conscious, everything was hazy and distant.

Pain.

Like an elephant riding in a tank sat on his chest.

Soft cries finally started piercing through the haze, and he blinked and forced his mind to snap back into gear.

If nothing else, he knew that not focusing his mind meant death.

Somehow, he summoned enough strength to pull it together and opened his eyes to find Tallulah sitting beside him, her head hanging down, chin against her chest.

His pixie.

Something inside him settled.

She was still alive, that was what was most important.

Another splash on his cheek made his own eyes water.

Tears.

Her tears.

His pixie was crying.

Those tears pierced him sharper and more effectively than the bullet had. He'd failed her. She'd been hurt, that he remembered. Remembered the sounds of her pain as she tried to hide it from him.

That hurt worst of all.

It was his job to protect and he hadn't.

His pixie had paid the price.

His body was jostled again, and once again pain took him under. Mercifully giving him a break from the crushing sense of failure.

Something soft was stroking across his forehead.

So gentle it was almost tickling.

There was humming too. A soft, gentle sound that matched the fingertips caressing his skin.

"Pixie?" he croaked, hating how weak he sounded. How was he going to get his pixie out of here when he could barely think, let alone move, let alone come up with any sort of workable plan?

"Gabriel? Are you awake?"

"Barely."

"Just rest." Her hand that had stilled when he'd spoken, resumed its tender caress.

There was no time to rest.

While he'd been out of it and had no idea what had gone on in the warehouse, he knew it was bad. His pixie was tough, she wouldn't cry over just anything.

"Where are we?"

"Van. I think O'Riley is taking us to his place. Or at least a place he owns."

The vehicle driving was what kept jostling him. If he hadn't lost so much blood, he wouldn't have needed to be told that.

Bracing his palms on the floor of the van, he attempted to sit up, get his bearings, clear his head enough to be what his pixie needed right now.

Small hands pressed on his shoulders, holding him down.

It was depressing that it worked.

Weak as he was, he didn't have the strength to fight off someone as small as Tallulah. That did not bode well for them.

Sinking down against the floor, he braced an arm under his ribs, breathing in and out slowly, determined to figure something out.

"How bad?" he asked, throwing a glance the pixie's way.

"How bad what?" She made that adorable little frown he knew he was going to miss when she was gone.

Assuming, of course, they both made it out of this alive.

"How badly are you hurt? Don't bother lying to me, pixie," he added when she immediately swung her gaze away from his.

"Not bad," she said, but although she'd returned her gaze to his, she was looking through him rather than at him, so Tank knew she was lying.

"Tell me."

"Gabe, it's not important, we have ..."

"It's important," he growled. He got that Tallulah was used to nobody caring about her pain, but he cared. Damn, did he care.

More than he would ever have thought possible given how little time they'd known one another, and under the circumstances they'd met.

But it was what it was, and now certainly wasn't the time to be trying to figure it out.

"Tell me," he repeated in a tone he knew brokered no argument.

"He just ..."

"What, pixie?" This time he gentled his tone, coaxing out the information he knew she wouldn't give up freely.

"Wanted me to crawl to him. I wouldn't so he ..."

"What did he do, Tallulah?" More a demand this time, but the anger brewing inside him was directed at Mac O'Riley and not his sweet little pixie.

Instead of answering, she held up her hands, and even in the dim light in the back of the van he could see her palms were bloody, the skin shredded.

Shot or not, if he could get his hands on O'Riley, Tank would tear the man to pieces.

Nobody hurt his pixie.

That's what he'd promised her at least.

Only he'd failed her spectacularly.

"Show me your knees," he commanded.

She sighed but shifted so he could see her knees, which had received the same treatment as her hands.

"What did he use?"

"Belt," she mumbled.

"His belt?" Given half a chance, he would give the man a taste of his own medicine. "What else?"

A shrug. "Just hit me a few times, nothing serious."

If torn clothing hinting at injuries beneath, and a bruised cheek were nothing serious, he'd hate to see what she considered to be serious.

Strike that, he absolutely wouldn't.

Tank got the feeling there was more she hadn't told him, but he didn't have the time right now to try to coax it out of her. They needed to figure out their next move.

"Do you know why they brought me along with you?" It didn't make sense. They should have killed him and left his body behind, not bothered to lug his unconscious self about. No guarantee he wasn't going to succumb to his injuries either. Seemed like more hassle than it was worth, although he was glad he was here. The thought of his pixie facing this alone was more than he could allow himself to think about right now.

"I don't know. I don't think he knows who you are though. I think he thinks you are just another bounty hunter."

Good.

Then he wouldn't be expecting to have the entire might of Prey Security bearing down on him.

Gunfire erupted outside and the van swerved, tossing them both about. Tank grunted and did his best to brace his body, but he was more worried about Tallulah. He managed to grab her as the vehicle came to a stop, but the resulting pain from her body slamming against his wound had his vision fading to black.

The back of the van was flung open, and Tank didn't give himself time to think of anything other than his pixie's survival.

Somehow, he got his body up off the floor.

Using his unsteadiness for him rather than letting it become a hindrance, he barreled at the man who came through the door, sending them both careening into the floor.

Thankfully, he landed on top because if the man's body had crashed into his, Tank knew it would have been lights out for him.

This man was no untrained goon. Simultaneously, he swung both at Tank's head and at his wound, going to incapacitate him as quickly as possible.

It worked.

Agony exploded inside him hard enough that he gasped, but as darkness once again came curling around him, he knew he'd given Tallulah a chance to run.

Hopefully, she was already out of the van, using the continued gunfire as cover to get herself away and someplace safe. She knew his brother was a safe person to go to, and if she could get herself to him, he'd get her back in Prey's hands. After that, his team would keep her safe.

The man stood above him.

A dark shadowy figure.

Since he couldn't identify any features, Tank saw in him the men who had ended his parents' lives.

He hadn't seen those men that night, but after they were found and prosecuted, he'd come face to face with them at the trial.

That was who he saw now as he looked death in the face.

As much as he didn't want to leave behind his brother or his team, especially his team right now as they were dealing with the whole Beth situation, or even his pixie, it would be nice to be reunited with his parents.

Another gun fired, this one so close the sound blasted through his head.

Tank braced for the coming pain, knowing this bullet would definitely end his life.

Only the pain never came.

Instead, the man who had been standing over him mere seconds before suddenly swayed, dropped to his knees, and then crashed to the floor.

Another figure took its place.

Tallulah.

Fear for her shoved away the pain long enough he could push himself up, where he saw his pixie, gun in hand, standing over the body.

"Pixie," he rasped.

She turned, her wide blue eyes glassy with shock, her entire body trembling. "H-he was g-going to k-kill y-you," she stammered.

She'd just saved his life.

Bright light suddenly flooded the van as his strength faded. He fought it, not wanting to leave his pixie to fight for both their lives alone, but he was powerless to stop himself from crashing into the vortex of unconsciousness.

~

April 21st
6:59 A.M.

Tillie swung the gun in the direction of the light.

There was only one thought in her mind.

One thing propelling her.

Protect.

Not protect herself but Gabriel.

If his wound was going to kill him outright, he would already be dead. As long as he got treatment before infection set in, he could live, be happy, and save other lives.

He had a chance at a life while hers was already over.

Whether it ended today or in a week, a month, or a year, there was one thing she knew for certain, Mac O'Riley had zero plans of letting her go.

On the contrary, he'd found himself a new toy.

Eyes accustomed to the dark as they were wanted desperately to close against the sudden intrusion of light, but Tillie fought against the urge. Gabriel had passed out again after giving them both a chance at survival. A chance she wasn't going to squander.

It was all on her, and she wasn't going to let Gabriel down, not after he'd risked everything for her and almost lost his life in the process.

None of the mercenaries or O'Riley's men thought she was any threat, but as soon as they saw that body, they would know that she was.

That meant if she didn't find a way to get free now, she might never get another chance.

To get herself and Gabriel out of here, she absolutely would kill these men, too, if she had to.

Protect herself and Gabriel, that was her only goal.

Her only focus.

Straightening her arms, she held the weapon steady. Not an easy thing to do when tremors of fear rippled through her entire body.

"Put the gun down," a voice ordered.

Yeah, right.

No way she was doing that.

Did he think she was crazy?

"Put the gun down, now."

Despite the fact she was aiming her weapon right at them, they didn't stop moving toward her. There were four of them dressed all in black with huge weapons—much bigger than her own—in their arms, pointed right at her as they tried to get to Gabriel.

Shooting a real person was so very different than shooting the paper targets at the range. Tillie had learned to shoot not long after she graduated high school. In college, there had been some people who had put two and two together and discovered her real identity.

After that, there had been several incidents where people accosted her, threatened her, even going so far as to break into her apartment. Not feeling safe alone, she'd signed up for lessons to learn how to use a gun and then purchased one when she felt comfortable enough. Over the years, she made sure to keep her training up, but nothing could really have prepared her for shooting a living, breathing human being.

One who wouldn't hesitate to kill her, but still a human being.

These men wouldn't hesitate to hurt her either. She could see it in the confident way they continued moving like they knew she didn't really have the guts to shoot them.

If it wasn't for Gabriel relying on her, she might not have.

Even if she killed them and escaped, Mac O'Riley would only send more mercenaries after her, staying might have seemed like the easier option.

But for Gabriel she would fight.

She wouldn't let these men hurt him, not after he'd saved her life and been shot because of her, she wasn't going to let him die.

At the same second she fired, someone lunged at her, somehow dodging her bullet and managing to wrap their arms around her, pinning her helplessly against a huge chest. Why did every single mercenary and bounty hunter have to be so huge? Couldn't they for once be small to at least even the odds for her a little bit?

One of his enormous hands circled her wrist and pried the gun from her grasp, and with it, her hope died.

They were going to kill her.

Her and Gabriel.

She'd failed him.

Panic flooded her system, bringing with it a rush of adrenaline, and Tillie went crazy.

She fought against him frantically, kicking, clawing, and flinging her body about. There was no pain in this moment, not even real fear, just a heavy sense of self-preservation. She was more cornered animal than human right now, with a single all-consuming goal.

"Stand down, pixie," a deep voice, heavy with pain, said weakly.

Gabriel.

Telling her to stand down?

Didn't he know these men would likely kill him?

They had a reason to keep her alive, but none to spare his life.

Probably the blood loss was affecting him and he didn't know what he was saying.

"Stop fighting, pixie," he repeated, "the cavalry has arrived."

Tillie stilled instantly.

The cavalry?

Gabriel's team?

Was it possible that they had somehow managed to find him?

They hadn't shot her or Gabriel. And now that she realized it, the man holding her wasn't actually hurting her, nor had he done anything to hurt her when she was flinging herself about like a wild animal.

Was it really possible that they were safe now?

Tillie hardly dared to believe that it might be true.

Thrown into overdrive by everything that had happened these last few hours, days, weeks, and months, her mind seemed to splinter from her body. The tremors wracking her frame grew to the point where she felt like she was about to shatter into a million pieces. Her head got kind of floaty, and she lost control of her limbs.

Sagging in the man's hold, he shifted his grip on her, gentling his hold and scooping her up so he cradled her against his chest.

"She okay?" Gabriel asked.

"Shock," the man holding her said. His voice was soft, gentle, and he seemed to be rocking her as though she were a crying baby. "It's okay, sweetie," he murmured against her ear. "We got you, you're safe now."

Safe.

The word felt so foreign.

So disconnected from her.

She was never going to be safe.

Ever.

The truth of that hit her hard and her shaking somehow seemed to increase until her muscles were jerking painfully. Even her brain seemed to spasm as pain pulsed between her temples.

"Give her the gun back," Gabriel ordered.

He shouldn't be making orders, he should be resting. Didn't he remember he'd been shot? And he shouldn't be worrying about her. He needed to conserve his strength because crazy as it seemed given how their weird relationship had started, he was the only one who made her feel safe and she didn't even know if he was going to be okay.

Cool metal touched her palm, and it was pure instinct that had her fingers curling around it. For some crazy reason, it did make her feel a little safer to have the gun in her possession, it meant she wasn't completely helpless.

How did Gabriel always know what she needed?

And why was she falling apart when he needed her to be strong?

"G-Gabriel was sh-shot," she stammered through chattering teeth. Try as she might, she couldn't seem to get her body to stop shaking.

"I know, sweetie. Rock there is working on him. Rock's a medic," the man holding her advised, his voice still calm and soothing like he knew he was speaking to the equivalent of a spooked horse.

"Gonna be fine, pixie," Gabriel rasped.

Fine.

What did that even mean anymore?

She'd said to herself she was fine for years, and it was always a lie, yet she continued to tell herself that as though in saying it she could make it true.

But she couldn't.

There was no way to be fine when you'd lived her life, but she was so afraid to admit that, even to herself, because she didn't want to be weak. Pretending she was tough was the only way she managed to survive, because if she had to admit that she wasn't strong enough to survive the aftermath of her father's killing spree, then her entire life would be a lie.

She wasn't strong.

Most days, she struggled just to put one foot in front of the other. Living in her father's shadow was exhausting and depressing, a never-ending shadow that there seemed to be no way to escape. Now she was living under another never-ending shadow and the combination of the two was enough to shatter all her pretenses, rip away all the lies she told herself, and leave her naked and completely without defenses.

It was all too much. All she wanted was one moment of peace where she didn't have to worry about anything else. Didn't have to be the daughter of a notorious killer, didn't have to be the woman with a crime boss after her.

Didn't have to be Tallulah Russel.

Too bad there were no reprieves in life, and she couldn't be anyone but herself.

CHAPTER

Fourteen

April 21st
   7:13 A.M.

Tank fought through the pain that begged him to hide in unconsciousness for one reason only.

His pixie needed him.

Fighting with one of O'Riley's men—brief though the fight had been—had not only sapped the last of his strength but restarted his wound bleeding.

If it wasn't for Tallulah's panicked breathing it would be so easy to let go. His team was here now. They were safe.

There was nothing he could contribute to their extraction, weak and bleeding as he was.

Well, not entirely true.

He could keep the pixie calm.

Proud, he was so damn proud of her. Terrified as she was, untrained as she was, she hadn't hesitated to kill to protect him. Would have taken out his team, too. To her, they looked no different than O'Riley's men, and for a moment, he'd been afraid she was going to kill them.

A true warrior, she'd held it together, endured hell while he'd laid uselessly beside her, but now that she knew she was safe, her mind had reached the limits of what it could endure. Tank didn't hold it against her. She'd been an absolute rockstar through everything, from him holding her captive, to battling her fear of heights, to standing strong in front of the man who wanted her dead. This woman had what it took to make it in his world, but it terrified him that he was even thinking that way.

He hadn't been looking for a partner.

Ever.

His parents' deaths had cured him of ever wanting to let himself get attached to another person.

The military was different. His team had become his family. His brother was still part of his life, but these men were who he spent most of his time with and he would die for them without hesitation.

There had never been another person who had even come close to entering that same zone in his heart.

Until this feisty little pixie.

The sound of gunshots jolted him fully awake, and he immediately turned to find Tallulah struggling to get out of Panther's hold. As the only one of them with a kid—seven-year-old Andy was the cutest, smartest, sweetest little boy Tank had ever met—he had mastered the art of calming down virtually anyone and usually got put on victim watch.

Normally, Panther had no trouble soothing them, but not today.

Today, his pixie was afraid, hurting, and wanting to cling to what made her feel safe.

Which was him.

When Panther set her on her feet, she scurried over to him.

But not to sit beside him.

Nope.

His pixie planted herself between him and the open door of the back of the truck like she wasn't surrounded by highly trained former Delta Force operators.

If Tallulah didn't find herself a sense of self-preservation soon, she really was going to wind up dead despite his best efforts to keep her alive.

"Stand down, pixie," he ordered again, but she either didn't hear him or ignored him. Tank would bet anything it was the latter.

"Panther, you stay on her. Pixie, you do whatever he tells you, no arguments, no hesitation."

"Won't let her get hurt, man," Panther assured him, already standing in front of the pixie. The look his friend gave him said he knew exactly how important Tallulah had become to him.

It was insane to him that a job he hadn't wanted, that had come at a time when he wanted nothing more than to be with his team and not some stranger who'd gotten herself into a mess, had turned into this.

Into a woman he was damn near obsessed with.

A woman he could never have.

Because he was still keeping secrets from her.

Ones his pixie wouldn't be able to forgive.

But at least she'd be alive, she'd be safe, and she'd be able to live the rest of her life without having to be constantly looking over her shoulder.

"Rock, you need to ..."

"I know what I'm doing, man," Rock interrupted him. "Relax. We got this. Won't let your girl get hurt. Believe it or not, we've done this a time or two."

Of course they had.

He knew that.

But this was no normal mission.

Trick and Scorpion were at the open van door, firing off shots at whoever was approaching. Panther was crouched in front of Tallulah's trembling form, and Rock was working beside him starting an IV with fluids and a transfusion.

Since he'd been in and out of it, Tank had no idea how long it had taken his team to get to them once his watch sent off the alert.

O'Riley had made a critical error in assuming that he was just another bounty hunter.

Other than pat him down to remove any weapons, all his men had done was bring him along with them when they took Tallulah to him. If they had put in even a little more effort, they might have discovered his watch. Designed to monitor the wearer's vitals, after being shot, his blood pressure would have dropped dramatically sending off an alert to Prey. His team would have mobilized immediately and the tracker in the watch would have been activated, giving them his position.

Had he told the pixie about the watch?

Tank honestly couldn't remember, and now wasn't the time to worry about it. He had to focus.

Only focusing was much harder than it should be.

His pain was increasing as well.

Shouldn't be since he was sure Rock was pumping him full of painkillers. They weren't working. His head was throbbing, and his skin felt too tight to fit properly over his skeleton and muscles. And why was it so hot in here?

"Hold on, man," Rock said, pulling out a syringe.

His hold on consciousness was fading and the world began to turn in sickening revolutions around him.

Turning his head, he threw up the meager contents of his stomach.

"Gabriel?" Cool fingers glided across his burning forehead. "What's wrong?"

"Fine, pixie," he forced out.

"He's too hot," she said, obviously not to him since she was staring anxiously at Rock.

"Infection," Rock said as he lifted a syringe, checked it, and then plunged it into Tank's thigh.

Although he was the one to receive the shot, he felt the pixie's hand tighten reflexively around his.

She was holding his hand.

He hadn't even noticed.

With his heart struggling just to keep up its diminished blood volume to his vital organs, the extremities were having to make do with all that was left, leaving them feeling slightly numb.

Now that he felt her small fingers curled around his, the soft sensation seemed to be all he could feel.

Pain faded.

As did the heat of fever.

This woman was sweet.

Too sweet for someone like him.

Someone who was using her.

She deserved better.

Deserved the world.

Problem was, the pixie didn't see it that way.

She believed she had to atone for her father's sins. Sins she had witnessed even if her conscious mind couldn't recall them.

Dedicating her whole life to making up for what her father had done meant she was missing out on living *her* life.

Who was the real Tallulah?

The one she hid behind the mask of a perfect citizen.

Over the last few days, he'd gotten glimpses of that real Tallulah. She was brave even when she was afraid, she faced her fears and didn't hide from them. She was sassy and funny. She had a smart little mouth on her, and although she seemed a little uncertain when it came to sex, she knew what she wanted and she took it.

Strong, smart, and sweet.

The trifecta.

Everything he shouldn't want but craved wrapped up in a tiny blonde, five-foot package.

"He's not going to die, is he?" Tallulah's panicked voice asked. "You can't let him die."

She was scared.

For him.

A half smile curled up one side of his mouth.

"Relax, pixie. Not going to die."

Tallulah ignored him although her grip on his hand tightened once again. "Is he going to die?"

"I'm doing everything I can for him, okay, blondie?" Rock said, his voice calm and reassuring, not that it seemed to go any way toward easing his pixie's anxiety.

"That's not an answer," she replied shrilly. "I don't want him to die."

"Pixie, look at me," Tank ordered. When she did, it gutted him to see those big eyes of hers shimmering with tears. "I am not going to die. Hear me?"

"Y-you can't know that," she whispered forlornly.

"Can so. Too stubborn to go out like this. Have faith, pixie."

"I'll try."

"You'll do it. One other thing I need you to do for me, pixie."

"What?"

Whatever Rock had injected into him was making quick work of sending him crashing back into the darkness, but he needed the pixie's word on this. "Promise me."

"What do you need me to promise?"

"To forgive me," he murmured.

The last thing he saw before he tumbled back into unconsciousness was his pixie's confused frown.

As the darkness swallowed him up, Tank clung to the feel of her hand on his and prayed that she might actually be able to forgive him for the sins she didn't even know he had committed against her.

∼

April 21st

   8:41 A.M.

Why couldn't she stop shaking?

Logically, Tillie knew the answer was because she was in shock, her body and mind both had reached the limit of what they could handle and so they'd kind of checked out.

That she was safe with Gabriel's team hadn't really sunk in yet.

Maybe because she didn't *feel* safe.

Was it just because Mac O'Riley was still out there and she knew he wasn't going to stop coming after her, or because these guys gave her a bad feeling?

She was pretty sure they didn't mean to give her a bad feeling. They'd all been very nice to her, gentle too. It was obvious they loved and cared about Gabriel, but that didn't have anything to do with her.

It was also obvious that they knew something had gone on between her and Gabe. More than was supposed to have given he'd been sent by their boss to pretend to kidnap her and hold her at the cabin until ...

And that was why she had the bad feeling.

What was the end of that sentence?

There had been no time for her and Gabriel to talk about much of anything because the whole time they'd been walking through the forest they had known they were being hunted. She knew that Gabe was Agent Dawson's brother, and she knew there was a leak at the US Marshals that had jeopardized her new identity. That much at least was true because Gabriel wasn't the only one who had come after her, so the new name she'd gotten in witness protection was already tainted.

Okay, she could buy that he'd taken her the way he had in case anyone else was watching her, he'd look like just another bounty hunter. And he'd said he had to keep her at the cabin because if he didn't she was likely to go running straight to the Marshals to help them find their mole, and he wasn't wrong. That likely would have been her first thought.

But drugging her, making her think she'd been abducted, keeping her chained up so she couldn't escape, that hadn't been strictly necessary.

If he'd explained everything to her and shown her proof, then she would have listened to reason.

Instead, he'd purposefully made her think she was being held ready to hand over to O'Riley.

Could that be true?

No.

She was being ridiculous.

Gabriel's team had come for them.

Well him?

Both of them?

Problem was she wasn't sure.

It was true that they'd carried their teammate to a vehicle when they'd eliminated the last of the threats. One of them had tried to pick her up, too, but she'd panicked and swung the weapon at him.

He—Panther she thought his name might have been—had been gentle, soothing, and hadn't pushed her on it. He hadn't seemed particularly worried that she was pointing a loaded gun at him, but then again, he was probably trained enough that he could have taken it from her if he really wanted to.

Instinct had told her not to get in the car with them, or maybe it was just her fear, but it wasn't like she had any other options.

So here she was.

Crammed in the backseat next to Gabriel, the weapon still clutched between her hands. The medic, Rock he was called, sat on Gabe's other side and was constantly checking the IV, taking his vitals, and tending to his wound. None of the guys seemed all that concerned about his injury, but she was terrified.

It was infected, she knew that much, and since it had missed his heart and lungs, and she assumed it had bounced off his ribs it had likely cracked or even broken them.

He must be in so much pain.

Tillie hated that.

Other people's pain was a huge trigger for her.

Just because she didn't have conscious memories of the night of her father's killing spree, it didn't mean she didn't remember the feelings. The echoes of screams still sounded in her head, and the look of absolute terror in eyes as they looked at her as though her tiny toddler-sized body had the power to save them. Their fear lived inside her like it had passed from their souls to hers when they passed away.

When she saw someone in pain, it set off all those old feelings. And she knew Gabriel, had spent days with him, knew that even if something else was going on here he was at heart a good man, one who had spent their time together at the cabin trying to keep her distracted from her fear. If he wasn't a good man, he wouldn't have bothered.

Unlike the small child she'd been that night, now she was an adult, she understood what was going on, well at least part of it, but she definitely understood that Gabriel could have died, and if he did, it would have been all her fault.

Lost in thought as she was, Tillie didn't realize that they'd stopped driving until someone opened her car door.

When they did, she gasped and swung the weapon in their direction, ready to eliminate anyone who was a threat to her. Or to Gabriel.

"Easy there, blondie, we're here," Panther said. His hands were up, palms out, in what she knew was an attempt to put her at ease, but it wasn't working. Nothing was going to put her at ease right now. Her entire life was in turmoil and she might never be safe again. What about that screamed ease?

"Here where?" she asked as she fumbled to unbuckle her seatbelt.

"Somewhere safe," Panther replied vaguely.

See.

This was *exactly* why she was having major trouble trusting anyone. All she kept getting were half-answers or no real answers at all. That told her absolutely nothing.

He leaned in and she panicked.

Swinging the gun up at him, he gave a small sigh, even as his eyes were twinkling with amusement. "Just going to undo your seatbelt, blondie. You going to keep threatening to shoot me every time I get close?"

Yes.

Although she didn't say that.

She didn't say anything because she realized that some of the guys had taken Gabriel out of the vehicle and were carrying him toward a small cabin. A different cabin than where they'd been before.

Her hands were still shaking, but she made herself lower the gun, and Panther leaned in and helped her with her seatbelt. As soon as he had it undone, she was scrambling out of the vehicle and hurrying after Gabe.

By the time she climbed the porch steps, Gabriel had been laid out in a bed.

Tears shimmered in her eyes as she looked at him. He looked so still, so vulnerable, lying there like that.

Anything could hurt him and there was nothing he could do about it.

It seemed like the most natural thing in the world to cross the small cabin and curl up on the floor beside the bed, placing herself between Gabriel and the other men who were pulling up seats at the table.

Stupid as it was, Tillie couldn't resist the urge to try to protect him, even if he didn't need it or she couldn't provide real protection. If these men wanted to, they could kill her without breaking a sweat. They were allowing her the illusion of having some control over her situation, but they all knew it was a lie.

She had no control.

Her life was swinging wildly about over a huge bottomless pit.

One wrong move and the thin thread keeping her up would snap.

Shrinking away from Rock when he knelt in front of her, it took all of her focus not to point the weapon at him. These men were Gabriel's friends, they weren't going to hurt her.

Perhaps if she kept telling herself that, eventually she would believe it.

"Need to check your wounds," Rock said gently, nodding at her bloody hands and knees.

Right.

Somehow, she'd completely forgotten them. Crazy since now he reminded her, they throbbed and burned. But she'd had bigger problems than her own discomfort. Worrying about Gabriel had consumed all the energy her brain had left.

Plus worrying over him meant she didn't have to think about what O'Riley had made her do in that warehouse.

That was something she wanted to erase from her memory and pretend it had never happened.

Letting anyone she didn't know touch her right now was beyond her.

Quickly, she shuffled back until she bumped into the bed. Her head shook back and forth with enough force her neck hurt, but she couldn't seem to stop.

"No!" The word burst out of her, and although she said no more than that, understanding filled the man's eyes.

"Okay, blondie, no one will touch you right now, you just try to get some rest, okay? I know you don't believe it, but you *are* safe here, and Tank *is* going to be all right."

As Rock walked away to join the rest of his team, leaving her clutching the gun and still shaking her head, Tillie allowed a single tear to escape.

No one knew what was waiting for them around the corner, and in her case, each corner seemed to conceal another horror, another trauma, another loss.

All she could think about was what awful thing would happen to her next.

CHAPTER

Fifteen

April 22nd
   3:44 A.M.

Waking was harder than it should have been, but somehow, Tank managed to pry open his eyes.

First thing that registered was that he was lying in a bed. Second was a white bandage taped to his chest, and vague memories of Rock treating him flittered through his mind. Third was an IV running from the back of his hand to a pole that had been set up beside the bed.

His bed it turned out. A quick glance around the small cabin showed it was his cabin. The guys had brought him home, probably the safest place in the world his pixie could be right now.

Pixie.

Another look around his cabin, and this time, he noted Rock, Panther, Scorpion, and Trick sitting around his table.

But no Tallulah.

Panic sent a jolt of energy through him, shoving away the lingering effects of whatever sedatives Rock had been feeding him to keep him out and give his body a chance to recoup its strength. There was no way his guys would hand her off to anyone else, he was sure about that. This meant if she wasn't here, she had been injured more seriously than he realized and they'd had no choice but to send her to a hospital.

As he shoved himself up into a sitting position, he saw her.

Sitting on the floor with her back against the side of his bed, her knees pulled up to her chest, and one hand still clutching the gun.

Even though she knew these guys were his team, that they were safe here, she had still put herself between him and his team, ready to protect him despite the fact she knew nothing was going to happen.

His heart did something weird in his chest. It filled with a warmth that spread through his body. This tiny little woman was ready to take on four highly trained killing machines with a single weapon, injured, and exhausted because she cared about him.

"Everything is going to be okay now, pixie. Told you to stand down already, we can trust the cavalry," he said.

At the sound of his rough voice, Tallulah scrambled off the floor and leaned over the bed. "You're awake." Tears shimmered in her eyes, along with obvious relief. "I was so scared you were going to die, and it would have been all my fault."

Her distress wrapped like a vice around his heart, making it hard to breathe. At every turn, this woman managed to pull emotions out of him that he had been positive he'd managed to eradicate in the aftermath of his parents' murders.

Not letting anyone in seemed like the smart move. Protect himself at all costs. His brother and his team, that was it, the only people he allowed himself to care about, and even that was taking a massive risk given their line of work.

At any moment, he could lose any one of them and it would hurt.

Badly.

But losing this woman he'd known only a few days?

That he feared had the ability to crush to smithereens his moral compass.

Losing her would snap his hold on his restraint, and he would become the killing machine he had vowed never to become. Taking a life as part of his job was one thing, but to go off the rails and start hunting

—even if it was evil, dangerous men—would make him into someone he wouldn't like. Wouldn't respect.

Someone who would be unworthy of his pixie.

"I'm not that easy to kill, pixie," he assured her. "And the only person whose fault it would have been is O'Riley's."

Tallulah didn't look convinced, but she took a step back when Rock came over and began to check his vitals.

"You were lucky," the medic said.

"Yeah," Tank agreed. It was true he was. He should be dead and had no idea why he wasn't. Luck was the only way to describe why the bullet had bounced off his ribs instead of plowing through his chest, piercing his heart, or puncturing his lungs. His gaze shifted to Tallulah, who was still between him and the other guys, and he couldn't help but smile. After everything she'd been through, she was more worried about him.

Then he noticed her hands.

They weren't bandaged.

Smudges of dry blood coated them, and since he'd seen them he knew it had to be agony for her to be clutching that weapon so tightly against her wounds.

Turning accusing eyes on Rock, he growled, "You didn't treat her wounds."

Rock held up his hands, palms out. "Tried, man, she didn't want to be touched."

This time he turned his gaze to his pixie. She'd averted hers and red was staining her otherwise pale cheeks.

What had happened in that warehouse?

Earlier in the van, he'd known she was keeping something from him, but he hadn't had the time then to push her on what exactly it was.

Now he needed to know.

Needed to know how badly he was going to punish Mac O'Riley when he got his hands on the man. Because no one got away with hurting his pixie.

Not even him.

And Tank knew when she learned the truth, the wounds he inflicted would be the worst ones of all.

"Go sit down, let Rock take a look at you," he ordered somewhat gruffly. Tallulah's almost imperceptible flinch didn't go unnoticed, and it made him feel like the lowest piece of filth on the planet.

There she'd been, sitting watch at his side, protecting him to the exclusion of her own health and comfort, and he couldn't even thank her.

Head down, she turned to follow Rock to the table, and it was pure instinct that had him reaching out to wrap a hand around her wrist, stopping her from leaving.

She'd been through enough, he couldn't add to that.

"Sorry, pixie, didn't mean to be rough on you. You saved my life, can't ever thank you enough for that, but ..." Tank scrubbed his free hand down his face, not sure how to explain it to her in a way she would understand and not take offense at. "It's my job to protect *you*. I failed, pixie. I'm so sorry. Can you forgive me?"

Tank didn't ask for forgiveness.

In his job, he did what was necessary to keep the good guys—whether that be his team, innocent bystanders, or someone he had been assigned to protect—alive, and the bad guys eliminated. There was no need to apologize for that, it was what he was paid to do.

But with his pixie ... he'd hurt her and there was no excuse for that.

Tallulah's face softened and she leaned over and touched a kiss to his cheek. "I understand. The order of things as you know it, as they exist in your world, has been thrown into chaos. But I'm still alive, and that's thanks to you—and them," she added with a glance over her shoulder at his team.

"Your big heart is going to get you killed one day, pixie," he said. As much as he respected her for caring for and about everyone who entered her orbit, he hated that it would wind up getting her hurt.

"I don't know how to be anyone else but who I am, Gabe," she said softly.

"Don't change who you are, pixie, just remember that not everyone you meet has your best interests at heart." Him included.

Because while Prey would do everything within its power to keep her alive and safe, none of them were on her side.

None of them truly had her best interests at heart.

Nudging her toward the table, he swung his legs over the side of the bed. "Go, get those hands and knees of yours taken care of. And next time, pixie, you make sure someone treats your wounds, you don't tell them no for any reason."

When she rolled her eyes at him, he fought back a laugh. His pixie didn't have an ounce of self-preservation, but she loved and cared with her whole being, and he loved that about her. He just couldn't stand seeing her hurting.

Never before had he experienced anything like it. From his parents' gruesome murders to his years in Delta and now at Prey, he'd seen and heard a lot of people in pain. It was never pleasant, even when those screams were coming from the enemy. But never before had he felt another's pain in such an internalized way.

"Your girl is as tough as they come," Panther said, coming up beside him as he walked slowly toward the table to join the others.

"She's not my girl," Tank replied automatically, but he felt a pang in his chest at the declaration. Did he want her to be his girl? Had he done something utterly ridiculous like fall for Tallulah Russel? And when had it happened?

When she'd gotten him in the groin when he'd abducted her? When she'd sassed him at the cabin despite her fear of him? When she'd told him she wanted to kiss him? When she'd shot a man to save his life?

Nothing had changed, she was still a job, and she was still in danger. Until O'Riley was caught she would never be safe.

"We need a new plan," he said, his eyes still watching his little warrior pixie.

"We have a plan," Rock reminded him. "We need to stick to it, use Tallulah as bait to get O'Riley then this will all be over."

Over.

Yeah, it would be over all right.

"No!" The word came out so loud and so viciously that everyone looked over at him. His eyes met his pixie's, and Tank knew he was fighting a losing battle.

There was no question about it, no doubt in his mind. He was falling for the pixie, and if Tallulah was his then he would protect her with his dying breath, and that started with not following through on Prey's original plan of using her as bait.

~

April 22nd
   4:03 A.M.

"Gabe?" Tillie shoved away from the table and walked on unsteady legs toward him. He sounded so angry, and she wondered what his friend had said to him to provoke such a response. Surely, it couldn't be good for him to be so worked up given his injuries. Really, he shouldn't even be out of bed. "What's wrong? Are you okay?"

"Isn't Rock supposed to be checking you out?" he growled, his dark eyes stormy with an emotion she didn't understand.

She cast a wary glance at the medic. All of these men were big, and they scared her. They were hard, and tough, and although they'd all been nice, she didn't know them, and they reminded her of O'Riley's men even if they were the good guys.

As much as she wanted to, she just couldn't shake the sense that something was off, and until she knew what it was and how it affected her, she couldn't relax.

"No more delaying. Go. Now," he ordered. He was all over the place since waking up, angry that she hadn't let anyone treat her wounds, then apologizing for being angry with her, but then not even a minute later being grumpy all over again. She knew he was hurting and weak and worried, as well as dealing with some guilt over being out of commission and not being able to get her away from O'Riley, but something else was going on here.

"But—"

"No buts, Tallulah. You look like a slight breeze is enough to knock you down, and you'll be lucky if those wounds aren't already infected."

He wasn't wrong about the slight breeze. Her entire body was trembling with the effort of remaining standing, and she wanted nothing more than to curl up in a big, soft comfortable bed and sleep for about a week.

Worried Gabriel's massive frame was also on the verge of collapse, she ignored him and moved beside him, slipping an arm around his waist to steady him.

"I'm fine," she murmured. "What made you angry?"

He pressed his lips into a thin line and refused to answer.

Fine.

If he was going to be a baby, she'd have to get answers somewhere else. She turned to Rock, noted his amused smirk, but ignored it. "Why is he angry?"

Instead of answering, Rock looked to Gabriel, who obviously communicated something with his glare because the medic merely started unpacking his first aid kit, laying out supplies on the table.

"Panther? What's going on?" she asked the man standing on the other side of Gabriel.

"Think you better go sit your cute little butt down at the table and let Rock take a look at those wounds," Panther replied, which was not at all an answer to her question. Not even close.

A growl rumbled through Gabriel's chest, and she frowned at him. He was even more confusing now than he'd been at the cabin when she first started getting an inkling that there was something she was missing.

There was still something she was missing, but it seemed she was the only one because all four guys were laughing now.

"I don't get it," she said, feeling utterly lost.

"He doesn't like anyone mentioning your butt, darlin'," Trick drawled.

"Oh." Her cheeks heated. Right now, she didn't want anyone looking at her backside, except maybe .... She cast a surreptitious glance up at Gabriel who was glaring at his friends.

Her head chose that moment to make her feel like they'd jumped on a rollercoaster without her permission, and a small moan escaped before she could stop it.

Any hope Gabriel wouldn't notice was, of course, in vain.

"Pixie?" Any anger in his tone was gone. Now he just sounded concerned as he brushed away the arm she'd wrapped around him and instead scooped her up.

"You shouldn't be doing that," Rock said, but sounded totally resigned.

"He's right," Tillie said even as she wrapped an arm around his shoulders and held on to him for dear life as her head continued to spin. "You shouldn't be carrying me."

"And you should be in bed, with your wounds cleaned and bandaged, and with an IV giving you painkillers, antibiotics, and fluids. Did you even drink some water?" Gabriel asked as he carried her to the table and set her down in a chair, pulling one up beside her and sitting down in it.

"Umm ..." No she hadn't, but she didn't want to have an argument with Gabriel about it when she could barely think straight and couldn't defend herself.

"Drink this, darlin'," Trick said, and she curled up her nose at the orange drink he held out to her.

"What is it?"

"Electrolyte drink. It will help replenish everything your body lost," Trick explained.

When she went to pick it up, Gabriel grumbled and nudged her hand away. "Hands on the table, pixie, palms up so Rock can see them."

She knew a command when she heard one, was also smart enough to know that these guys had reached their limit, and would now enforce that she let them take care of her. Maybe if she just kept reminding herself that none of them were going to force her onto her knees and make her do something she didn't want to do then she could do this.

As she laid her hands on the table, palms up like Gabe had ordered, Tillie knew they were shaking badly enough that everyone would notice.

Which of course they did, she knew because she felt the protective male energy in the room grow by like a million percent.

"Drink." A straw touched her lips, and almost absentmindedly she opened her lips and took a sip of the too-sweet liquid. When Gabriel set it down, he immediately moved closer so their thighs touched, and slung an arm around her shoulders, urging her to rest against him.

"Belt?" Rock asked gently as he began to wipe away the dirt and grime stuck in the gashes.

"Y-yes," she stammered. He was wearing gloves and that helped because she couldn't feel skin against her skin.

"How did the wounds get dirt in them, sweetheart?" Rock asked.

"H-he wanted me to c-crawl," she replied. There was no way Tillie was telling them what else O'Riley had made her do. That was a secret she planned on taking to her grave.

"I'm sorry, pixie," Gabriel whispered as he pressed his lips to her temple and held them there.

His touch helped, and so long as he didn't move she was able to hold her hands still while Rock carefully cleaned her palms, then applied antibiotic ointment and wrapped them in bandages. It would mean she wasn't able to do a lot for the next few days, but honestly, her hands hurt so badly that she didn't really want to use them anyway.

"Knees next, pixie," Gabriel said, spinning her in the chair so she was sitting sideways, then settling her so her back rested against his chest. One of his thick arms circled her waist, his hand resting against her stomach, and she finally felt safe again.

She had no idea how he managed it, but this man possessed the ability to take away everything she was going through and make her feel like it was all going to work out okay.

Ripping the holes in her yoga pants so he could get access to her knees without having her remove them—something which she greatly appreciated—Rock went to work on those wounds.

"Why did you get angry before?" she asked Gabriel, to distract her from the stinging agony in her legs that made them feel like they were being struck all over again.

"He doesn't like our plan," Rock replied.

"Your plan?" Tillie asked.

"Leave it," Gabriel growled.

"No, I want to know," she insisted. It was her life they were talking about, after all. For Gabe and his team, this was a job, but for her it was life and death.

Gabriel growled again, but Rock merely laughed, then sobered as he looked at her. "O'Riley isn't going to let you go, blondie, not for anything, I think you know that. The only way you'll ever be safe is to remove him from the equation. Permanently."

"How do we do that?" she asked. Gabriel gave another growl, and she absently stroked his thigh, calming him. She was too lost in thought to see the other men exchanging glances.

"They want you to play bait," Gabe snarled, throwing mean-looking glares at his friends.

"Bait?" she echoed, twisting so she could look over her shoulder at him.

"As in, risk your life again on the chance that we get this guy. I won't allow it," Gabriel said.

"Excuse me? You won't allow it? When did you become the boss of me?" Tillie asked but she couldn't deny she kind of liked the growly possessive look in his eyes right now. It was so nice to have someone standing in her corner after so long standing there alone. Could he really care about her? As in a more than a job way?

"You have a death wish, pixie?"

She huffed a chuckle despite the nausea churning in her belly. As badly as the idea of facing O'Riley again terrified her, the desire to end things and finally be free, was tempting.

Too tempting.

"This has to end, Gabe, and I think I'm the only one who can end it."

CHAPTER

Sixteen

April 22nd
4:34 A.M.

Surely, they had all gone insane.

The pixie included.

He might have been the one who was shot, lost blood, and was battling an infection, but it seemed like he was the only one capable of being logical.

"She's not doing it," Tank told his team. It didn't matter that this had been the plan all along. Get custody of Tallulah Russel, make it look like she'd been taken by another bounty hunter, keep her restrained so she believed she was being kept ready to be handed over so her reactions would be believable when it was time to make a deal with Mac O'Riley.

Although the pixie would make a compelling witness in the case of the murdered maid, none of them would put it past the crime boss to find a way to buy his way out of trouble. That would be a whole lot harder to do when he made a deal to purchase the star witness for the prosecution, backed up by members of the well-respected Prey Security.

The plan had never set well with any of them. Nobody liked using an innocent even if she had inadvertently gotten herself into the mess to begin with. But in the end, it was the only way for Tallulah to truly be safe.

The ends justify the means and all that.

But that was before he knew her. Had spent time with her. Witnessed firsthand her strength and courage. Knew how she hid the real her behind a curtain of perfection in her never-ending quest to make up for her father's crimes.

The worst part was, he now knew that if they'd told her of the plan, she would have agreed to it, and maybe even been able to pull it off believably.

Only now, the thought of her in danger made him queasy.

"Don't dismiss me," Tallulah fumed beside him.

Since the thought of his pixie willingly walking into the lion's den had him a step away from losing his mind, he ignored her and focused on his team. "Come up with another plan. I won't let you use her." As far as he was concerned it was as simple as that.

"Won't *let* them?" his pixie spluttered.

"You're cute when you're mad, pixie. But you have no training which makes you a liability." Tank actually thought the opposite. Yes, she had no training, but she was anything but a liability. She had saved his life back in that van, point blank, no questions asked. If she hadn't grabbed that gun and shot that man, he'd be dead, and she would likely still be in O'Riley's clutches.

But he had to find a way to keep her as far from O'Riley as he could.

Right now, nothing was more important to him.

"You are unbelievable. I saved your ungrateful self, didn't I?" Tallulah snapped.

"She's got you there, Tank," Rock said, clearly amused. "Don't worry, we'll make sure your girl doesn't get hurt."

"I'm not his ... oh ..." Tallulah peeked up at him through her long lashes and he'd give almost anything to know what was running through her head right now.

Just because he was feeling damn possessive of the pixie, it didn't mean she wanted him in any way. Even if she did when she knew that he'd been using her this whole time, she would never believe that he truly cared for her.

Tank threw a glare his friend's way, the last thing they needed right now was for him to be distracted by his feelings for Tallulah.

Rock just shrugged, packed up his first aid kit, and went to join the others in the sitting area, leaving him and his pixie alone.

Wasn't like they hadn't been alone before. Most of the time they'd spent together, it had been just the two of them, but Tank was feeling vulnerable, exposed, like he had already given too much away and now the pixie could see right down deep into his soul.

"Ignore Rock, he just likes to stir up trouble," he said quickly.

"Oh." Now she looked hurt and confused. Women. What guy understood them? Certainly not him. "So ... you don't like me?" There was a hesitation in her question, like it took major effort on her part to ask it.

"I ... it's not ... we're ..." he stammered, and stammering wasn't something he ever did.

"He likes you, darlin'," Trick called out.

"I'm going to take great pleasure in killing you all," he growled, but his team just laughed at the threat they knew he'd never follow through on.

"Gabriel, I like you too," his pixie said softly, resting one of her small hands on his forearm.

Damn.

There she went again, showing him up. She had more courage in her little finger than he did in his entire body.

He sighed and scrubbed his hands down his face. This was all so crazy. Women were usually a one-and-done thing for him, he didn't fall for them, and he certainly didn't fall for them in a matter of days.

How could this be happening?

Besides the obvious that she was going to hate him when she learned the extent of her involvement in their plan, the life he lived was hardly conducive to long term relationships. How could he ask Tallulah to sign up for that when her life had been anything but stable? She deserved a man who would be there for her every night, who would help around the house and taking care of the kids. Who wouldn't be gone for days, weeks, or even months at a time, who wouldn't miss birthdays, and holidays, and other special occasions.

Yet he couldn't deny that Tallulah had him feeling things he had no business feeling.

"We don't have a lot in common." If he could convince her that she didn't want anything to do with him, maybe it would make all of this easier.

"We have one thing in common. We like each other. It's crazy, and makes no sense, and I don't understand it. It ... scares me, but ... I don't think I want to walk away until I do understand it."

How could he possibly deny her that?

Denying himself was one thing, but not giving Tallulah anything her heart desired seemed impossible.

"Can't deny I crave you, pixie," he admitted, "but I don't know how to do ... this." He waved his hand between them.

"You think I do? I've dated before, but I never felt for them anything even close to what I feel right now. It's definitely overwhelming, but maybe it could be amazing, too." Shy but hopeful eyes looked up at him, and he knew in that moment he was prepared to do whatever it took to make this woman his, and offer her everything he had in return.

"Pixie, *you* are amazing," he said as he reached out and brushed his knuckles across her cheek. "I don't want you hurt."

Her small hands clasped his, and he quickly turned them so he cradled hers and she wasn't putting pressure on her wounds. "I don't want to get hurt either, but O'Riley is never going to let me go. I want my life back, I want a chance to see what this weird and crazy thing is between us. But I don't want to do this alone. I'm so tired of being alone. I can do this with you, I trust you, Gabe. I know you'll keep me safe, protect me. Please, Gabriel, I need you."

This was a bad idea, he knew that it was. There were so many things that could go wrong. But how could he not help this beautiful woman get her life back, even if he had to walk away from her when this was done, when she was safe?

Because that was the inevitable ending.

Once she knew the truth, Tallulah would no longer trust him.

No longer need him.

He felt that loss deeply.

She'd never really been his, and yet, when she was gone she would leave a huge hole in his heart.

"Fine. I'll be there. We'll do this," he agreed. "But right now, we're both going to get some sleep. You haven't slept in days, and even before that, you can't have slept well cuffed to me."

"I did ask you to uncuff me," she teased, and her ability to forgive left him in awe of her.

"Knew my pixie would fly away if I let her." Tank stood and picked her up, carrying her over to his bed, barely feeling the tug in his chest from his wound. It wasn't because of the painkillers Rock had given him, it was because this woman managed to make everything better just by being there.

"What are you doing?" she asked when he set her down on the mattress and pulled back the covers, sliding in beside her and covering them both up.

"Sleeping."

"Why am I in your bed?" Although she asked the question, she made no attempt to climb out.

"Because we both need sleep. We're both exhausted and both at the end of our ropes. And I need you here, in my arms," he admitted, as close as he could come right now to saying how far he had already fallen for her.

Instead of answering, Tallulah yawned and snuggled close against his side, already drifting off to sleep. This wasn't going to last, but Tank was going to enjoy every second of his pixie's light while he could.

April 23rd
    7:39 A.M.

Peace.

There was something about this place that made her feel like she had entered another world. One without pain and suffering, one filled with the gentle, soothing peace of nature.

Tillie could stay here forever.

"Breakfast is served."

She glanced up as Gabriel walked out onto the porch carrying a tray with more food than the two of them could hope to eat in a day let alone a single meal.

"You really should have let me help," she said, standing to reach for the tray.

"Uh-uh, sit yourself back down. You know what Rock said, you're supposed to be resting those hands," Gabriel told her.

"You were *shot*," she reminded him. Although looking at him, you wouldn't be able to tell that just two days ago he had been shot in the chest, lost a whole ton of blood, and gotten an infection.

Standing there in gray sweatpants and a black T-shirt that molded to his chiseled physique, he looked the picture of strength and power. She knew there was a bandage taped to the wound beneath that T-shirt, and that Rock had given him antibiotics to take for the next several days, but Gabriel looked ... like perfection.

Everything she needed right now.

As much as it terrified her to go up against O'Riley with this ruse, she knew she could do it as long as she had this man in her corner.

It felt like she could do *anything* so long as she had this man in her corner.

"Sit, pixie," Gabriel ordered, and she dropped down onto the porch swing without conscious thought. For some reason, now that she knew Gabe wasn't going to hurt her, that he was one of the good guys and not the mercenary she'd thought him to be, she didn't mind when he ordered her about.

In fact ...

When she thought of him ordering her around in the bedroom it made her aroused.

"Okay, pixie, I've got to know what just made you blush," Gabriel said as he sat beside her on the large wooden porch swing and set the tray in between them.

"Umm ..." No way was she going to tell him that the idea of him taking complete control in the bedroom left her a throbbing mass of pure desire. "It's nothing."

Gabe arched a brow. "Nothing, huh? So, if I drag you over onto my lap and kiss you it won't at all be connected to whatever has you brighter red than these strawberries?"

She squeaked when he somehow managed to grab her, lift her without disturbing the tray, and set her on his lap. The thick ridge in his pants told her he wasn't just thinking about kissing her, and as much as her body throbbed in response to the thought of that huge erection filling her up, she glanced over her shoulder. "We can't, Gabe. We're outside. What if your friends see us?"

"They're in their own cabins," he said, nuzzling her neck and making her moan and tilt it to the side to give him better access.

"Their own cabins? You guys live out here? I thought this was just like the cabin you brought me to before only someplace else, like a safehouse or something. This cabin is yours?"

"Yep. Built it myself," he said proudly.

"It's amazing, like something out of a storybook."

As a child the idea of living in the woods, surrounded by trees, flowers, streams, and animals had always been an appealing one. It was so quiet, so peaceful, and without a million sets of eyes watching you suspiciously as though they expected you to break out a knife at any second, you could just ... be.

That's exactly how she felt right now.

Despite the danger she was in and the plan to play bait that she had agreed to, she felt free out here.

"It's a great place to live," Gabriel agreed.

"And your whole team lives here?"

There was a moment's hesitation, and Tillie thought maybe she had somehow inadvertently asked the wrong thing, but then his dark eyes grew serious, and he held her gaze. "Yeah, they all live here. We all have our own cabin and then there are some common areas we share. Panther's seven-year-old son lives here, and so does Axe's wife."

"Axe?" She didn't remember meeting him. There had only been four men, Rock, Panther, Scorpion, and Trick. Who was Axe?

"He's our team leader. Well, he was until a few months back when he asked me to take over for him." Gabriel sighed and there was genuine concern and affection in his eyes when he spoke. "Beth—Axe's wife— she disappeared. Couldn't find a trace of her, and believe me, we have the best people in the world working with us. It was like she just went poof and disappeared into thin air. Then just as mysteriously as she disappeared, she reappeared. Same day I got assigned your case."

"The poor woman." Tillie couldn't think of anything more horrible than being snatched away from the people who loved you. "What happened to her? Where was she?"

"She doesn't know."

"Doesn't know?"

"Amnesia. Doesn't remember any of us, or Axe, or who she is, or her life before or during her disappearance. Nothing. It's all gone."

Okay, so there was something worse than being snatched from the people who loved you. Not even remembering them was just awful. So awful she didn't even want to think about it.

"Poor Axe," she whispered. Fighting back tears, her heart broke for the man.

"This is hell for him, but we're all there for him. For both of them. We might not be a family built on DNA, but we couldn't love each other more if we were."

As nice as that was ... "I don't think I quite understand exactly who you guys are. Are you military?"

"You've heard of Prey Security?"

"Yes, of course. Who hasn't?" The world-renowned company and the billionaire siblings who owned it were known across the globe.

"We're one of the teams who work for Prey. Bravo Team. The guys and I used to be in Delta together, but we had to get out. Eagle Oswald offered us a job and a chance to stay together, and we jumped on it."

"And this is what you do? Protect people like me?" Although she'd heard of Prey, she didn't quite have a mental picture of what it meant to work for them.

Instead of answering, Gabriel palmed the back of her head, his fingers almost absently massaging her scalp. "I didn't do a very good job of protecting you though did I, pixie?"

There was so much guilt and remorse in his expression that her eyes teared all over again. "It's okay, Gabe. I know if it wasn't for you and your team, O'Riley would have me right now."

"It's not okay, pixie. Tell me what he did to you in that warehouse."

This time she didn't get all hot and bothered at his order.

This time shame filled her.

For the most part, she'd been able to block what O'Riley had made her do. Hadn't been hard, she'd been too busy worrying over Gabe, fighting for her life, and then sleeping away most of the day before as exhaustion finally caught up with her.

But now, with Gabriel asking her point blank what had happened, how could she erase it from her memory?

"Tell me, pixie," Gabe said again, the command in his voice clear, but there was also a whole lot of tenderness.

That was what had her hanging her head, resting her forehead on his broad shoulder, and admitting the truth.

"He brought in little Mac," she said softly.

"His son was there?"

"Yeah. Guess he's decided it's time to inflict more horror on the child. To warp and twist him into a mini-version of himself. The boy was so scared, and he's so small."

"You were scared, too," Gabriel said fiercely. "And you're tiny compared to O'Riley. What did you do to keep the boy safe."

Maybe it should surprise her that Gabe knew whatever she'd done she had done so to protect the child, but it didn't. From the very beginning, he seemed to be able to read her and know what she needed before she did.

"O'Riley gave little Mac a gun, the boy was crying, pleading, but his father didn't care. He wanted me to crawl, thank him for not killing me outright. I refused." When his big chest vibrated with a growl, she began to absently pet him, above his wound, right over his heart. "That's why he whipped me. When he had his son there, I knew I'd do whatever he wanted. He knew it, too. And when he told his innocent little boy to shoot you if I didn't do what he wanted I didn't have a choice. He told me to kneel before him, and ..." she trailed off, assuming the end to the sentence was obvious.

The growl that roared through Gabriel was something she'd never heard before.

Hoped to never hear again.

For a moment, she couldn't tell if he was angry with her or scared for her.

Then he crushed her against his chest, and she knew.

Scared for her.

Not just scared, terrified, even though he knew she was here and she was okay. She had survived.

"Don't you *ever* put me or anyone else above your own survival again," he growled.

"Gabe, you know I can't agree to that," she said gently. "I can't be anyone other than who I am. And who I am is someone who will *always* put the people I care about before myself. Just like you do."

His hold on her tightened until it was almost too much, but since she knew he needed to hold her as much as she needed to be held, she didn't protest or try to pull free.

"I don't deserve you, pixie, but I'm too selfish to let you go."

Before she could decipher those cryptic words, his lips crashed down to meet hers and everything else faded away.

CHAPTER
Seventeen

April 23rd
8:02 A.M.

This was it.

No going back.

Once they crossed this line, Tank knew he would never be able to let the pixie go. Even when she learned the truth, that he had always intended to use her and put her life in danger, he would fight for her.

Get down on his hands and knees and beg for forgiveness if that's what it took.

Didn't matter that he hadn't known her then or that he'd only been following the orders he'd been given, Tallulah would feel betrayed. She'd handed him her trust, not an easy feat for someone who had been through what she had, and he'd stomped all over it.

Damn. If his team had arrived at the cabin before the other bounty hunters all of this could have been avoided. They would have made contact with O'Riley, waited until the money had been transferred, then capture the man when he came to pick up Tallulah. She never would have had to run for her life, almost drown in the waterfall, be captured, hurt, and sexually assaulted.

She wouldn't be here in his arms right now, offering him free reign to her huge, warm heart.

He never would have gotten so attached that he couldn't think straight.

When his pixie's hands fumbled at the waistband of his sweatpants, a little of his common sense clicked back online.

They couldn't do this out here, not after what she'd just been through.

Somehow, he managed to tear his lips from hers. "Pixie, we can't do this."

Her face fell, the heat and desire bleeding away, replaced by disappointment and uncertainty. "You don't want me?"

"Pixie," Tank groaned. "I want you more than oxygen, more than I can bear. I'm aching to feel you come all over me, but you just went through something horrific, and I don't want to push you into doing something you aren't ready for."

The smile she gave him was so soft he felt its tenderness deep down to the parts of himself he'd locked away that night as a boy listening to his parents' horrific murders. "Gabe, what O'Riley did to me was outside of my control. I wanted to stop it, but I couldn't, not without you getting hurt, not without that innocent child having to do something he can never come back from, the first step in him becoming his father. But this I want. This I need."

That was all he needed to hear.

When he went to pick her up, take her inside, do this right, the way his pixie deserved, she placed her hands on his shoulders and stopped him. "No, here."

"Anyone could come by and see us."

"You said your friends are in their cabins. I want to do this here, freely, no inhibitions. I don't always want to be the girl who has to be perfect to make up for things she didn't even do. I want to just be me. Me and you, out here in the forest, like this I feel like we're the only people in the whole universe. I've never felt like this before, I feel like all the chains that have always been tying me down are gone. How did you do that?"

The wonder in her eyes was beautiful, but in reality, he hadn't done anything other than cause her pain. She'd found her own way to let go of those chains, she'd found her power, and come to the realization that she had no sins to atone for.

"All you, my sweet, beautiful pixie. You found your strength, the strength that was there all along, but you weren't looking in the right place to find it. Tell me what you want, pixie."

"I want you to take me. Don't hold back, treat me like you would any other woman," she said as she ground her hot center against his erection. Already he could feel the wetness soaking through her panties and the pair of leggings she'd put on this morning.

"You're not like any other woman, pixie." Tank needed Tallulah to understand that. She wasn't some random woman he'd picked up because he wanted a warm body rather than his hand for once. If she was, his team never would have brought her here to their home.

She was special and she deserved to be treated as such.

Still, he wasn't averse to a little sex on the porch.

Anything to keep this look of wonder in the pixie's stunning blue-green eyes.

"You're not like anyone I've ever met. You're this mixture of sweet and compassionate, and tough and strong. You're totally an alpha, but at the same time, you've gone out of your way to be a softie to me. I ... I'm falling, Gabriel," she admitted.

"Oh, pixie, I've already fallen."

With that, he gripped her hips and tipped her backward, keeping hold of her as she squeaked and giggled so she didn't hurt her hands by holding onto him.

Pressing his nose between the apex of her thighs, Tank breathed deep.

An intoxicating aroma immediately filled his senses, and he knew he would never be able to get enough of her.

Tank wasn't usually a praying man. His prayers the night of the home invasion had gone unanswered, and he'd held a grudge.

Stupid really.

But now he knew he couldn't not pray. Pray that somehow when she learned everything his team had planned his pixie was able to forgive him because he didn't know how he could ever let her go.

"These have got to go." Balancing her with one hand on her backside he slid her leggings and her panties down her slim legs. She wasn't wearing shoes, so he slipped them off and tossed them out into the grass surrounding his cabin. "No going back now, pixie."

"Don't want to go back." The way she said it told him she meant more than sex outside on his porch. She meant in life. Tallulah was finally learning to embrace who she was and stop worrying about other people holding her accountable for her father's actions.

His pixie had found her wings and now it was time for her to fly free.

"Good, because I'm not letting you go, pixie. We go through with this and you're mine."

Tank held her gaze, giving her one last chance to back away, but she didn't.

Instead, she locked her eyes on his as he cupped the backs of her knees and hooked them over his shoulders then buried his head between her legs and swiped his tongue across her center.

"D-don't stop, Gabe," she pleaded as he touched the softest of kisses to her thighs, her entrance, her tight bundle of nerves.

"Remember those words, pixie," he warned as he supported her weight with one hand while his other scooped up the evidence of her arousal, coated his fingers with it, and slipped one inside her.

Damn she was tight.

And hot.

And pure perfection.

While he stroked inside her, catching the spot that he already knew drove her wild, his lips closed around her bud, and he sucked and licked until she was squirming and writhing in his hold.

Never once did she break eye contact and it was insanely erotic knowing she was getting off on watching him get her off as much as she was from what he was doing with his hands and mouth.

Tank knew exactly when she was about to fall apart.

Her entire body went taut, she sucked in a ragged moan and then screamed his name with a ferocity that spoke of her newfound freedom.

But he didn't stop.

He increased the pace of his thrusts, and his mouth sucked hard, flicked his tongue faster against her bud.

"Gabe ... Gabriel ... Tank ... I can't ... enough." She gasped as she continued to ride out wave after wave of pleasure.

"You told me not to stop, pixie, and I won't." Not giving her time to recover from her orgasm, he shifted her down, shoved his sweatpants and boxers out of the way and impaled himself in her in one thrust.

His pixie gasped and moaned as he filled her, her internal muscles still quivered with the last of her pleasure, almost setting off his own release, but he wasn't coming until he got her off again so they could share that ride.

Grasping her bud, he rolled it between his thumb and forefinger, tweaking the no doubt overly sensitive bundle of nerves.

Tallulah squirmed on his lap. "Oh ... Gabe ... no ... it's too much ... I can't ..."

"You can do anything, pixie. Come for me again. Now, pixie, let me see you fall off that ledge." He thrust into her harder, like he wanted to own her, possess her, imprint himself on her so she had no choice but to forgive him and keep him in her life.

"Oh ... I can't ... ah ... I ... I ... I'm coming." She gasped right as her body clamped around him as pleasure hit her hard, sending his own orgasm exploding through his body.

Time had no meaning as he continued to thrust into her, continued to work her bud, continued to ride that wave of pleasure. It was more than pleasure though, it was the sense of connection that he felt. They hadn't just had sex they'd made love. Shared something special. Something he wanted to hold onto and never let go.

When the wave finally ebbed, he tucked her close against his chest, not wanting to let go of this moment just yet.

"Gabe, we didn't use protection," Tallulah said as though it only just occurred to her.

"Ah, sorry, pixie. I knew you were clean and on birth control, but I should have asked. Sorry. I am clean too though, and you only just recently had your shot so we didn't make a baby."

"Oh. I think I'll be offended about that invasion of privacy later, right now, I'm too happy and relaxed," she said as she snuggled closer, his length still buried deep inside her. "Don't let me go, 'kay?"

"Don't plan on it, pixie, don't plan on it." As he wrapped his arms around her, cocooning her against him, Tank once again sent up a prayer that he could keep his pixie.

～

April 24th
    8:47 P.M.

Tillie hoped she knew what she had gotten herself into.

The magic of the day before was gone, although she would hold onto those special moments, use them to ground herself, hold it together, when she faced the terror about to come.

Terror she had invited upon herself.

There was no one but herself to blame for this mess. She'd gone against her boss' orders knowing full well Mac O'Riley was a dangerous man, and she had agreed to play bait when Gabriel's team had suggested it.

Too bad she hadn't come up with this idea right back at the beginning when she first learned there was a bounty on her head, and she had to go into witness protection. If Gabe's brother had suggested that she go to Prey and ask them to help her set up a sting, she could have avoided all this mess.

And yet ...

If it had gone down that way, she wouldn't have connected with Gabriel like they had.

Would she go back and undo the last several days knowing it would mean she wouldn't have found a connection she thought existed only in fairytales?

No.

Tilly knew that she wouldn't.

Love had never seemed to be in the cards before. She'd looked, tried dating, hoped that there might be somebody out there for her, but she'd never really believed it.

Not until a crazy contradiction of a man had broken into her house, drugged her, then cared enough to clean her up when she got sick.

"You smiling, pixie?" Gabriel asked as he came up and slipped an arm around her waist, drawing her up against him.

She came willingly, happily even. Didn't even care that his team was right there watching them. It seemed like the most natural thing in the world to curl her fingers into his T-shirt and tug him down so she could brush her lips across his.

Could she ever get enough of kissing him?

Nope.

Definitely not.

Not when he tasted like happiness and freedom.

Was that even a flavor? Not really, and yet that was absolutely what she tasted, what she felt, whenever he kissed her.

And they'd done a lot of kissing yesterday.

A lot more than kissing, too.

In between him showing her around the impressive property, meeting the guys when she wasn't so strung out that she felt the need to hold a gun on them, and him feeding her more food than she'd ever eaten before in a single day, they'd made love at least a dozen times. From the bed, to the jacuzzi tub, to his huge walk in shower, to the couch, in front of the fire, to the kitchen table—in her mind that was eww because you ate there, but in reality had been pretty hot when he'd tossed her down on it and ravaged her body, making her come four times in quick succession—they'd christened about ever surface in his cabin.

"You can back out if you want," Gabriel whispered against her lips.

Only they both knew she couldn't.

Scared or not, this was her best chance at having a life.

Her best chance at having a future.

With this man.

One she desperately wanted.

For the first time in her life, she felt like she could be herself. Gabriel knew who she was and it didn't seem to matter to him, he liked her anyway, trusted her anyway. Because he had to trust her if he agreed to let her play bait and work with his team, she knew his team was everything to him.

Tillie drew in a breath and then straightened her spine. They'd gone through everything in detail. She knew that Gabriel would be with her the entire time. The rest of his team would be watching their backs. She was sure that nothing could go wrong so long as she had these big, strong warriors at her back.

As long as she had Gabriel at her back.

"No, I don't want to back out. Besides, it's too late to back out now, the plan is already in motion."

Gabriel sighed, and she could tell he was less than enthusiastic about the whole thing. He'd made his position clear, the idea of using her as bait worried him. Okay, it more than worried him. When they had their meeting last night over dinner, he'd pretty much freaked out, and she could tell it amused his friends no end that he was getting that bent out of shape about her. In the end, she and his team had talked him into it. Actually, it had been more his team than her. She was pretty sure the only reason he was going along with this whole thing was because they hadn't given him a choice.

Still, it helped a lot to know he believed she had what it took to do this.

All her life she had lived with the crushing weight of other people's opinions of her, but Gabriel's view of her wasn't crushing, it was freeing.

Because he believed in her.

That mattered more than that he was attracted to her or even that he liked her.

"Let's get this over with," Gabriel said, gathering supplies and ushering her out the cabin's door. Their plan was for him to pretend he had been a bounty hunter all along and that he hadn't appreciated the other mercenaries swooping in and taking his payday. So, he'd gotten her back with the help of some of his friends and now intended to hand her over to O'Riley for the reward like he had wanted all along.

With her stomach in knots, Tillie followed him out, reminding herself that even though she wouldn't see them, Gabriel's team were going to be right there watching over them. The whole time. She was never going to be alone. Gabriel would remain by her side, and as soon as the money was transferred, so there was no way O'Riley could wriggle out of his crimes, Bravo Team would take him and his men into custody and hand them over to the cops.

Easy.

Easy peasy.

Easy peasy lemon squeezy.

Nothing was going to go wrong, and when this was over, she would finally be free of O'Riley. And there would be nothing standing between her and Gabriel, and they'd get a chance to explore this thing between them. Because as much as it scared her, it scared her even more to walk away without knowing what could have been.

If it was nothing, okay, no big deal, she hadn't lost anything.

But if it *was* something, then maybe she could have the future she'd always dreamed about. A husband, children of her own, a happy, normal, boring life.

No, life with Gabriel wouldn't be boring. Not ever. This was his life, putting himself in danger to protect others, it was something she would have to get used to. Images of his big body lying so still, stained with blood, flooded her mind and she knew that any day, any mission could end with him lying that very same way, only maybe not as lucky.

The next bullet could hit his heart or his lungs, end his life and take him from her.

"Hey." Gabriel's large hand caught hers, turning her to face him. "I won't let him hurt you again, okay?"

"I know you won't." Tillie smiled up at him then carefully rested her head on his chest, avoiding his wound. Maybe she'd been selfish in wanting him to be the one to play this out with her. He'd been hurt because of her, almost killed. What if O'Riley did kill him this time? "Maybe you should ..."

"Don't," he warned. "No one else is going to watch your back because no one else will watch it like I will." His hands moved to settle on her hips, and she tilted her face up to meet his as his lips captured hers.

The kiss started out soft, but then Gabriel yanked her closer so she was plastered against his chest, and deepened it. His tongue swept into her mouth, and one of his hands curled possessively into her backside as the kiss grew steamier.

How did this man manage to affect her so much when she'd known him for such a short time?

When he finally released her, they were both breathing hard, both turned on. Her panties were wet, and she could feel his hard length between them.

"Later," he murmured as his knuckles brushed across her cheek.

"I can't wait. Can't seem to get enough of you."

"Already addicted, pixie. You're positive?" His dark eyes probed hers and she tried to hide her nerves. She was scared but she was doing this.

When she nodded, he pulled her wrists behind her back and secured them with zip ties. Tillie had to fight not to panic. Knowing part of the plan involved tying her up and actually being tied up were two different things.

Two *very* different things.

Next came a piece of duct tape over her mouth and she felt her heart rate accelerating. Gabriel scooped her up and put her in the trunk of the car, securing her ankles with another zip tie.

Then he pulled out a syringe and a small vial.

He was going to drug her?

That wasn't part of the plan, at least not as far as she'd been aware.

Fear raged inside her. What was he doing?

"I'm sorry," he whispered, then the needle pierced her skin, and the world immediately began to grow fuzzy.

Was this still a plan to save her, or had Gabriel been playing her all along and just betrayed her for real?

CHAPTER

Eighteen

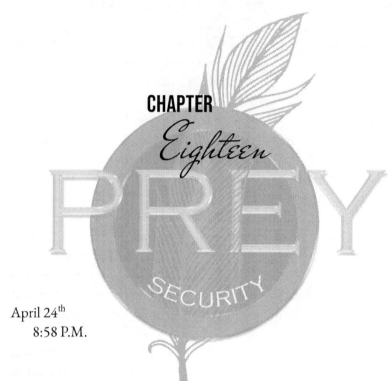

April 24th
8:58 P.M.

Doing the right thing shouldn't be this hard.

This was, without a doubt, *the* hardest thing Tank had ever had to do in his entire life.

The betrayal and raw fear in his pixie's eyes when she saw that vial of sedatives had sliced deeply through his heart.

Knowing there was a chance she would never forgive him for this and actually seeing it play out weren't even in the same universe.

That single moment had destroyed the connection they had been building. A connection that was still small and fragile. They had managed to overcome how he'd treated her when they first met, and for some reason, neither of them seemed to care that these feelings had come out of nowhere and at the speed of light. Trust had been building, and affection was already there. Their attraction burned up the sheets and pretty much any other surface in his cabin, and there were the first sparks of what could turn into love.

Now all of that had gone up in smoke.

"Sorry, man," Rock said, clapping a hand on his shoulder. "We know how hard this is for you."

Looking down at his pixie's unconscious body, bound and gagged, knowing she'd so trustingly allowed herself to be used without really knowing or understanding the stakes, shredded any self-control he had.

"You know do you?" he growled, rounding on a man who had been his friend—his brother—for more than a decade. "You know what it's like to utterly destroy the woman you care more about than your own life? You know what it's like to take her trust and absolutely decimate it? You know what it's like to use her best qualities against her to get what you want without her consent, knowing you're destroying a piece of her soul she will never get back? You know what it's like to lie to the woman you're obsessed with? You know what it's like to sell your soul to the devil because that's what it feels like I've done tonight. You know what it's like to be in love?" he roared the final question because there was zero point in denying he hadn't somehow managed to fall in love with his pixie, and he knew that he'd destroyed her and any hope he'd had of a future with her.

"Yeah, man," Rock said softly, withdrawing his hand. "I know what it's like to completely destroy the woman you love with every fiber of your being. I also know what it's like to attempt to earn redemption so you even stand a chance at deserving her." The man glanced at his chest, where there was a tattoo under his T-shirt. One he'd never explained to any of them, but one they all knew had great significance to the man.

And now Tank felt like the lowest of the low.

Not only had he betrayed Tallulah, but he'd swung a low blow at his friend who was only trying to be supportive.

They all knew there was a woman from Rock's past that he had never gotten over, who he was trying to prove his worthiness to. None of them ever asked questions because that kind of stuff was personal, and they all knew that if he wanted to, Rock would talk to them about it.

Hanging his head in shame, he dragged in a ragged breath. He was losing his mind here. "Sorry, man. That was uncalled for. I know you got a woman out there who you're in love with. I shouldn't have said any of that. Know you were just trying to help."

"It's okay," Rock said.

"No. It's not. I was lashing out, shouldn't have done that. I just ..."

"You love her, and even though we won't let her get hurt, she doesn't know that," Rock finished for him.

"Keeps running through my head, how she's going to feel when she wakes up. She's going to be scared, confused, and angry, and I won't be there to reassure her. Sedatives make her sick. She's going to wake up feeling nauseous, probably throw up. I knew that. I gave them to her anyway. What does that say about me?" Because he didn't want his pixie suffocating on her own vomit if she did indeed throw up he loosened the tape at her mouth so it was barely hanging on and wouldn't keep any vomit trapped inside her mouth where it could block her airways.

"That you're willing to do whatever it takes to keep your girl safe," Panther said.

"Yeah, at first, she's not going to get it. No one is saying we like what we're putting her through," Trick added. "But she's in a bad spot, and if we don't pull this off right, if she doesn't absolutely look terrified out of her mind, then O'Riley will bail without paying. No way she can do that if she thinks we're on her side. You know that, Tank. She's going to be looking to you for reassurance and comfort. O'Riley isn't stupid. He'll see that and know something is up. If we don't get the money transferred into our account, he'll find a way to wiggle out of these charges like he has everything else. If that happens, not only will he go on hurting others, but your girl will never be safe. Ever."

"This is it. The only way," Scorpion reminded him.

"We're doing this *for* Tallulah even if she doesn't know it yet. She will. Once you explain you can start working on earning her trust and forgiveness," Rock said.

"And if I can't?" Tank wasn't kidding himself, there was every chance his pixie was already lost to him.

"Then at least you know she's alive and safe, and you'll find a way for that to be enough," Rock replied.

"Think you can earn your girl's trust and forgiveness?" he asked his friend.

"Pray every day I will," Rock said softly. "But this isn't about me and my situation, this is about you and that strong woman there." He gestured to Tallulah's still form. "I didn't hurt my girl because I was trying to save her life, I did it because I was selfish and grieving and so very guilty that lashing out was all I knew how to do. I don't deserve her forgiveness, although I'd take it in a heartbeat, but you deserve to be forgiven. This whole situation is messed up, but you're trying to do the right thing for her. I think in time Tallulah will see that."

Tank wished he was as confident.

But he'd made his bed and now he had to lie in it.

Reaching out, he gently eased away a lock of blonde hair that had gotten stuck to the duct tape. Then because he knew he might never get another chance, he leaned down and pressed his lips to her forehead, holding them there, breathing in her scent, trying to memorize everything about her.

There was no more delaying. He hadn't given her a large dose of the knockout drugs because he knew they'd make her sick, just enough to keep her out long enough for him to do this.

The sound of the trunk lid closing seemed to ring through his soul with a finality that terrified him.

Still, he climbed into the car and started driving toward the meeting place. If everything went smoothly, this would be a quick in to convince O'Riley that the shooting had been about the mercenaries who took Tallulah from him and nothing to do with the crime boss. Once he had the man's trust, the transfer should happen quickly and then they'd round up O'Riley and his men and hand them over to the cops.

Easy.

He hoped.

He prayed.

Because if a single thing went wrong, it would be his girl paying the price.

As he drove, he prayed his pixie stayed out of it for the whole exchange. If she woke up safe back at his cabin, he'd have a much easier time convincing her how sorry he was for keeping this part of the plan from her than if she woke up in the trunk of the car, or worse while they were with O'Riley.

The arranged meeting place was an hour away from the compound, but the drive felt so much shorter.

Far too soon he was pulling up outside another abandoned warehouse. His team was watching, ready to come in as soon as the money was transferred, but in this moment, Tank felt so very alone.

Counting to ten, he gathered himself and slipped into his role. The success of this mission depended on his acting skills so he couldn't afford to mess up.

"O'Riley, I got your package," Tank yelled out as he stepped out of his car.

Nobody answered him, but he knew he wasn't alone, he could sense the presence of others, feel eyes on him. O'Riley was here and he was likely making sure Tank had come alone before he was going to show himself.

Refusing to do anything that would set off a single suspicion in an already suspicious man, he leaned against the side of the car and tried to look bored when he felt anything but.

What he felt was a buzz of nervous energy he hadn't felt on a mission since the very first one he'd undertaken with Delta. Back then, he was green and didn't quite know what he was getting himself into.

But he'd pulled it together, kept his emotions separate from the mission, achieved his goal, and today could be no different.

For now, Tallulah had to be just another mark for a greedy bounty hunter.

A full two minutes later, he saw O'Riley approaching, flanked by two bodyguards who leveled weapons at Tank.

He straightened and watched them approach. This had to be the worst plan in the entire history of plans, but it was all they had. He'd been outvoted by everyone from his team, to Eagle, to Tallulah herself, and it was far too late to back out now.

"What are you doing here?" O'Riley asked. The crime lord had a smug smile on his face, amusement crinkled his eyes like the whole thing was funny to him, like buying a witness whose only crime was standing up against him was no big deal at all, and that only fueled Tank's rage.

"I have something you want."

"You tried to protect her earlier," O'Riley said.

"I tried to protect my interests," Tank corrected. "I'm a mercenary, I go where the money goes. I found the girl first, this was my payout, I can't allow someone else to steal what's mine. Sure you can relate."

O'Riley eyed him shrewdly. The man was good at what he did, skilled at reading people and deciphering the best way to get them to comply. "I suppose I can understand that. The girl tried to take something from me, after all. Where is she?"

"Trunk," he said simply. As one of the bodyguards approached, Tank rounded the car and popped the trunk.

Inside, his pixie blinked up at him, from the looks of things her head was pounding, and he could tell by the way she was curled in on herself that her stomach was churning. Since there was one of O'Riley's men right there with him, he couldn't say anything, couldn't even risk shooting her a wink or something to let her know that she was okay.

Doing his best to keep her shielded while also keeping O'Riley's attention, the betrayal in his pixie's eyes hit him like a physical blow, and he hated himself for doing this to her. Forget what Rock had said earlier, he didn't deserve her forgiveness.

∾

April 24th
   10:18 P.M.

Tillie felt ill.

Sick to her stomach.

And it had nothing to do with her body's reaction to the sedatives she'd been given.

It had everything to do with the man standing by the open trunk like he didn't have a care in the world.

Like he hadn't just betrayed her, sold her out.

Like he hadn't taken her heart and methodically chopped it into a million pieces.

Pieces she had no hope of reassembling into anything that would look like a normal and working heart.

She had woken up in the trunk while the car was still moving. The drugs did nothing to dull her memories, and everything had immediately come roaring back. How very stupid she had been to agree to play bait when she didn't even really know those people.

Once again, she had let her heart get her in trouble.

If she could just learn to stop trying to please everyone, stop trying to always do what she believed was the right thing even if she knew it would get her in trouble, then maybe she could finally find the peace she so desperately craved.

She'd thought she'd found that peace with Gabriel.

How wrong she'd been.

It should have been a giveaway when Gabriel was so reluctant to agree to the plan. At least he had the good grace to feel uneasy about betraying and drugging her.

Not that it helped her right now.

Certainly wouldn't keep her safe.

And he hadn't felt bad enough not to go through with what he knew was wrong. Just because she had gotten herself into this mess, had no one else to blame for going ahead with talking to O'Riley's son, she didn't deserve this. Her heart had been in the right place, and it was the right thing to do, and it was beyond unfair that she was going to wind up paying for her choices with her life.

Even worse was that now no one cared enough to stop O'Riley's innocent little boy from being groomed and molded into a criminal madman like his father.

Her stomach churned and she had to swallow down bile. The last thing she needed right now was to throw up with the tape over her mouth. Not only was she tied up and stuffed in the trunk of a car, but if she vomited, she would wind up choking on it and suffocating.

Not how she wanted to die.

Although what was coming was no better.

Probably worse in fact.

Maybe she should allow her body to throw up the contents of her stomach and just get death over and done with. O'Riley might be disappointed he couldn't play with her, but in the end, what he wanted more than toying with her was for her to be dead.

Pain lanced through her chest as she looked up at Gabriel. He was standing very close to her, and she noted that he had his body kind of angled weirdly, unnaturally.

Why was he doing that?

It hurt so bad to look at his handsome face, remember how it had looked buried between her legs, how he'd watched her as they spent time together. Why had he gone to all that trouble to play her like that if he didn't care about her? Was it just for sex? Surely a man who looked like Gabriel did wasn't hurting for a woman's company.

She was so confused.

Her head pounded with a vicious headache, not just because of the drugs she'd been given, but with the pain that came with trusting someone only to find out it had been a mistake.

When O'Riley's face appeared beside Gabriel's, it was pure instinct to shrink away from him. It was stupid since she had nowhere to go, but this man terrified her. She'd had a little taste of what horrors she could expect from him, and she didn't want to see what else he had in store.

Agreeing to play bait when she thought there was no chance of falling into this monster's hands was one thing, but now she knew she couldn't expect any kindness or protection from Gabriel which meant she wasn't bait anymore. Now she was just a way to make money.

"How lovely to see you again, my darling Tallulah. Mac Junior will be so thrilled to have you back with us," O'Riley said, giving her that evil, smarmy smile that made her insides go so cold her body began to shiver.

Gabriel's jaw went tight, his mouth pulling into a straight line, and she could have sworn she saw fury dancing in his dark eyes.

Huh?

He cared that O'Riley was going to hurt both her and his son?

He knew that already. She'd told him what the man had done to her, she still bore the open sores from his belt, and the psychological scars he'd inflicted making her put her mouth on him would last a lifetime.

There was no way he could care.

If he did, he wouldn't have drugged her.

Unless ...

Could it be possible that he hadn't turned on her?

Maybe there was a logical explanation for why he'd drugged her without telling her.

Right now, her brain wasn't functioning clearly enough to figure out what the reason might be, and since she wasn't going to be stupid again—she was going to figure out how to stop letting her heart guide her if it killed her, *before* it killed her—she wasn't going to blindly trust him.

After all, maybe she was only seeing what she wanted to see and Gabriel truly didn't care what O'Riley did to her.

A man she didn't recognize leaned down as though to pick her up, and Tillie pushed as far back into the trunk as she could. As awful as it was in here, it was by far preferable to anything that would happen to her out there.

Before the man—who she assumed was one of O'Riley's top men—was able to grab her, Gabriel nudged him out of the way, standing between her and the men who wanted to hurt her. Again, she was confused by his behavior. Her heart said there was more going on here than she knew, but her head screamed at her to stop being stupid, and for once take things at face value and not live in her fantasy land where good always triumphed.

"Uh-uh," Gabriel said. He sounded more like the man she'd met those first days in the cabin, cool and aloof, totally in control, with that annoying mocking lilt to his voice.

From the way his eyes narrowed, she knew O'Riley also wasn't impressed by Gabriel's attitude.

"No touching till I get my money," Gabriel said. "I already had her snatched away once before I got what I deserved, I'm not letting that happen again. You want her, you pay up."

"What's to stop me just grabbing the girl and finishing you off now?" O'Riley asked. "After all, I believe you are vastly outnumbered."

Only if Gabriel's team weren't nearby.

Were they?

It all depended on whether or not Gabriel had betrayed her. If he had, then his team hadn't come with them. If he hadn't, then they were out there somewhere, watching, waiting, ready to come in when the time was right. Even if they were out there it didn't mean they were here for her. They might have come just to make sure Gabriel was safe.

"Hmm, well, I mean, I guess you could try," Gabriel said in that smug tone that said he had an ace up his sleeve he hadn't yet revealed.

"I could more than try." O'Riley huffed. The man didn't like anyone showing him up and making him look like a fool. If Gabriel wasn't careful, he was going to get himself killed. Whether he'd betrayed her or not, she didn't want him dead.

"If you did, you'd have to be prepared to be taken out with me," Gabriel said, dropping his bombshell.

"What do you mean?" O'Riley snapped.

"I mean, if you kill me we all go boom."

Since his back was to her, Tillie couldn't see what he was doing, but whatever it was it got muttered curses and gasps from O'Riley and his men.

What game was Gabriel playing here?

"A little insurance policy," Gabriel said. "I know your reputation and I know you've been known to screw people over to get what you want. Not going to get screwed over again. You either pay me the money, or if you kill, me the bomb goes off, and we all die."

"Why would you be willing to die over this?" O'Riley asked.

"Why not?" Gabriel shrugged. "Got nothing specific to live for. Bounty hunting pays the bills but it's not like it's a dream career, more something I fell into. Can't say I want to die today, but also, not adverse to the idea. So, ball's in your court, O'Riley. You transfer the money and take the girl, or we all go boom. What's your pleasure?"

CHAPTER

Nineteen

April 24th
   10:34 P.M.

While he typically punished anyone who had the audacity to try and out maneuver him, O'Riley could see the humor in the situation.

You had to respect someone who made bold moves. He himself had managed to take an already well-established empire and grow it exponentially by not being afraid to make big and powerful moves.

Go big or go home.

What was the point of life if you didn't take risks?

Mac had always wondered how people lived in their safe, boring little lives. They may as well be dead if they were too afraid to get out there and really live, because really, they were dead already.

Fear was not an emotion he was acquainted with. Never in his life had he felt fear. At least not that he remembered. Perhaps as a very small child he might have, but he had always known his father was bigger and badder than any monster out there and that had helped him sleep safely at night.

As an adult, while he hadn't felt fear himself, he knew what it looked like in others. Knew what it sounded like, screams of pain and unrivalled terror. Knew what it smelled like, urine and sweat.

And it was not an emotion the man standing before him, threatening to blow himself up if he didn't get what he wanted, was currently experiencing.

Since he didn't really have time to hang around and discuss things, and he had no intention of dying today, or losing his chance at capturing Tallulah Russel, he gave a long, deep sigh. Better to just give this man what he wanted and get himself out of here. Already there had been too much carnage potentially linked to him for his liking. Taking risks didn't mean being stupid, and he was glad he had allowed the bounty hunters who brought the woman to him to transport her. Otherwise, he would have lost a lot of good men today. Loyal men. Men who wouldn't hesitate to throw themselves in front of a bullet meant for him.

The kind of men you needed to build an empire like his.

While he had brought this man along with Tallulah with the hopes of turning him into a valued employee, he was now rethinking that plan. He might appreciate someone like himself who wasn't sidelined by fear, and who stepped out and claimed what they wanted, made those bold moves that all great men did, but he didn't want one working for him.

Loyalty and obedience were the two main requirements he wanted in his soldiers, and this man lacked the obedience gene. He was a free spirit and while he might be someone Mac would call on if he needed such services, it wouldn't work in a full-time employee.

"Fine," he agreed. "You get the money. No need to be making threats."

"Not threats, just insurance," the man said.

He still didn't know who this was, or what his name was, and given he wanted to get the girl and get out of here as quickly as possible, it wasn't time for twenty questions. Still, they had a little time to talk while the money was processed.

"I presume you have your bank account information?" he asked it as a question even as he knew a man like this wouldn't come without all the relevant information.

"Sure do," the bounty hunter agreed cheerfully. He certainly wasn't fazed by the fact that he was surrounded by a dozen armed men who all had their weapons pointed at him.

"Please, pass it along to Friedrich and he'll process the payment for you." Mac nodded at his right-hand man who was standing beside him, and Friedrich immediately pulled out a tablet.

As he gave the information, the bounty hunter made sure to stay close to the trunk of the car, blocking their view of the woman, and Mac found himself both more intrigued by this man and more irritated. It was obvious he took his job seriously, and that he was good at it. But Mac also knew the man had friends because he'd been in no condition to get himself and the woman out of that truck.

No one had survived the assault, but it was presumed there had been at least four other men there from the position of the bodies and the quick and organized way the ambush had been executed. Were they part of a team of mercenaries this man worked for? Had he somehow managed to make contact with some colleagues who owed him a favor perhaps? He'd come alone tonight, so he hadn't promised anyone a cut of the reward money. Mac knew how these men worked, and if he had promised them a cut they would be here too.

"Did you sample her?" he asked, deliberately moving around the bounty hunter so he could get a look at the woman he'd just secured. Even bound as she was in the back of a trunk, she was stunning. There had been fear in her eyes, but as soon as she looked at him it shifted to defiance.

Damn, he couldn't wait to get her alone and begin her training. She was going to be an absolute pleasure to break, and he hoped he could keep her alive long enough to present her to his son on the night of the boy's thirteenth birthday.

The man laughed like the question amused him. "Is it a problem if I did?"

"No, not really." As much as he would prefer no one else had touched the woman, it wasn't like he had purchased her as a virgin. This was personal, he wanted her for revenge, punishment, to send a message, but now he wanted more as well. Still, he didn't expect that the woman was pure. What woman was?

"Didn't force her," the man said. "Didn't have to. Told her what she wanted to hear, and she couldn't spread her legs fast enough." When the bounty hunter leered at her, tears filled the woman's turquoise eyes and the fine tremors rippling through her body increased to shakes.

"I have no doubt that soon she'll be willingly spreading those legs for me, won't you, dear. I'm sure there will be sufficient motivation to have you offering yourself to me on a silver platter." He curled a hand around one of her knees. Although he couldn't see the wounds beneath her leggings, it was enough to know that they were there. Soon her body would be littered with his marks.

A whimper escaped through the tape covering her mouth, and O'Riley smiled as he squeezed her knee hard and watched as her body jerked and she tried to pull away.

Only there was nowhere for her to go.

Lazily, he trailed his hand up until it was between her thighs. Her shaking increased as he reached for the bundle of nerves that was supposed to bring a woman pleasure and pinched it as hard as he could.

A muted shriek came from the woman and her legs reflexively pressed together.

Of course, that did nothing more than trap his hand right where he wanted it.

No woman of his received pleasure. As far as he was concerned, a woman didn't need pleasure. Sex was either for reproductive purposes or for the man's pleasure. When he slept with his wife, he never concerned himself with whether or not she enjoyed it. Same when he was with one of his mistresses.

Things would be no different with Tallulah. He would train her in all the ways she could pleasure him, and then his son, but she wouldn't be receiving any pleasure. Pain was what her future held, as much pain as she could take and then more. Until he owned her mind as well as her body.

Shoving his finger inside her as far as it would go with her clothing in the way, she squirmed, trying to expel the intrusion, but bound as she was there was nowhere for her to go. Mac couldn't wait to touch her, feel her without the barrier of clothes.

Soon.

Once the payment had gone through, he could bid the bounty hunter farewell, take his new prize possession, and head home. It had been a long day, a long few days on the back of a very long and trying few months, and he was looking forward to some downtime. Especially now that he had a new toy to work with and train.

"A little bit of sweet talk and she's putty in your hands," the bounty hunter said on a laugh. Then he winked at the woman, and tears began to trail down her cheeks.

Crying, while definitely an appealing quality in one of his toys, was only going to lead to her suffocating if her nose blocked up. Removing his hand from between her legs, he reached over and pulled the tape from her mouth.

"Thank our friend for bringing you safely home," he ordered her.

Despite the tears which continued to roll down her cheeks, a spark of anger and defiance lit her eyes.

Mac didn't hesitate—any hesitations when it came to discipline led only to an unruliness—just slapped the woman's cheek. Her head snapped to the side, the red handprint already standing out in stark contrast to her pale face.

"You'll get out, get down on those knees, and show him how grateful you are," he ordered. While he wasn't a fan of sharing, he some-times ordered his toys to touch or be touched by some of his men to remind them that he was in complete and utter control of them and their bodies.

"Not really a fan of an audience when I get off," the bounty hunter said.

Before he could persuade the man, perhaps offer him more money if a gorgeous woman's mouth on him wasn't enough motivation, Friedrich nodded at him.

"Money is in the account," his right-hand man announced.

"Perfect," the bounty hunter said, pulling out a cell phone and taping away on it. A moment later he grinned and held out his hand. "Pleasure doing business with you, Mr. O'Riley. Enjoy your new plaything."

He looked down at the woman who was staring in shock at both of them like she couldn't quite believe the hand fate had dealt her. She was gorgeous, fiery, stubborn, and defiant, the most perfect plaything. "Oh, I intend to."

CHAPTER

Twenty

April 24th
10:53 P.M.

This must be what Hell felt like.

Standing by doing nothing while Mac O'Riley assaulted his pixie was the worst kind of torture. Physical pain Tank could take without blinking. Wasn't pleasant, but there was an easy way to separate your mind and body so you didn't feel its full impact.

There was no way to separate your mind and body when the woman you loved was cowering in the trunk of a car, bound at the wrists and ankles with no way to protect herself, while being sexually assaulted by a despicable monster who fed off her fear.

A monster who would soon be dead.

Because Tank didn't think he was strong enough to just cuff the man and hand him over to the cops. Even with their airtight care, he wouldn't put it past this slimy crime boss to find a way to wiggle out of the charges, pay someone off, tamper with evidence, or something.

Tank couldn't allow that.

For putting his hands on Tallulah, the man deserved death.

Preferably a long slow one, but he'd take what he could get.

For standing by and letting it happen, Tank deserved that same penalty.

There was no way he could ask the pixie for her forgiveness. He wasn't deserving. Doing what he had to to keep her alive was no excuse for standing by and allowing her to be hurt all over again.

He should have stopped it.

Somehow, someway, he should have been able to stop it from happening.

Throwing another wink at Mac O'Riley but really aiming it at Tallulah and praying she got his hidden message, he waved. "Hold on tight, things are about to get crazy," he said to her, hoping O'Riley assumed he was telling the now bought and paid for woman that she was about to experience hell at his hands.

There was no time to look and see if his pixie realized he was talking to her and telling her to be prepared because all hell was about to break loose.

Unfortunately, his team couldn't come in right this second. O'Riley had brought more men with him than they had anticipated, and that was just asking for someone to get hurt, likely his pixie since she was right in the middle of things. There were just too many armed men here it would be a bloodbath.

Instead, they would wait until the men got into cars then ambush them a little way down the road, split up O'Riley's men so they were less effective.

As he turned and walked away to get back in his car, he felt Tallulah's eyes following his every move. He didn't have to be looking at her to know what she was thinking.

She was thinking how could he walk away and leave her behind?

Telling her the extent of what his team had planned would have assuaged her fears, but it would have turned this into a disaster. There was no way she would have been able to not let on that she trusted him. Not on purpose, but his pixie wasn't an actress, she wore her heart on her sleeve, she was too good for this world, too pure, and much too good for him.

Hold on, pixie. Just a little longer and I'll be coming for you.

It took all his willpower to climb into the driver's seat of his car and turn the engine on. A glance in the rear vision mirror showed that one of O'Riley's men had pulled Tallulah from his trunk and had her slung over his shoulder.

That was his final view of her as he drove away from the warehouse.

A few minutes later, he was meeting up with the rest of Bravo team. As soon as he joined them he jumped out of the car. "We good to go in?" he asked immediately. Once they had the okay from the cops that the money was in the account and the cops had what they needed to finally take down the crime boss, this would all be over.

"We got the okay to do the takedown," Trick told him.

All four of his friends were grinning at him and he appreciated that they hadn't hesitated to welcome Tallulah into their family. None of them had ever brought a woman back to their compound before or had a woman they cared enough about to bring to their home. None of them had ever expected to bring a woman back there. Part of the whole having a target on your back thing meant keeping a low profile, not exactly conducive to a relationship.

Once he'd met Tallulah none of that mattered.

It didn't matter that he had no experience with serious relationships. Didn't matter that he was asking her to take on a lot to be with him. Didn't matter that he had no idea how they were going to make the practicalities work. All that mattered was that he would be with her.

Now all that mattered was that he get her back alive.

"Then let's go do it," he said, more than ready to go get his girl.

A round of hooahs went out and then he and his team piled into vehicles and went to set their trap.

The road was quiet, lined with trees, and they positioned themselves just around a tight bend. There would be no time for O'Riley's men to do anything until it was too late. Tank fully expected there to be a firefight and a whole lot of bloodshed, but it wouldn't be Bravo Team whose blood would be shed tonight.

They had just gotten themselves into position when they heard the sound of approaching vehicles.

A moment later, they saw the headlights and Tank's hands tightened almost convulsively on his weapon. The next few minutes were critical.

One wrong move, one mistake, even a tiny one, could mean that Tallulah would wind up hurt or worse.

She'd be in O'Riley's vehicle, which would be the most protected. If they didn't act quickly enough, there would be time for O'Riley to figure he may as well just kill her and be done with it.

Not going to happen.

He was bringing his girl home.

Almost time, pixie. Just a couple more minutes and I'll be there.

No sooner had he sent up that silent prayer than the cars were upon them.

Bravo Team took out the first two cars before they even knew they were under attack.

The next car in the convoy slammed into the car ahead of it before it could stop or veer off.

By then, though, the remaining vehicles knew something was going on and began shooting back.

Bullets were flying in all directions. One plowed into the tree he was using for cover right where his head would have been. These guys were good, well trained, and even though they had already disabled three cars worth of men, Bravo Team was still outnumbered.

Didn't mean his money wasn't on them though.

Difference between them and O'Riley's men was that they were there for the money, O'Riley paid them very well to do his bidding. But he and his team were here because someone they cared about needed them.

There was no more powerful motivator in the world than fighting for a loved one. It was often even more powerful than fighting for your own life because seeing someone you loved in pain was a whole new level of torture.

After several minutes of gun fight, the night suddenly went quiet.

Deadly quiet.

The only men left standing were Bravo team.

Slowly, weapons still raised in case someone was attempting to lure them into a trap, they approached the line of wrecked vehicles.

Even though he ached to run off and search each vehicle as quickly as possible to find Tallulah, he forced himself to move methodically. Clearing one vehicle at a time, his team watching each other's backs.

With each one they cleared without finding his pixie his panic grew.

It wasn't until they reached the last vehicle without any signs of her that he realized what was wrong.

There were two less cars than there had been at the warehouse.

Of course, he had surveyed it as he was driving in and while he was hanging around pretending to wait for the money to go through for his job. He'd taken note of exactly how many men were there and how many vehicles. There had been seven. Now there were only five.

O'Riley hadn't come with the others. Whether it was because he had a feeling something might be up or just because he was overly cautious Tank had no idea.

Nor did he care.

It didn't matter why O'Riley wasn't here, it only mattered that he wasn't.

Wherever he was he still had Tallulah.

Their plan to use her as bait had backfired. Instead of getting their hands on one of the most wanted criminals in the country, he was still in the wind, and he had the bait.

Bait that was something the monster wanted to hurt and destroy as much as possible, probably was already hurting and destroying right at this very moment.

Bait that meant the world to him, who he would give anything to get back.

Literally anything.

Yet, he might not get her back. They had rolled the dice and lost, only the stakes were so very high and the loss would wind up destroying him.

～

April 24th
    11:27 P.M.

. . .

Watching Gabriel drive away and leave her behind was one of the lowest moments of her life.

And given her life that was saying something.

But she wasn't a small child anymore who didn't truly understand what was going on, nor could she hope that her tiny little mind would block everything out for her because her mind was all grown up now. And unlike in the warehouse last time when she'd been whipped and forced to pleasure O'Riley, there was no one there to protect, no one to give what was happening to her meaning, no one there for support even if they were unconscious.

Now she was truly on her own.

There was no one coming riding in to save her. This was her life now and she had to accept it.

From now until he tired of her, she was Mac O'Riley's plaything. He would hurt her, humiliate her, make her do things she didn't want to do, and he knew the perfect way to make her do whatever he wanted. All he had to do was bring in his son and she would do anything she could to try to protect the child to the best of her ability.

The man who had pulled her out of the trunk of Gabriel's car carried her over to another vehicle. While she expected to be tossed in the trunk again, instead, the back door was opened, and she was put in the back of a small limousine.

She'd never been in one before, never had a need to. She hadn't gone to prom, and she didn't have friends close enough to be invited to be in a wedding party. Of all the ways or reasons she had thought she might find herself in a limo, being the kidnap victim of a psychopathic billionaire crime boss wasn't one of them.

"We'll be home soon, dear," Mac said as he joined her in the back of the limo. "It's a bit of a drive, but I'm sure we can think of something to do to occupy ourselves."

Tillie was sure she could think of plenty of things to do to occupy herself during the drive, but all of them revolved around killing this man.

Never before had she been a violent person, all the times people had accused her—to her face or behind her back—of being like her father she had known they were wrong. She didn't hurt people she helped them, she couldn't even kill bugs when she found them in her apartment.

The only person she had ever hurt was the man in the van who had been going to kill Gabriel.

Now, though, she felt a powerful urge to rip this man to pieces with her bare hands.

She didn't just want him dead, she wanted him to suffer.

If that made her a bad person then so be it, but she was pretty sure most people would feel the same way about a man who had done to them what O'Riley had done to her.

She couldn't do that of course. Even if her wrists weren't bound behind her back, she wouldn't be able to kill him. Tillie just didn't think she had it in her, but maybe she could entertain herself with thoughts of how wonderful it would be if the tables got turned and O'Riley got a taste of his own medicine.

"I very much enjoyed our last ... tryst, I'd love a repeat," O'Riley said with a smarmy smile.

The man was going to take great pleasure in inflicting pain on her. Since she couldn't stop him from doing it, she would likely acquiesce to protect Mac Junior, all she could do was deny him his fun. She could give him her body, but he would never own her soul. That she would protect with everything she had.

All her life she had been fighting alone, she was used to it, could handle this. If O'Riley thought he could break her he was sorely mistaken, but she'd play the role of perfect toy to perfection. An Oscar worthy performance.

"I think you know where I like you," he said.

How he thought she was going to be able to move to kneel before him in a moving car with her wrists bound behind her back and her ankles bound she had no idea, but she did know he didn't care if she injured herself in the process.

On the contrary, he likely hoped she *would* hurt herself.

Moving kind of like a caterpillar, Tillie inched her way across her seat and then flopped like a dead fish onto the floor.

As she struggled to get a grip on something to get upright and on her knees, she was aware of O'Riley's amused expression as he watched her. It would be so easy for him to reach out and help her, but he liked her struggling, it made him feel superior.

Only thing he was superior on was being an evil criminal genius.

Finally, she managed to get up on her knees, not an easy feat at all in a moving car, and she shuffled across the limo floor until she was in front of O'Riley. Once she got there, she immediately yelped as dozens of sharp things poked her already battered and flayed knees.

O'Riley grinned. "Thumb tacks aren't just for putting up displays, they've got dozens of uses. Uses you'll become intimately acquainted with over the next several days and weeks as you undergo your training."

There was no use complaining about the pain in her knees. The more she showed her distress the more turned on he became. If she denied him that pleasure, she at least held onto a little piece of power.

Power she wasn't sure she could utilize in any effective manner, but she'd try.

Because if O'Riley thought she was just going to go down without a fight he was sorely mistaken.

Going along with what he wanted to protect his son was not the same as him being crowned the winner.

His large hand tangled in her hair, and he shoved her head into his lap. Her stomach revolted as his length prodded at her mouth. The very last thing she wanted to do was let it pass between her lips, but he was thrusting it toward her like an unskilled, desperate, hormonal teenage boy.

Just as she had no choice but to take him inside her, the car suddenly slammed to a stop.

Although his length poked her in the nose as she was thrown forward anything was preferable to it going in her mouth.

The door was thrown open, and two of O'Riley's men reached inside. One whispered in his boss' ear, and the other reached out and cut the zip ties binding both her wrists and her ankles.

What was going on?

Had they reached O'Riley's place already?

No, if they had, the car wouldn't have stopped like that, something else was going on.

Before anyone could say anything else, gunfire erupted.

Tillie had no idea who was shooting at who or who started it, but the next thing she knew someone was grabbing her and dragging her out of the back of the limo. Whatever was going on it was good news for her.

Anything that got her away from O'Riley was good news, and if this was some rival group coming to attack him, she was going to look for a chance to run.

This could be her only opportunity to escape, and she had no intention of wasting it.

As she was set on her feet, she barely even noticed the burning, tingling pain of proper blood flow returning to her deadened limbs because she saw who had attacked O'Riley.

Gabriel and his team were here.

Firing at O'Riley's men.

Coward that he was, O'Riley wasn't fighting, he was hurrying away with a bodyguard.

This time he wasn't getting away. She was done living her life in fear of him coming after her. She was done letting men like him do whatever they wanted at the expense of anyone who got in their way just because they had money and power.

No more.

The man dragging her away after O'Riley turned to yell something at his friend. He didn't see her as any sort of threat, she was just the woman who had tried to go against his boss and failed and was now paying the price.

A nobody.

A nothing.

Nothing to worry about.

He had no idea how wrong he was, but he would soon find out.

Tillie's shaking hands reached for his gun, which was tucked into the waistband of his jeans, taking his own weapon to use against him. Served him right for thinking she wasn't a threat.

She'd show him.

She'd show everyone who had ever put her down because of who her father was, treating her as less than human, as someone who deserved to be ridiculed, mocked, and taunted. Who could be used for their own purposes. Who didn't matter.

She mattered.

Maybe not to anyone else, but that didn't make her worth any less.

Swinging the weapon at him, she tried not to see him as a human and instead just as someone who wanted to hurt her.

He was a threat and threats had to be eliminated.

She fired.

Red.

Blood.

Her body rebelled at the sight, but she fought against the terror crawling over her like a blanket of fire ants.

Tillie aimed the gun again.

"O'Riley!" she screamed.

The man stopped, turned in her direction, and she began to fire it, over and over again until there were no bullets left in the clip.

Red.

Blood.

It wasn't until it no longer fired that she realized the burning pain that had covered her a moment ago was now centered in her chest.

Unlike when Gabriel had betrayed her, this pain wasn't from putting her trust in someone who had used it against her.

This time it was from a bullet.

CHAPTER

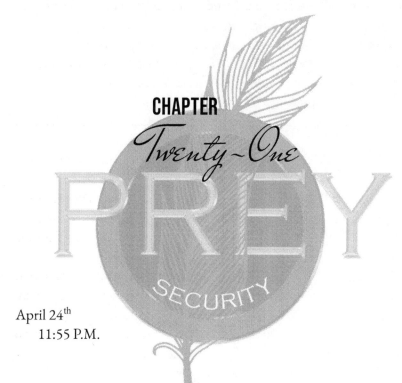

Twenty-One

April 24th
   11:55 P.M.

"No!" Tank screamed the word as he watched in horror as his pixie dropped to the ground.

The last of O'Riley's men had been taken out by his team, and Tallulah herself had taken down the notorious crime boss. While he couldn't be prouder of her for taking part in saving herself, she wasn't supposed to be hurt.

This mission had gone to hell.

From start to finish it had been one great big mess, and now the woman he loved was lying drenched in blood on the side of the road.

Tank closed the distance between them at a run and dropped to his knees by her side.

Red.

Blood.

So much blood soaked her front, gushing from her chest like an ominous hourglass counting down the seconds until his pixie's time ran out.

As he pressed his hands to the wound, fighting what felt like a losing battle to keep her alive, Tank couldn't help but think of Tallulah's nightmares. Red. Blood. That's what she'd told him filled her dreams. The blood of the innocent people her father had killed had haunted her for almost three decades.

Now her own blood was spilling out of her.

Blood that would haunt him for the rest of his life whether she lived or died.

Beneath him, Tallulah moaned in pain, her lashes fluttering against her too-pale cheeks.

"Hold on," he ordered her as though by command, he could keep blood pumping through her body instead of gushing out through the hole the bullet had torn as it pierced her chest. "Don't you dare die on me."

Her eyes opened almost impossibly slowly, filled with pain. So much pain. Tank knew part of it was because of the physical pain she was in, but he couldn't wipe from his mind the betrayal that had been there because she thought he had really been going to turn her over to O'Riley.

That would stay with him forever.

His punishment for everything he'd put her through.

On the other side of Tallulah, Rock dropped to his knees and immediately began rifling through his pack for first aid supplies.

Their eyes met.

The concern in the medic's decimated any hope he had.

Rock was the only thing standing between Tallulah and death.

"I would never betray you, pixie. Never. Not for any reason. The drugs were to make you doubt me, so that O'Riley wouldn't know you were being used as bait. He wouldn't have believed us otherwise. I tried not to give you too much because I know sedatives make you sick, but I was hoping you'd be out until you were safe back at my cabin. I'm sorry, pixie. Damn, I'm so sorry. I wanted to tell you, but we decided it would be best if you looked at me like I had betrayed you if you woke up. Well, the guys decided." The idea of her thinking, even for a short time, that he had betrayed her had come dangerously close to causing him to lose his mind.

"Sorry," she mumbled.

"You have nothing to be sorry about, pixie. Nothing. I'm the one who's sorry. So damn sorry."

Tillie shook her head, winced, then murmured, "Sorry I have to leave you."

"You're not going anywhere," he growled. He couldn't let that happen. No way would he survive losing her, especially like this.

Her death would be his fault.

Even if she lived, he would never be able to forgive himself.

As much as he wanted to beg and plead with her to forgive him, he also didn't want her wasting her energy on him.

She needed it to fight for her life.

"Don't have a choice," she whispered, her voice so weak it was barely more than a hint of sound, her breathing harsh. Breathing had become a struggle for her, and he wished there was a way he could give her his oxygen.

There was nothing he wouldn't give her.

Nothing he wouldn't do.

If it was possible, he would go back in time and take that bullet for her. Scratch that, if he could he would go back in time and outright refuse to allow Tallulah to play bait regardless of the plan, regardless of his team, regardless of her own desires to help.

Keeping her safe should have been his number one priority, and if she lived, he would spend the rest of his life putting her first.

"We always have choices, pixie," he said. One of his hands pressed against her wound, with his other, he cradled the back of her head, his thumb stroking her temple, needing to maintain as much contact as he could. "And right now, your choice is to fight. Not to give up. To do whatever it takes to keep breathing. To stay with me."

"Wish we ... had more time."

Fear tightened its hold on him.

It felt like a physical being, one standing before him deciding his fate with no care to what Tank wanted. It was going to curl its claws around his pixie and snatch her away from him. Steal what was his.

"Doesn't sound like fighting words, pixie," he rebuked. "Don't give up, please. I'm begging you."

Begging absolutely wasn't above him right now.

He'd beg her, he'd beg the universe, he'd beg God. Whatever it took to keep the woman who had somehow managed to wriggle her way inside his heart, a space he had reserved just for his brother and his team, a space he thought was impenetrable to anyone else.

But not his pixie.

She used those magic wings of hers and just flew right on in.

"Don't want ... to go," she wheezed.

Her strength was fading, and fast. Rock had set up an IV, was giving her fluids and pushing plasma into her, putting a quick clot pressure bandage over her wound in an attempt to slow the bleeding, doing whatever he could to save her. Tank could hear sirens in the distance, but they weren't going to get there in time. He knew it. Felt it.

"I know you don't, pixie. I'd do anything I could to keep you here, anything to take this from you. If I could I'd be the one to take that bullet."

"Don't want you hurt," she murmured.

"I deserve it, pixie. For lying to you at the beginning, and then continuing to withhold information. I don't deserve your forgiveness or your kindness." Her love was more than he could hope for. "I'm sorry. I failed you. Can't lose you, pixie, I can't."

Nothing in his life had felt this painful.

How the hell was he supposed to survive losing her like this?

Why couldn't they have gotten to her sooner?

Why hadn't they done the takedown at the warehouse instead of waiting to ambush O'Riley and his men?

Why hadn't he clued her in from the beginning so that the whole mess hadn't even started?

So many whys.

Whys that would haunt him for the rest of his life.

"Don't leave me, pixie," he pleaded.

But her eyelashes were fluttering, more blood was flowing from her wound, the pulse in her neck growing weaker by the second. He was about to lose her.

Leaning down Tank touched his lips to hers. If this was his pixie's final moments, he didn't want her to be alone. This wasn't a journey he could take with her, he couldn't hold her hand as she crossed over, she'd have to do that alone. But he could be here. Holding her, loving her, praying, and begging for her to stay.

For him to have a chance to do things right this time.

Sirens got louder, flashing blue and red lights filled the night.

Ambulance and cop cars pulled up around them and the buzz of activity throbbed through his head.

EMTs tried to push him away from his pixie, and although he shifted so they could get access to her wound, he kept a hold of one of her hands, needing to be able to touch her.

In minutes they had rebandaged her wound, were giving her blood, and had her loaded onto a stretcher.

Maintaining his grip on her hand, he went with them to the back of the ambulance.

When one of the paramedics tried to stop him from following the stretcher in, he about lost it.

"Sorry, man, family only," the medic said. That he did indeed look apologetic didn't help in the least.

"She doesn't have family," he exploded. If this man tried to keep him from his pixie's side, he was going to explode.

"Sure she does, Tank."

When he looked around, he saw Rock, Scorpion, Panther, and Trick all standing behind him. A wall of warriors who had his back.

Had Tallulah's back.

They loved her and accepted her because she was his.

Yeah, she had family. A family who would go to any lengths to protect her. More than that, would go to any lengths to make sure she knew she was loved and cared about. That she belonged.

"We *are* her family. And I'm not leaving her alone when she's fighting for her life. If she doesn't make it, she's not dying alone in the back of an ambulance with strangers."

Tank knew he'd won even before the medic nodded his permission. With assurances from his team that they'd meet him at the hospital, he joined Tallulah in the ambulance, and held on to her small, delicate hand, praying for a miracle.

~

April 25th
   2:12 P.M.

"Miracles do happen."

Those were the first words Tillie heard when she fought through the fog and blinked open heavy eyes.

She had no idea what they meant.

No idea what had happened.

All she knew was pain.

It pressed heavily against her chest, engulfing her in a ball of agony she would do anything to escape.

So, when darkness curled around the corners of her mind, she surrendered to it without a fight.

For some time—could have been minutes, hours, or days, time had no meaning in this place—she floated.

Drifting along, calm, free from pain, peaceful.

Although there were no conscious thoughts, there was an understanding that leaving this place meant inviting pain back into her world.

Not just physical pain, but the agony of knowing someone you had fallen for had used you in the most horrible of ways.

So, she stayed here.

Floating along.

Hiding from the world in a cocoon of darkness.

Sometimes she heard voices. They whispered above her in a language she couldn't understand. Or maybe it was just that she didn't want to understand.

She didn't want to feel.

Just wanted to be.

But like all good things they eventually had to come to an end.

The bubble she was resting in began to shimmer before popping, and against her will her eyes popped open.

Beside her bed sat Gabriel. One of her hands was cradled in his much larger one, and there was a clinging quality to the fingers that wrapped around hers. Almost as though he were afraid to let go of her in case she disappeared. There were bags under his eyes, he had a scruffy beard that said he hadn't shaved in days, and he looked exhausted.

Pain radiated off him.

But it was different from her pain. Beyond the physical, her pain came from knowing Gabriel had been going to betray her all along, that everything else that happened felt like a lie. His looked more like guilt.

He should be guilty.

He'd played her.

Used her.

Treated her like she was nothing, the same way she'd been treated all her life. Like she didn't matter, like she wasn't important, like she was something that could be talked about and used without consequence.

That Gabriel had treated her that very same way filled her with an emptiness she had no idea how to fill.

Why was he still here?

If her memory was working correctly, and she assumed it was since she could remember every horrific detail from the moment she met this man until now, Mac O'Riley was dead. Killed by her hand. No longer a threat to her, no longer a threat to anyone, which meant Gabriel's job was finished.

So was this thing that had been between them.

"You should be dead," Gabriel told her. His voice was rough like his throat was sore, and now that she looked closer his eyes were red rimmed.

Had he been crying?

Over her?

After she'd been shot, she remembered him beside her, apologizing over and over again for hurting her. But being sorry she'd been hurt as a result of his games wasn't the same as being sorry for making her develop feelings for him that had been real on her end even if they'd been a lie on his.

"Doctors don't know why you're not," Gabriel continued. "Said it was a miracle. Or a wish."

Tillie vaguely remembered saying she wished they'd had more time right before she took what she had been sure was going to be her very last breath. There had been so much regret, so much uncertainty and confusion, and she had wanted a chance to find out if everything had been a lie. She had been so sure that she'd felt her feelings reciprocated, but Gabriel's betrayal changed everything and now she doubted everything. Including herself.

When she opened her mouth to ask the first in a long line of questions that were buzzing inside her still slightly foggy head, all that came out was a croak.

Immediately, Gabriel reached for a glass of water on the table beside her bed and held the straw to her lips. "Drink. Just a sip until we see how your stomach handles the water."

The water was cool and refreshing as it slid down her throat, and it gave her some much-needed strength. "How long?"

"Have you been here?" When she nodded, he said, "Eight days. Eight very long days." The toll those days had taken was etched into his face, his eyes, and his tone.

Did it mean he did care for her, or was it more lies?

Problem was, she honestly didn't know anymore.

Gabriel had proven to be a very skilled liar, and even if she forgave him for the betrayal, how could she ever trust him again?

"O'Riley?" She was almost afraid to ask, but she had to know for sure that he had died from his injuries.

"You killed him." There was a note of pride in Tank's voice, and it almost made her smile.

"So, it's over."

With O'Riley dead, she no longer needed to stay in witness protection, not that it had done her any good anyway, but where did that leave her? Gabriel had told her that he and his team had made a strategic decision to drug her to make sure she was believable, and although the lie hurt because her fear had been real when she'd woken in the trunk of the car, wondering if Gabriel was going to betray her, she got it. Truth was, she probably would have kept looking to Gabriel for reassurance and that might have tipped off O'Riley.

But everything else wasn't so easy to understand or accept.

"It's over," Gabriel echoed.

"Was it all a lie?" she whispered.

"Damn, pixie. No. Of course not."

"But from the beginning, you were going to use me as bait. That was the plan all along. I know I agreed, and I honestly was good with it, but ... drugging me to make me doubt you, that hurt."

A lot.

Made her doubt everything they had shared.

That pain lodged in her damaged heart. She didn't think it would ever go away.

Breaking contact with her, Gabriel dragged his fingers through his hair then rubbed them over his red rimmed eyes. "That was the plan. At least at first. Once I knew you, once I fell for you, I couldn't go through with it. I tried everything to convince you not to play bait. No one ever felt good about the plan, about using you, but in the end we all knew it was the only way you'd ever be safe."

"The end justifies the means," she whispered bitterly. It sucked to be the means, especially given that she'd almost lost her life several times and had been forced to do horrible things for the sake of the man using her.

"No," Gabriel said fiercely. "It doesn't. I hate that I used you. I won't ever forgive myself for what you went through because of me. But, pixie, nothing else was a lie. I swear it. I never intended to fall for you, but I did. Couldn't not. You're everything I don't deserve. You're goodness, and light, and your heart is so damn big I'm terrified for you because I know how easily it can be used against you. Falling for you was real, and so easy I swear I don't even know how it happened."

Everything that had happened over the last few weeks and months, ever since she'd witnessed O'Riley kill that maid, had shaken her, drained her, and left her with nothing left.

Nothing to offer Gabriel right now.

Despite his words, she still had major doubts. He had lied to her from the beginning, willingly used her even if he said he hadn't liked the plan, and put her in danger more times than she could count. He'd played the perfect mastermind manipulator, getting her to develop feelings for him that he could exploit. Even if he had wanted to back out, he'd still lied to her almost up until the end by drugging her without her permission or knowledge.

How was she ever supposed to trust him again?

Worse, how was she ever supposed to trust herself?

Because she had stupidly fallen for his games, and believed in him even when her instincts were telling her there was more going on than she knew.

"Pixie—"

"I need some time," she blurted out, cutting off whatever he'd been about to say. Right now, she needed space to figure out the mess of confusing emotions tangled inside her. There was no way she could do that with the horrible ache—both from the bullet and his betrayal—in her chest. "I'm sorry, it's just everything in my head is all messed up, and …"

"And I ruined this special bond we were building," he finished what she was unable to say.

"I'm sorry," she whispered again, not really sure what she was apologizing for only knowing that she felt pain. So much pain. Hers, Gabriel's, it was just too much.

"Told you already, pixie, I'm the one who's sorry, you did nothing wrong." Gabriel reached out and took her hand, squeezed it, then leaned over to touch a kiss to her forehead. At the door to her room, he paused. "You gave me the most amazing gift, your heart, I'm sorry I damaged it. I'd do anything to take back the pain I caused, anything to help heal it."

Then he turned and left.

Tillie wanted to call him back, ached to do so, but she also knew she needed time. Time to figure out the mess in her head, she'd almost died, killed several people, and fallen in love with a man who had hurt her so very badly.

Despite the pain he'd caused, her feelings were still there, she didn't know how to just turn them off.

Tears streamed down her cheeks, a sob tore through her aching chest, and when unconsciousness came calling, she answered and slipped away into the darkness.

CHAPTER

Twenty~Two

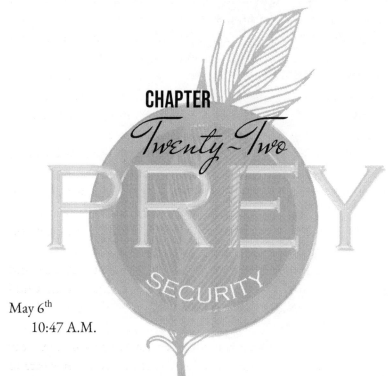

May 6th
10:47 A.M.

Life had lost its color.

As a boy, sitting cramped and hot in his attic, with his little brother beside him, he'd listened to his parents' screams as they were tortured. They'd refused to say where their sons were, adamantly sticking to the story that the boys were at a friend's house, even with the overwhelming evidence that they'd been in their beds when the home invaders broke in, and Tank's world had become dull.

There were moments of color. His feelings of accomplishment when he made Delta, pride when his brother became a US Marshal, the beauty and tranquility of this place, the home he shared with the men who had become his brothers.

There were dark colors, too. Angry reds as he experienced the horrors people could inflict on one another, the sting of betrayal, the anger at having to give up his life—a life he'd fought hard for—because there was a target on his back.

But all of those colors had been dull. Like water had poured down upon them and it had all leeched away.

Only it wasn't water that had caused the color to leech out of his world, it was blood.

The memory of being found hiding in the attic by the cops when concerned friends, family, and colleagues who hadn't heard from his parents in days called for help, and being carried through the house was seared into his mind.

His parents' bodies might have been blocked by officers trying to protect him and his little brother, but he'd seen enough.

Seeing the living room where he used to play video games, watch TV, have family game nights, and had played with his Lego when he'd been younger drenched in blood was something that couldn't be forgotten. Couldn't be wiped from your mind's eye.

Then, in one moment, a sassy little pixie burst into his life and brought with her a world of color. Tank hadn't even realized how dull his world had become until he saw the contrast to what Tallulah brought with her.

She'd been through so much and yet her heart and capacity to love and care about others was huge. He knew part of it was her desire to make up for her father's actions, but honestly, she was just a good person who couldn't not care about those who crossed her path. Her ability to put others above herself made her the most wonderful kind of person, but it also terrified him because he'd seen how it had gotten her hurt.

The need to be there to stand between her and anything that might cause her pain was strong, but she'd asked for time, and he was trying to give it to her. It had been four days since he left her in the hospital, four days of not seeing her, not being there to make sure she took her painkillers on time, was eating enough, and not pushing herself too hard.

Four days of torturing himself by ringing the hospital every hour or so to get an update on her condition.

Four days of walking around with an ache in his chest to rival the pain he knew was in his pixie's chest.

Pain he'd put there.

So many regrets, if he could just ...

"Oh," Beth gasped, her slender hand flying to cover her mouth as he walked down the dock to find her lying in the sun on the wooden pier.

"Sorry, sweetness, didn't know you were out here." Tank had been walking around in a fog these last four days, and hadn't made the effort he should have to go and check in with Beth to see how she was doing.

"I ... umm ... like the sound of the water," she said softly, nervously, her large brown eyes glancing from him to the water, where her gaze stayed. Small tremors wracked her thin frame, and he wished he could go to her, comfort her, but knew right now it wouldn't be appreciated.

He was a stranger to her.

Seeing her like this, it was hard not to remember how she'd looked, how terrified she'd been when they first found her six years ago. She'd been a tiny waif of a girl, barely an adult, tortured and abused to the point where she could barely function. Their team—Axe in particular—had taken her under their wing, kept her here on the compound, given her time and space to recover, and in those months of recovery, she had cemented herself in all their hearts. She was the team's baby sister.

Well, baby sister to everyone but Axe who loved her more than life itself.

"How you doing, sweetness?" he asked, making sure he didn't move any closer, not wanting to spook her.

"Umm, okay?"

It was obvious she was nervous and twitchy, not comfortable around him anymore because she didn't know that there wasn't anything he wouldn't do for her. Upsetting her was the last thing he wanted to do. "Want me to go, sweetness?"

"Umm ..."

"It's okay. I'll leave you to enjoy the water." Besides, he could mope and sulk just as well anywhere else.

Just as he turned to leave, she called out, "Wait. Stay. Please. I ... I think I'd like some company."

Without a word, he turned back, walked down to the end of the dock, kicked off his shoes, and sat, dangling his feet in the cool lake. Beside him, Beth fidgeted and he knew she was battling her instincts to run, but to her credit, she didn't. She stayed where she was, bare legs hanging over the edge of the peer. The T-shirt she wore was one of hers, but it hung off her tiny frame. Tank remembered how he could feel each of her ribs when he'd held her that night she'd shown back up here.

But Beth was a fighter, and he knew if anyone could come back from this it was her.

"Are you okay?" she asked after several minutes had passed in silence.

Surprise had him jerking to look at her. After everything she'd been through, everything she was still going through, why was she worried about him?

Damn, what was it about a sweet woman that made her so appealing?

No wonder Axe had been smitten with Beth from the moment they rescued her. She was so similar to Tallulah, they both loved fiercely and with everything they had. They were both so much braver than he could ever hope to be.

"Hanging in there, sweetness."

"Are you ... thinking about her?"

"Tallulah?"

Beth nodded.

"Yeah."

"I ... saw you two together. The other day. Down here at the lake. I was walking around the lake and you two were here on the dock. You were laughing and talking, you looked so happy," she said wistfully.

"I didn't know what happiness was before her."

"I saw you kiss her," Beth admitted. "The way you looked at her, the way you held her, I could tell you love her a lot."

"Didn't plan on it happening, it just ... did."

"Was ... was that how it happened? For me and Axe?" There was fear in her voice as though she wasn't sure she wanted to know the answer, but courage too.

"For him, yeah. He knew the second he saw you that you were it for him. Took you a while longer, not a surprise given what you'd been through."

"It's so weird to hear about my life, it feels so ... distant. Nothing to do with me. I ... I want to feel it, but at the same time I'm ... terrified."

"Normal, sweetness," he reminded her.

"The girl ... Tallulah ... she must be scared too. She had to give up her life because someone hurt her, and then ..."

"Then I hurt her too," he finished for her because she was too nice to say it herself. Beth might not remember who she was, but she was still the same sweet woman she'd always been. "If you were me, what would you do?"

"With Tallulah?" Beth sounded surprised that he would ask her opinion, but right now, there was probably nobody who better understood what his pixie was going through.

"Yep."

"You want my opinion?"

"Of course."

"Well ..." she hesitated, then drew in a long, slow breath. "I wouldn't want it to always be about me. I'd want to know about you. Not just that you're sorry, but I'd want to understand ... you. What made you who you are. If I could understand, then maybe I wouldn't feel so lost and alone."

Tank knew they weren't just talking about him and his pixie, but her and Axe too. "Axe hasn't told you anything about him?"

"No. The doctor the bird man sent told him that I needed to remember on my own. He's told me things about my past to see if it helps jog my memory of who took me and why, but he hasn't told me anything about him, who he is, what made him this man, what our lives together were like." Her brow furrowed. "Why are you smiling like that?"

"Bird man," he snickered.

Beth blushed adorably. "My memory can't seem to hold onto anything."

"Eagle would get a huge kick out of you calling him bird man."

She huffed a chuckle, but it turned into a sigh. "My body remembers weird things. I can cook my favorite dishes even though I don't know they're my favorites. I remember how to play the flute, but I have no memory of learning. And I knew to come here even though I don't remember any of you or ever being here before. I don't know who I am,

I don't remember my life, I have no anchor ... Tallulah ... what does she do for you?"

"She gives me wings to fly," he said without hesitation. "Allow myself to fall in love and accept the fear of losing that love."

"And what do you do for her?"

"I ground her. Her wings help her fly high, but she doesn't know how to figure out who she is. I think with me she feels safe to find that person she hides by putting everyone else first."

"Then that's what you need to do. Show her how you can ground her, show her how she helps you fly. Don't let her go, okay? Being alone is the worst feeling in the whole world. If you find your other half, you cling to it."

Beth's words of wisdom were exactly what he needed to hear, he just didn't know how to prove to Tallulah that he deserved a chance.

~

May 13th
10:32 A.M.

"Argh," Tillie screamed in frustration.

Being injured was the worst.

She felt so helpless, and at a time when she was already feeling like her life was spinning out of control, it was the last thing she needed.

Not that there was ever a good time to be shot in the chest and almost bleed out.

But this had to be the absolute worst time ever to get hurt and need help. All she wanted was to shut herself away from the rest of the world, maybe lick her wounds a little, sulk a bit, and wallow in the huge pit of misery that was her life.

Which actually made her feel worse because her friend Ariel had given up everything to come and help her out. How ungrateful was it of her that all she wanted was to be alone?

With no family of her own, and things with Gabriel all confusing and strained, she'd needed someone to come and help her when she was discharged from the hospital three days ago. Tillie had a couple of friends from work, people who even though they knew who she was, who her father was, and what he had done, still managed to be nice to her. One of them was Ariel Emerson.

Her social worker friend was just a year younger than Tillie was, and a gorgeous woman with long, dead straight, silky black hair, big golden-brown eyes, and snow white skin that reminded you of the fairytale princess with the same name. Ariel was sweet and shy, but it was obvious from the shadows lurking in her eyes that she had also suffered a tragedy that had shaped her and the person she had become.

Maybe that was what had bonded the two of them.

In a world where you couldn't trust anyone, it was nice to find a kindred soul, and without any other options, Tillie had reluctantly called upon her when the hospital insisted she would need someone to help her for the next few days at least.

"What's wrong?" Ariel asked, coming hurrying into the room.

"Dropped the remote," Tillie said with a huff. The smallest things were suddenly major obstacles that seemed almost insurmountable. The remote had only dropped off the arm of the sofa. Normally, she'd just lean down and snatch it up, but the pain in her chest meant any movement was painful, let alone trying to lean down and pick something up off the floor.

"Here you go." Ariel crossed the room, scooped it up, and handed it over. "What are you watching?"

Tillie shrugged disinterestedly. Truth was, she wasn't watching anything. The TV was on and maybe it was on a show she liked, she couldn't even remember what she'd put on, but she wasn't paying it the least bit of attention.

Her mind was fully occupied by thoughts of one Gabriel Dawson.

The man was a tank in more ways than one. Not only was he huge with muscles that would have any woman swooning, but he had barreled into her life, plowing through her and all but destroying her.

Only she wasn't destroyed.

She was still standing, and *she* had been the one to end the life of notorious Mac O'Riley. There was a certain level of power that came from knowing she had been the one to take control of her own life. For once, she'd managed to take down the monster trying to toy with her. It felt great, empowering, and yet it didn't solve any of her problems.

"You know," Ariel said slowly as she dropped down onto the armchair and tucked her feet up underneath her. "I'm a good listener."

"I know you are." It wasn't that she thought Ariel wouldn't listen. Or that she wouldn't give solid advice. It was just that everything was so messed up in her head that she wasn't even sure she could articulate all that she was feeling.

Even if she could articulate it, she was worried Ariel would think she was crazy.

What kind of woman could still have feelings for a man who had drugged her, kidnapped her, kept her chained up, lied to her from the beginning, and then betrayed her even if it had just been to try to keep her alive?

It made her feel so stupid, and yet she couldn't just erase her feelings.

If she could, it would make things so much easier. A full stop could be placed at the end of this chapter of her life, and she could move on. No more thinking about Gabriel, no more dreaming about him, no more second-guessing every interaction they'd had, attempting to pull it apart and analyze it to death.

"I know we haven't talked that much about anything but work," Ariel said, "but I know what you're going through. Kind of. Not that I know all the details about what happened with you and the crime boss … or the guy from the hospital. But I know what it's like to not be able to stop loving someone who hurt you."

Curiosity piqued. Tillie took a welcome break from being stuck inside her own head. "I'm a good listener, too."

With a wan smile, Ariel began to rub at the scars on her arm. Scars that Tillie had, of course, noticed since they snaked up and around one of Ariel's arms from wrist to shoulder, but never asked about. Not everyone's dirty laundry was out in the open, free to be aired for all to see because, after all, a serial killer didn't deserve anything more. And if his innocent daughter got hurt in the process, oh well.

"Let's just say that I once thought I had everything, and in one second it was all gone. I lost it all. My best friend, the boy I loved, the respect of everyone I knew. A single lie tore it all apart, and even though it's been thirteen years it doesn't hurt any less."

"That is not good news." Tillie sighed. "Was kinda counting on the whole time heals all wounds thing."

Ariel huffed a laugh. "Yeah, that would be awesome if life worked like that."

"Men."

"Men," Ariel agreed.

"Who needs them?"

"Not me. That's for sure. More trouble than they're worth."

"Think if we keep saying that out loud it will eventually not be a lie?"

"Not a chance."

Ariel offered her a smile and Tillie found herself smiling back. Even though the two of them were more what she would have considered acquaintances, Ariel was the only person who had come to mind when she needed some help as she recovered. They weren't close, but maybe a true friend had been hiding in plain sight.

Now that she saw it, she realized that she and Ariel had a lot in common, and they both needed someone. They both needed not to be so alone.

"It's a crazy story," she warned.

"Should I make popcorn?" Ariel teased.

"Well, I was going to say no, but actually popcorn sounds amazing. Caramel popcorn, my favorite snack ever."

"No way. That's my favorite too."

"Guess we have even more in common than we realized. I could really use a friend. Not just because I need help right now, but because ... I'm tired of being lonely," Tillie admitted.

"I hear you. It sucks. I haven't had a real friend in so long. I'm ... scared to let anyone in like that again in case they hurt me."

Ignoring the pain in her chest, she reached over and took Ariel's hand, squeezing it gently because her palms were still a little tender after O'Riley's assault. "I won't hurt you. Trust me. I know what it's like to have no one to rely on, that's been my whole life. Sure, it taught me to be tough, and honestly, I'm not sure if I could have survived the last few months if I hadn't learned how to rely only on myself. But it's exhausting having to figure everything out on your own, no one to bounce ideas off, no one to talk things through with. No one to care if you're struggling or not. I'd never do anything to hurt you, Ariel. That's a promise."

Tears shimmered in the other woman's eyes. "I ... I'm not sure I even remember how to be a good friend."

"You remember. If you didn't you wouldn't have dropped everything to come and help me when I needed someone, packed a bag, and moved into a hotel to stay with me. You already are a friend, and to be honest, the best one I've ever had." Releasing Ariel's hand, she planted hers on the side of the couch and slowly inched into a standing position. "You ready to go make caramel popcorn and listen to an insane story?"

"I'm ready." Ariel stood, too, and linked arms.

"Good, because I need someone to tell me if I'm utterly crazy to even be thinking about a future with a man I don't even know if I can trust."

"I'm not sure I'm the right one to be helping you make decisions like that when I am yet to figure out a way to get over a teenage crush that never even turned into anything more," Ariel warned.

"If there's one thing I learned since meeting Gabriel, it's when love gets its claws into you, it doesn't let go. And I can't figure out if that's a good thing or a bad one."

CHAPTER
Twenty~Three

June 2nd
   3:15 P.M.

"That's it. We've had enough. It's time for something to change."

Tank had been sitting on the porch of his cabin staring out at nothing, now he blinked and saw his whole team, and Beth, were approaching.

One month.

It had been one month to the day since the last time he'd seen his pixie. The day she'd woken and stayed awake, and he'd finally felt his heart settle in his chest, thinking he wasn't going to lose her, only to have it shattered into a million pieces when she told him to leave.

Was she thinking about him?

Looking for him?

Just because she'd been here, it didn't mean she knew exactly where here was or how to find this place. Nor did she have his number, so even if she wanted to see him, Tallulah didn't have a way to get in contact.

Every night he dreamed that she was trying to find him but

couldn't, but every morning he woke up to nothing but silence and an empty cabin.

Losing his damn mind, that's what was happening.

"How much longer are you going to wait?" Rock demanded.

As if he didn't ask that question every day. As though all he thought about wasn't what he'd say if she gave him another chance, how he'd convince her that he'd never lie to her again. As if Beth's words of wisdom didn't replay constantly in his mind like they were stuck on a damn loop.

"She asked for time," he said dully. They'd had this conversation every day when Rock came by to check on him. What else could he do though? As badly as he wanted—needed—to see her, he had to respect her wishes. All he'd done was bring her pain, at least this time, he could do as she asked and show her that he could put her first.

"You've given her time," Scorpion reminded him.

"She'll reach out when she's ready." He hoped. He prayed.

"She doesn't have your number, brother. And have you ever thought that maybe she's waiting for you to come to her? Fight for her," Trick said.

"Tallulah doesn't play games like that."

"I don't mean like a game. I mean she felt betrayed, like you didn't really care about her, and everything was a lie. Maybe she needs you to prove that you do care about her."

He thought he was doing that by staying away.

Proving to her he could respect her wishes and put her first.

Had he made a huge mistake?

"I don't want to see you hurting anymore, man. Or punishing yourself. You wanted to tell her about the drugs, you wanted to come up with a plan that wasn't using her as bait. I know you feel guilty, and I get why she's upset. But you fell for her, and she fell for you, that has to mean more. It's time, yeah?" Panther said.

"Don't mess this up," Axe said, casting a glance at Beth who had her arms wrapped around her stomach, but who stood straight and firm with the others. "Trust me, life can change in a second and you'll regret not going to her."

In the end, it was Beth's encouraging smile, the stark pain and loss in her eyes, that made up his mind. The woman had lost everything, including herself, and yet she still had the capacity to love and care about others. Her brain might not recognize him or any of them, but her soul knew them. How could he not grab onto this chance at happiness, at a future filled with color, when Beth would give anything to get her life back?

Axe was right, life could change in an instant, and it didn't often offer you second chances to fix your mistakes.

A couple of hours later, he stood outside the door to the hotel where Tallulah was staying, praying he was doing the right thing.

If he wasn't, then he was only pushing her further away.

"Oh." Tallulah's mouth dropped open as she opened the door to find him standing there. She looked pale—too pale—and she'd lost weight since he last saw her—too much weight. She was lucky to be alive, but her recovery would be long and slow. Broken ribs sucked and she'd had three cracked by the bullet that almost took her from him. Add in the massive blood loss and he knew she shouldn't be standing here before him.

"Please say I've given you enough time," he said roughly. The need to touch her, hold her, claim her, was overwhelming. She was his and he never wanted to have to walk away from her again. Wasn't sure he could even if she asked him to.

"I haven't heard anything from you since you left," she said, a slight wobble in her voice.

"You asked for time."

"I know, but ..."

"Damn," he muttered, scrubbing his hands over his face. "I shouldn't have stayed away so long, should I?"

"I thought you ... I don't know ... I didn't know what to think."

"Tried to do the right thing, pixie. Wanted to be here more than anything. It was pure hell to be away from you, but you asked for space, and I wanted to show you that I can put you first. I won't let you down again, pixie. That's a promise."

From the indecision in her eyes, he could see she was battling against her heart and her mind. He had her heart, he knew that, what he needed was her mind. He needed her to trust him, to know she could rely on him. Never again did he want to see the sting of betrayal in her eyes.

Once was more than enough.

"I want to believe you, so badly, but ... I'm scared to. Every time I think about you, I miss you so much it hurts, but then I remember waking up in that trunk alone and sick and thinking you were really going to sell me to O'Riley. I don't know how to get past that, Gabriel. I want to but I don't know how."

There was so much misery in her stunning eyes, and he wanted nothing more than to pick her up and hold her, offer her the comfort he hadn't been able to so far. But she hadn't made any move to reach out to him, and he wasn't sure she was ready yet for his touch.

"I know, pixie. I won't ever forgive myself for lying to you."

"I don't want that either. I just want ..."

"I want to show you something." Unbuttoning his shirt, he turned so his back was to her. "My parents were murdered by home invaders when I was eleven. My mom hid me and my brother in the attic, then she and my dad were tortured horribly for not telling those men where we were. Listening to their murders, it changed me. Changed my world. Drained the color out of it. Made me scared to let anyone else in because I know in vivid detail what it's like to lose them. Then along you came. Flying into my life and bringing a trail of color with you."

When he heard her gasp, he knew she had seen the tattoo on his back.

"You gave me wings, pixie. Shared your pixie dust with me so I could fly. These wings are yours." Letting his shirt drop he turned to face her so she could see the other tattoo he'd had done. "This one is for you, pixie. A rock over my heart because I think while you gave me wings to live again, I've given you a safe place to stand, solid ground for you to figure out who you are without the shadow of others drowning you out. You and me, marked on my body for life. I don't ever want to be without you, pixie, and I'll do whatever it takes to prove I won't let you down again."

A sob burst out of her, and Tank took a step toward her, placed his hands on her shoulders and kneaded gently, prepared to take things slow, go at her pace. When she sunk down against him, he took the first full breath it felt like he'd taken since he walked out of her hospital room.

Finally, where he wanted to be.

Where he was supposed to be.

Here with this woman in his arms.

Careful not to jostle her and hurt her, he gathered her up and cradled her against his chest. For a long moment, neither of them spoke, there was nothing to say right now. All he wanted to do was hold her and give thanks that he hadn't lost her forever.

"I'm sorry, pixie."

"I know. I forgive you."

"I'll earn your trust back."

"I know that too. We can do this and figure this out." A smile touched her lips. "I missed you."

"Oh, pixie, I can assure you, not more than I missed you."

∾

June 2nd

5:55 P.M.

Tillie wasn't so sure about that.

Because she'd missed Gabriel something fierce.

Just because he'd hurt her didn't mean her feelings vanished, it just meant they got tainted by his lies. Not tainted enough that they couldn't work through it though. And they didn't have to rush, they had all the time in the world. They didn't know each other very well, and the time they'd spent together had been intense and crazy. It would be nice to kind of take a step back and do the whole get to know you thing without people hunting her. During that time, she could learn to trust the real Gabriel, and they could build something awesome between them.

Something solid.

A boyfriend and a best friend.

In the last few weeks, Tillie had gone from being all alone in the world to having people in her life. Actual people who cared about her and who didn't care that her dad was a serial killer.

It was amazing, and awesome, and she never ever wanted to forget this feeling.

"H-hmm." A throat cleared behind them and they both turned, her still cradled in Gabriel's arms.

Oops.

She'd totally forgotten that Ariel was still here.

"Oh, sorry." She shot her friend a sheepish look. "Ariel, this is Gabriel or Tank, I don't know what he wants you to call him. And Gabriel, this is Ariel. We work together, and when I needed someone to help me out when I was discharged from the hospital, she came to stay with me to help out."

Gabriel made a growl of displeasure that she assumed had to do with the fact that he hadn't been the one here looking after her. But truth was, she'd needed that space. Needed to put some distance between them to figure out if her feelings were real and if she was crazy to give him a second chance.

To soothe him, Tillie touched a kiss to his cheek, and noted that his tense body immediately responded by relaxing.

"Nice to meet you," Gabriel said to Ariel, who offered him a kind of awkward smile. Her shy friend didn't do well with new people unless it was at work, then she was cool, calm, confident, and always in control. Tillie got that. It was so much easier to exude confidence when you believed in what you were doing rather than when you just had to be yourself.

"Umm, yeah, uh, nice to meet you too. Tillie told me a lot about you."

"Mostly bad I assume," Gabriel said wryly.

Ariel's cheeks pinked. "Oh, umm, no I didn't mean it like that."

"Sure you did," Gabriel said, cheerfully this time, mischief dancing in his dark eyes. Seeing him relaxed and playful like this reminded her of being at the cabin, when he used to tease and provoke her. At the time, she'd thought he was a psychopath who was toying with her like a cat playing with a mouse, but now she knew it was his way of trying to make things a little easier for her.

It was that one tiny little thing that told her he was, at heart, a good guy. And when he'd made the plan to use her as bait, it wasn't like he'd known her. She'd just been a stranger who'd been stupid enough to think she could go up against a crime boss who had half the city on his payroll and win.

Although she wasn't going to lie, the tattoos were a totally cool gesture and one that she loved.

"He's teasing you, Ariel," she said, putting her friend out of her misery.

Cheeks reddening further, Ariel looked at the floor. "Right, umm, I knew that."

Gabriel laughed. "Sorry, I couldn't resist. I'm sure she did tell you how I messed up, but I'm glad you were here for her. Grateful that you did what I should have done. Thanks, Ariel. You should know that I owe you big time for helping my pixie."

"I was happy to be here for her," Ariel said. "I'd do it again any time she needed me."

"I'm glad she has a friend like you," Gabriel said.

"I'm glad to have a friend like her." When Ariel's gaze met hers, they exchanged mutual gratefulness. Ariel had told her about her past, and Tillie's heart broke for what her new best friend had been through. There was no way she wouldn't prove to Ariel that she could be a friend that she could depend on. One day there would be an opportunity for her to repay Ariel's kindness by dropping everything and being there for her when she was all alone and had no one else to turn to.

"I'm just as lucky," she said.

"I think I'll let you guys catch up," Ariel said. "And I'm guessing you won't be staying at the hotel anymore."

"Well ..." Tillie looked up at Gabriel. Just because she wanted them to give being a couple a real chance, it didn't mean Gabriel wanted to stay at the hotel and take care of her while she recovered.

"If you think I'm not going to stay here with you you're crazy, pixie."

"I guess it's okay for you to go home then," she said to Ariel, kind of glad to have this time with Gabriel. Not that she didn't appreciate every single second of the time she and Ariel had spent together. They'd forged the beginning of a true friendship that could last a lifetime, and it was the first real friend Tillie had ever had.

Kind of pathetic she knew, but when you bounced from foster home to foster home, and therefore school to school, it was hard to make connections. Add in that someone always managed to know who her father was, and no one wanted to be friends with the daughter of a serial killer. It had made for a lonely childhood, but that was behind her now. She had Ariel and Gabriel, and all of Gabe's team as well.

"I'll just go grab my bag and get out of here," Ariel said.

While her friend went into one of the suite's bedrooms to gather her things, Gabriel carried her over to the couch, sat down, and snuggled her on his lap. It felt so good to have those strong arms of his wrapped around her. This was a safe place, which was kind of crazy given that while he had protected her as best as he could, he'd been the one to place her in danger. In the end she'd saved him, and then herself, but she knew that Gabriel would do anything for her.

Her very own personal avenging angel.

"I'll talk to you soon," Ariel said as she came back into the suite's sitting area, bag slung over her shoulder. There was a clear question in her voice, and Tillie knew just like it would take time for her to trust Gabriel, it would take time for Ariel to trust her.

"Absolutely. I'll text you later tonight," she assured Ariel.

"I'd love to hear from you if you're not too busy," Ariel said, casting a glance at Gabriel.

"I'll never be too busy to check in with my friend who dropped everything to be here for me."

"I'm glad things are going to work out for you guys." The smile Ariel gifted them both with was warm and genuine. Despite what she'd been through, she was such a sweet, caring woman, and Tillie was proud to have her as a friend.

"I hope you find the same happiness," Tillie said.

Ariel's smile turned sad, but she nodded and headed out the door only to pause and pick up Gabriel's shirt. "Oh, umm, you left this out here."

Now it was Tillie's turn to feel her cheeks turn bright red because all she could think of was Gabriel stripping out of the rest of his clothes and making love to her. It felt like forever since she'd felt him inside her, filling her to the brim with all the emotions she'd spent a lifetime denying herself.

He was right, he was her rock, her solid ground, a place to stand without having to worry about anything dragging her down while she figured out who she was. He made her feel safe enough to throw away the covers she used to hide her pain and just be her.

The real Tallulah.

Gabriel's pixie.

The sound of the door closing drew her attention, and she realized Ariel had left and she hadn't said goodbye.

Best friend fail.

"Gabe," she said softly, hopefully, her gaze roaming his bare chest.

"We can't, pixie. I want to. Want to bury myself inside you and never let you leave, but you're hurt, recovering from major surgery and a bullet wound that should have ended your life. Sex is off the table for at least another few weeks."

Too bad he was right. As much as she wanted him, there was no way her body could handle that right now. Not even if they went slow and gentle. And who was she kidding, there was no way she wanted slow and gentle with this man.

Nope.

She wanted it all.

For now, she'd just have to settle for a tiny slice.

Cupping his cheek, her fingertips brushed over the rough stubble lining his jaw while her thumb swept across his bottom lip. "We could at least kiss a little, that won't hurt my ribs."

"Pixie," he warned.

"Please, Gabe. Let me feel your lips on mine."

"Damn, pixie, I'm a complete sucker when it comes to you. You have me wrapped around your cute little finger. Can't seem to say no to you."

When his lips captured hers, his hold on her so gentle, it brought tears to her eyes. Tillie pressed her palm against his chest, above his heart, above the tattoo he'd put there for her. With each beat of his heart her certainty grew.

She'd found her other half.

Found her place in the world.

She was home.

CHAPTER
Twenty~Four

June 3rd
   11:09 A.M.

"Are you sure about this? I mean absolutely positive? Because it's a big step."

Tank was grinning as he set the box down on his table and turned to face Tallulah. "You've asked me that at least a dozen times this morning. I'd ask if you thought I was a liar, but given our history, I already know you'll say yes."

Giving him one of her classic eye rolls, his pixie huffed. "I don't think you're lying this time. I just think maybe you haven't thought things through all the way."

"So stupid then?" he teased.

"Yes. I absolutely think you're stupid," she deadpanned, but then her expression turned anxious. "It's not that though. I just think that maybe you suggested this because you're scared of losing me. These last few weeks have been beyond intense, and I know I almost died, you did too, but that's not a good reason for us to move in together so soon."

Hooking an arm around her waist, he carefully tugged her against him, mindful of the fact she was still in pain. "Not why I asked you to move in."

"Then why?"

"Because I can't stand the thought of being away from you. My job is crazy and unpredictable. If we make this work, and I already know we will, then there are going to be long stretches of time when we're apart. I think we both know that life is short. Anything can be waiting around the corner. We've both been through a lot, both lost a lot, both thought that this wasn't in the cards for us. Now that we've found it, I don't want to waste a second. I want you here with me. Where I can see you, touch you, kiss you, anytime I want."

To prove his point, Tank hooked a finger under her chin and nudged until she was looking up at him, then leaned down and pressed his lips to hers.

"Coming through," Panther announced cheerfully.

"Yeah, coming through," Andy's little voice echoed.

Tank scowled as he looked up, not happy with the interruption. Sure, it was nice of his team, and Panther's little boy, to help move Tallulah's meager possessions into his cabin, but damn, they had the worst timing.

Panther grinned at him as he and Scorpion carried a large wooden chest through his front door. Buzzing around their feet was seven-year-old Andy, carrying a box of what looked like old photo albums. Behind them came Trick and Rock, wrestling a huge leather armchair up the porch steps.

"And that's another thing," Tallulah said. "You can't just be buying me things. I don't have a job, remember? How am I going to pay you for the armchair, and all the clothes, and the bookcase, and the hundred or so books you bought? Which, by the way, I know you went through my kindle and overnighted paperbacks of pretty much every book on there."

"You think I care about money, pixie? Money means nothing to me. Eagle pays us well, and what do I have to spend that money on? Most of the furniture in here I made myself because I needed something to do when we weren't out on a mission. I want you to have things that you like around you, things that make you feel safe and comfortable here. Like this is your home too."

"But you're ... spoiling me."

"So?"

"I don't ... I've never been spoiled before. It feels weird."

"Get used to it."

When he released her and stepped away, she frowned. "You can't just tell me to get used to it."

"Why not? O'Riley is dead, you can go back to doing social work once you're healed, then if it makes you feel better, you can contribute to the costs of running this place."

"Of course, I'll contribute," she snapped, like the very idea of freeloading offended her.

Only he didn't see it as freeloading. He had a ton of money sitting in the bank doing nothing. Why shouldn't he spoil this woman who had never had anyone care enough about her to even notice the things she would like, let alone spoil her with them? And it wasn't like he'd gone overboard or anything. Okay, so he had. A little. But they were building a whole life here.

"Don't think you're going to win this fight, darlin'," Trick said.

"It's not a fight. Just facts," he said. "You really want to go back to that house witness protection set you up in? It wasn't your home, and your old place from before is already leased to someone else. I want you here, but if you don't want to be here, we'll figure something else out." Leaving the compound and his family would be hard, and the idea of living in a city didn't appeal, but whatever made his girl happy.

Her eyes softened. "No, it's not that. I don't care about that place. It wasn't ever going to be a real home, and this place ..." She paused to glance around his cabin. "This place could be the home I always dreamed of. It's just ... I guess I have to get used to having someone care about me. It's weird, but ... good weird. Definitely good weird."

"You got a whole family now, blondie," Scorpion told her. "Five big brothers who will rip to shreds anyone who hurts you."

"I used to dream about having brothers and sisters, but I never thought it would ever happen," she said, a note of wonder in her voice. This was all new for her. New for him, too, but even though he'd lost his family he's always had his brother by his side, never been truly alone like his pixie had been.

"Well, you got brothers now, so you need anything at all, just come tell your favorite brother all about it," Rock teased.

"Why are you the favorite?" Trick asked.

Rock shrugged. "Why wouldn't I be? I saved her life, remember?"

"Because we all know *I'm* always the favorite," Trick shot back, amusement dancing in his light brown eyes.

"I want to be a brother too," Andy squealed, jumping about and almost knocking a vase off the table. Panther always seemed to anticipate his son's moves before the boy did anything, and reached out and grabbed the vase, steadying it before it toppled over.

Tank had never really thought about kids in his future. Since he hadn't planned on ever being serious enough with a woman to have a child together, he'd just sort of assumed it wouldn't happen for him. He'd been totally content to play Uncle Tank to Andy, and any kids his teammates might have.

Now though ... now he could already picture Tallulah's belly swollen with their child growing inside her.

Given her job, it was a no brainer that she loved kids, and what she'd been prepared to sacrifice to protect O'Riley's young son told him that she likely would love to have children of her own one day. Not that he was in any rush. For now, he wanted to spend time just the two of them, getting to know one another, building a foundation that a life could be built on.

But one day, when they were both ready, he'd love to have a whole bunch of kids running around the cabin, the sounds of their giggles already echoing in his mind.

"You can be a brother, squirt," Rock told the little boy. "But I get to be the favorite."

Tallulah gave Rock an eye roll, but then her eyes narrowed. The day was warm, and they'd all shed their shirts as they moved in the pieces of furniture he'd chosen for Tallulah, and the few possessions she'd kept when she entered witness protection. When he followed her gaze, he found it focused on Rock's tattoos. He could have sworn the color drained out of her face, and he wondered what that was all about. She clearly wasn't anti-tattoo because she seemed to love the ones he'd gotten. When they went to bed last night, she'd pressed dozens of kisses to the skin surrounding them. She also seemed to like Rock. Although she'd been nervous of all his team at first, once she realized they weren't going to hurt her she seemed to warm up to all of them.

What was going on?

Why did she look like she'd just seen a ghost?

Before he could figure out what had just happened, Axe came storming into the cabin looking like he was seconds away from murdering someone.

"What's wrong?" Scorpion asked. All humor fled the room. Even Andy sensed it and moved to stand close to his father's side.

"Eagle just called," Axe replied, his voice tight with barely controlled emotion.

"And?" Trick asked.

"Leonid Baranov went off the radar," Axe snapped.

Everyone froze. Tallulah didn't know that name, but she could tell something was wrong and moved to slip an arm around his waist and press her cheek to his chest, offering her silent comfort and support. Pulling her closer, he held on tight because Axe had just dropped a bomb that ripped their world apart.

"When?" Panther asked.

"Last summer," Axe replied.

"Beth was taken last summer," Tank said slowly as they all put the pieces together. The man responsible for a young Beth being snatched as a child, held captive for most of her life, and used as a sex slave had evaded the authorities for decades. A well-known human trafficker with dozens of connections—read blackmail—that kept him above the law, the man had painted a target on Bravo Team's backs, forcing them to leave Delta Force and join Prey.

Still, despite the fact he remained almost untouchable, Eagle kept tabs on the man, and as soon as they could pin down a location, they intended to take him down once and for all.

If Leonid Baranov was responsible for snatching Beth a second time, taking her away from her husband and the people who loved her, then nothing would stop Bravo team from tracking him down and making him pay.

Rock has only ever loved one woman, he's waited over a decade to get a second chance with her and in the blink of an eye its gone in the second book in the action packed and emotionally charged Prey Security: Bravo Team series!

Ruthless Scars (Prey Security: Bravo Team #2)

Also by Jane Blythe

Detective Parker Bell Series

A SECRET TO THE GRAVE

WINTER WONDERLAND

DEAD OR ALIVE

LITTLE GIRL LOST

FORGOTTEN

Count to Ten Series

ONE

TWO

THREE

FOUR

FIVE

SIX

BURNING SECRETS

SEVEN

EIGHT

NINE

TEN

Broken Gems Series

CRACKED SAPPHIRE

CRUSHED RUBY

FRACTURED DIAMOND

SHATTERED AMETHYST

SPLINTERED EMERALD

SALVAGING MARIGOLD

River's End Rescues Series

COCKY SAVIOR

SOME REGRETS ARE FOREVER

SOME FEARS CAN CONTROL YOU

SOME LIES WILL HAUNT YOU

SOME QUESTIONS HAVE NO ANSWERS

SOME TRUTH CAN BE DISTORTED

SOME TRUST CAN BE REBUILT

SOME MISTAKES ARE UNFORGIVABLE

Candella Sisters' Heroes Series

LITTLE DOLLS

LITTLE HEARTS

LITTLE BALLERINA

Storybook Murders Series

NURSERY RHYME KILLER

FAIRYTALE KILLER

FABLE KILLER

Saving SEALs Series

SAVING RYDER
SAVING ERIC
SAVING OWEN
SAVING LOGAN
SAVING GRAYSON
SAVING CHARLIE

Prey Security Series

PROTECTING EAGLE
PROTECTING RAVEN
PROTECTING FALCON
PROTECTING SPARROW
PROTECTING HAWK
PROTECTING DOVE

Prey Security: Alpha Team Series

DEADLY RISK
LETHAL RISK
EXTREME RISK
FATAL RISK
COVERT RISK
SAVAGE RISK

Prey Security: Artemis Team Series

IVORY'S FIGHT

PEARL'S FIGHT

LACEY'S FIGHT

OPAL'S FIGHT

Prey Security: Bravo Team Series

VICIOUS SCARS

RUTHLESS SCARS

Christmas Romantic Suspense Series

CHRISTMAS HOSTAGE

CHRISTMAS CAPTIVE

CHRISTMAS VICTIM

YULETIDE PROTECTOR

YULETIDE GUARD

YULETIDE HERO

HOLIDAY GRIEF

Conquering Fear Series (Co-written with Amanda Siegrist)

DROWNING IN YOU

OUT OF THE DARKNESS

CLOSING IN

About the Author

USA Today bestselling author Jane Blythe writes action-packed romantic suspense and military romance featuring protective heroes and heroines who are survivors. One of Jane's most popular series includes Prey Security, part of Susan Stoker's OPERATION ALPHA world! Writing in that world alongside authors such as Janie Crouch and Riley Edwards has been a blast, and she looks forward to bringing more books to this genre, both within and outside of Stoker's world. When Jane isn't binge-reading she's counting down to Christmas and adding to her 200+ teddy bear collection!

To connect and keep up to date please visit any of the following

Made in the USA
Coppell, TX
03 March 2024

29697174R00141